# Galaxy of the Damned

## Book Four of The Space Frontier Series

Michael D'Ambrosio

# Galaxy of the Damned

**Book Four of The Space Frontier Series**



For information address:
Helm Publishing
P.O. Box 9691
Treasure Island FL 33740

www.publishersdrive.com

ISBN 978-0-9830109-6-8

Printed in the United States of America
Published in the USA

# Dedication

In Loving Memory of My Mom and Dad. I'll Miss You Both.

# Table of Contents:

# Chapter One

# Reunion

Inside the Communications Room on the eleventh floor of the crystal palace on the planet Calamaar, two female alien creatures intently watched one of several large screens over the central monitoring system. Cintilla and her sister, Pinta, were nearly twins except for the plumage of webbed skin, fanned out across the rear of Cintilla's head. The Calamaari were tall, zombie-like creatures with ashen facial features and crooked rows of sharp, pointed teeth.

Pinta retreated behind Cintilla and glanced at the two guards who stood at attention in the rear of the room. She felt reassured by their presence.

"Saris' friends will find him for us," declared Cintilla. "A little insurance just in case he forgets our arrangement."

"Why do we waste our time on this criminal?"

"If he restores my son's health, then he has shown his true desire for peace."

"And if it is a trap? What if Goeth is already dead? He may be buying time for the humans to launch an invasion against us."

"The humans do not have the resources to mount an attack against us in this sector."

"Perhaps he has a pact with the Weevil."

"The Weevil make deals with no one. They are predators by nature."

"And how long can we afford to wait? As long as he's out there, he is a threat to our security," Pinta argued impatiently.

"Not much longer. Time is running out on the truce. His friends on Orpheus-2 will need to find him for a resolution to our agreement if they hope to avoid a war with us."

"I'll put our forces on full alert."

"For what?" Cintilla replied arrogantly. "There is no threat."

"To put him out of his misery!" exclaimed Pinta. "We are going after him, now."

Cintilla leaned into Pinta. She snorted angrily as she realized her sister just undermined her authority. She suspected a coup was under way and hoped her disregard for Pinta's threat would deter the support of the guards.

"We still have a truce! We'll do no such thing until I know of Goeth's fate."

"With Saris dead, there is no truce, dear sister."

Pinta pressed a button on top of the control cabinet and six more guards entered. All eight guards surrounded Cintilla with pulse rifles aimed at her head. She reluctantly surrendered to the guards.

Cintilla's eyes glowed red with hot rage. "What is this treachery, Pinta?"

"You are weak, sister. I will rule Calamaar and my first objective is to kill Saris. Then I will exterminate the humans."

As the guards escorted Cintilla to the door, Pinta laughed hysterically.

Cintilla held the door briefly and glared back at her. "I swear, you'll pay for this, Pinta!"

"No, it is you who will pay."

"What shall we do with her?" asked one of the guards.

"Take her to the mines. Find a nice abandoned pit for her to spend the waning hours of her life."

Cintilla hissed and spit at her before the guards shoved her through the doorway.

Outside the palace, Cintilla was shoved into the back of an armored truck and joined by two guards. A third guard locked the rear door and drove the truck away.

"This is treason!" Cintilla warned the guards.

"We're sorry but she's taken control. We have to follow orders."

Cintilla stared out the barred window on the back door. She watched the white palace disappear from view.

"Saris, I never thought I'd say this, but I'm counting on you." She thought to herself. "How ironic is that?"

She sat down and lowered her head dejectedly.

**********

The palace on Yord exhibited signs of major repairs from the disrepair that it fell into. The grounds were secured in hopes that Will and Shanna would one day return to rule. Huge wooden gates were installed with a high-tech locking device to prevent a future breech by insurgents. The outer walls were less ornate than before with carvings of patriots who died that fateful day defending Yord during Rourke's insurrection.

The underground base was sealed off since security concerns became minimal during the period of peace that started when Will's truce opened the shipping lanes to Orpheus-2. Its numerous bays lay empty in the dark. The inside of the surrounding maintenance shops were dusty and covered in spiders' webs that created a ghostly atmosphere

On the surface, expeditions left the transportation hub weekly to search for Shanna through the mountainous regions of Yord over the two years since she left but with no success. The key to restoring Yord and the profitable alliance was to find Shanna and then Will. Without Shanna, Will would never return.

Inside the palace, Bastille and Jack spent numerous hours in a side office using the communication equipment to query their contacts from passing ships for information on a possible location where Will might be but to no avail. Only myths of a renegade cruiser marauding Weevil supply ships and depots in the tenth sector lent credence to Will's ongoing assaults against his sworn enemy, the Weevil.

Bastille sat alone at one of ten tables in a large meeting room, sipping wine from a wooden cup. He wore a black kilt and collared shirt with his head shaved and a pony tail. Each ear had a piercing and a tattoo of a winking woman's face adorned his left arm.

Jack entered the room, located next to the foyer inside the palace's main entrance. He wore jeans and a T-shirt, with his thick mane of hair tied back.

"We've got problems, Bastille."

"I see that. Not one of our supposed allies showed for the meeting."

"Not much of an alliance is it?"

"It's not a problem so long as the truce is in place."

"But you know as well as I do, Bastille, alien truces don't usually last very long. A change of leadership or regime and all bets are off."

"Financially, Yord is failing," Bastille pointed out. "We need to find Will before things get any worse."

They mulled over the situation. One of the servants entered the room with a wooden cup of wine on a tray. She held the tray out and offered him the cup.

Jack accepted it graciously and dismissed the young girl.

"How did we get stuck in the middle of all this, Jack?" groaned Bastille. "We're not politicians. We're warriors!"

"No kidding. This is killing Maya. She's not very good with people skills and she's fed up with the petty behavior by the few leaders of the alliance that are left."

"We have to do something soon! I hate what we've become."

Two rough looking men entered the room, much to Jack's surprise. Each was dressed in a denim jacket and pants with tattoos on each arm, piercings in each ear and shaved heads.

Jack stood up and extended his hand in friendship. "Well, well. It's been a long time, my friends."

Each of the visitors shook hands with them.

"We have some information you might be interested in," said the taller man, Ivan.

"Talk to me," replied Jack anxiously.

"We stopped in a small shopping district at the southern edge of the Kamonga Mountain Range for supplies. We saw a woman with a child that may have been Shanna. I called to her but she disappeared inside one of the shops. We searched but she vanished."

"Do you think it was her?"

"I'm reasonably sure. She tried not to be noticed or followed for that matter."

Jack shook Ivan's hand enthusiastically. "Thanks so much. I owe you big time for this."

"I could use your help, come to think of it."

"Just ask."

"We have some illegal items on board that we confiscated from an alien ship."

"Say no more. The less I know, the better."

Jack glanced at Bastille for support.

"I'll arrange for your passage without inspection," replied Bastille.

Ivan shook Bastille's hand, then Jack's gratefully. "It's good to do business like we did in the old days," he remarked.

"And much simpler," added Jack.

Bastille immediately made a call via transmitter while Jack escorted the men to the palace entrance.

**********

Maya sat in the palace garden with both her young girls. She wore a long casual dress, accenting her shapely figure with her shoulder-length blonde hair tied back in a pony tail. As the girls bounced a ball back and forth to each other, she stared sadly at the flowering shrubs, a constant reminder of seasons past. Things were never the same after Will and Shanna departed.

Since their disappearance two years ago, Jack and Maya organized a democracy to run Yord. It was a weak ruling committee that pretty much kept things as they were. Other races no longer came there to trade. New governments were formed by the former allies and excluded Yord's people. In the event of an attack they were alone to defend themselves. The people of Yord prayed that one day their heroes would return and bring life and security to the once bustling trading hub of the galaxy.

Jack burst through the doors into the garden and startled Maya. "A friend of mine thinks he saw Shanna!"

Maya sprang to her feet excitedly. "Where?"

"At a small supply center along the southern edge of the Kamonga Mountain Range."

"Get a crew together! We're leaving immediately."

"I'm already on it. I'll meet you on board the *Leviathan*?"

Jack rushed back inside the palace.

Maya ushered the girls inside the palace as well.

Sara, Maya's friend and aid, met her in the hall and sensed her urgency. "Can I help you with something, Maya?"

"Yes, you can," she said hurriedly. Maya kissed each of the girls on the cheek. "We have an urgent mission that's come up and we need to go out on the *Leviathan.* Would you join us and tend to the girls?"

"Of course, I will."

Sara led the two three-year olds away while Maya rushed up the stairs to the security officer's desk. The officer, a tall woman of about twenty-five, blond hair and blue eyes, stood at attention.

"Relax, Silva," said Maya.

The woman took her seat and eyed Maya attentively.

"We're going out on the *Leviathan.* Something important has come up."

"Any special instructions, Ma'am?" the officer asked.

"Just maintain standard procedures for locking down the palace at night. I'm not sure how long we'll be gone but I'll be in touch."

"Yes, ma'am."

Maya rushed down the stairs and exited the palace. A camera followed her across the courtyard and the gates opened automatically when she approached.

Just outside the west wall of the palace was the transportation hub where numerous ships were docked. At the far end, a specially designed berth was built to house the *Leviathan.*

Maya nearly fell as she raced up the ramp to the ship's hatch. Jack caught her and the two staggered backwards into the ship.

"Whoa, young lady!" Jack said giddily.

"Is Sara on board with the girls yet?"

"Sure is."

"Then let's get going!"

Maya slapped the red 'close' knob for the hatch. It sealed quickly with the whooshing sound of air from its long pistons.

Jack pressed the intercom switch and informed Bastille that they were ready to depart.

On the flight deck, Bastille and Celine piloted the huge ship from the hub. Celine wore her hair tied back in a wide pony tail, dressed in a black vest and a kilt, like her love, Bastille.

Within a few hours, the *Leviathan* hovered over a large mountain range on the desolate side of Yord.

Jack and Maya sat at the communications console in the Comm/Nav Room on the second level.

Jack studied the infra-red scanners on one of the monitors as they scoured the mountains for signs of life.

"They tell me there aren't many folks out this way," remarked Jack. "During the winter season, the mountains are treacherous. Avalanches are prevalent with the heavy snows."

"I guess Rourke would never have found Marina out here," surmised Maya.

"Obviously, if Shanna has Marina, then she found Keira out here. Keira took one heck of a risk to get this far."

"As did Shanna to find her."

Jack pointed out the small trading depot on the scanner. "That's where Ivan spotted her."

Maya leaned over his shoulder and eyed the monitor. "There are only a dozen or so residences out there. It shouldn't take too long to check them out."

Jack pressed the intercom button and turned a selector knob to 'open speaker'.

"Bastille, we're going down. Hold your position until you hear back from us."

"Roger."

Jack and Maya stepped onto the transport platform.

"Go ahead, Bastille. We're ready," announced Jack.

A green flash illuminated the steel platform and the two of them vanished.

They arrived at the rear of the small supply center which once was a barn and silo. Maya grabbed Jack's arm and ushered him inside. She was excited about the possibility of finding Shanna after all this time and this was the best lead they had yet.

Inside the supply center, there were several aisles of crates and one aisle of shelves which held perishables and consumables.

Maya grabbed a box of chocolate bars as she approached the counter.

Jack frowned at her until she replied defensively, "It's for my nerves. I'm really on edge right now."

Jack massaged her shoulder with one hand.

They were greeted by a grizzled old man behind a wooden counter.

Maya placed the box on the counter with a silver coin.

"Anything else asked?" asked the man.

"We're looking for someone," answered Maya. "A young lady with blonde hair. She probably had a small girl with her."

The man rubbed the stubble on his chin and sat down on a stool. He seemed to be waiting for something.

Jack became frustrated by his greed. He added two more silver coins on the counter.

The man smiled through broken teeth. "I'm starting to recall someone like that. Is she in trouble?"

"Why? Does that raise the price?" chided Jack.

Maya placed her hand on Jack's. He sighed and turned away.

Maya placed two more silver coins on the counter. "Please, sir. It's really important."

The man reached under the counter and unlocked a small file cabinet. He retrieved a cigar box from inside one drawer, opened it and slid the coins into it.

Maya grabbed the man's arm firmly. "Alright, Mister, I'm done playing." She placed her hand on the pulse pistol holstered on her waist.

The man glared at her and pulled his arm away. "The girl lives with a couple up on the west face of Benton Creek Mountain - about a three mile walk. Now get out of my store."

"Was that so hard?" remarked Maya cynically. She took the chocolates and left the store.

"Yeah, was that so hard?" taunted Jack and followed her out of the building.

The man spit on the floor and locked the file cabinet.

Maya and Jack followed a trail to the mountain and entered the woods.

"You know, Maya, if Will and Shanna return and take charge of Yord, I'd really like to do something different."

"Like what?"

"I'd like to start a new parts depot someplace away from Yord."

"And what am I supposed to do?"

"I could use a partner."

"I'd love to," she replied cheerfully. "We might actually have time to raise our girls instead of having Sara do it."

A few hours later, Jack noticed a small house halfway up the slope of the snow-covered mountain. "What do you think?"

Maya gazed at him with hopeful eyes. "Let's go find out."

They hiked up to the small weather-worn chalet on the side of a tall, snow-covered mountain.

Jack and Maya glanced at each other as they approached the door. Maya rapped on it gently while Jack surveyed the surrounding terrain nervously.

"Are you alright, Jack?" she asked, amused by his now evident anxiety.

"I'll let you know in a minute."

The sound of a latch sliding against the door added to the tension. The door creaked as it slowly opened.

Shanna emerged holding Marina in her arms. Still with the innocent look of a young girl, her hair was now waist-length. She matured significantly from two years ago and looked quite maternal, wearing a plain brown denim gown and long-sleeve sweater. "Maya?" she blurted in surprise.

"Shanna!"

"Maya! Jack!  What are you doing here?"

"Looking for you," answered Maya, looking relieved.

Shanna became teary-eyed and hugged her with one arm.

"Hello, Shanna," said Jack.

"Jack! I can't believe you're both standing here."

Shanna hugged him, too. "What are you doing here?"

"Looking for you and for quite some time. Why else would we come this far?"

"I missed you all so much. How did you find me?"

"It wasn't easy," answered Jack. "We've questioned every trader and traveler that came through the palace district."

"Will you come back with us?" asked Maya. "It would mean a lot to everyone."

Shanna hesitated and looked back inside. A handsome young man with long blond locks appeared behind her.

Jack and Maya's hearts sank at the sight of him. They assumed that Shanna had found another to replace Will.

"Ah, these must be your friends," the man remarked.

"This is Rory," announced Shanna. "He's the main reason I was able to find Keira and Marina."

"Hello, everyone," Rory replied pleasantly.

Shanna continued, "This is Jack and Maya. I told you about them."

Jack shook hands uneasily with Rory. "Nice to meet you."

"Hello," said Maya disinterestedly.

"Can you give me a few moments?" Shanna asked Rory.

"Sure," he replied and left the doorway.

Shanna stepped outside and closed the door. She looked at them sheepishly for a moment.

"A lot has changed since I left Will," she explained uneasily. "I never would have found Marina without Rory's help."

Maya and Jack were speechless.

"Marina needs her parents in her life and she was growing up like an orphan."

"But Will is her father," Maya answered sadly.

"And she'll always know that."

There was an uncomfortable moment of silence.

"How is Will?" Shanna finally asked.

"He was really broken-hearted the last time we saw him," answered Jack. "He went on a spree with the Weevil and the Calamaari. He and the boys got a couple of Calamaari racers (cruisers) and pissed off the Weevil and the Calamaari at least once a day."

"Where is he now?"

"We think he's somewhere out in sector ten near a trading station called Orpheus-2," answered Jack. "No one has seen him in a few years. The last message we got from him was that no matter what, he would always love you."

Shanna broke into tears. "Do you think we can find him?"

"We can start with Orpheus-2. I'm sure someone out there knows something about where he's at."

"Rory!" Shanna shouted.

Rory and his wife Margot exited the house.

"What is it?"

"I have to go. It's time."

Rory and Margot approached them.

"Thank you, Margot, for everything," said Shanna sadly.

Margot hugged her and kissed her cheek. "Good luck, Shanna."

"We enjoyed having you with us," added Rory. "You've become like family."

Rory and Margot hugged Marina and kissed her.

"I can never repay you for what you've done for us," Shanna said humbly and they hugged again.

Shanna turned to Jack and Maya. "Let's go find my husband. We have a family to reunite."

Jack pumped his fist in the air. "Yes!"

Maya placed her arm around Shanna's shoulders and escorted her away from the chalet.

Jack tapped his transmitter. "We've got Shanna! Bring us home, Bastille."

"Well, Hallelujah!" Bastille replied.

A few seconds later, the four of them were transported on board the *Leviathan*.

Shanna and Marina sat down in the main quarters of the *Leviathan* with Jack, Maya and Celine.

"Why did you leave without talking to us, Shanna?" asked Celine. "We were all concerned about you."

"I didn't want to put any of you, including Will, in a position where you'd have to choose sides in this."

"I think you underestimated Will," replied Maya.

Bastille joined them. "Hello, ladies." He hugged Shanna and gazed at her adoringly. "It's so good to see you again, Shanna. You have no idea what an impact you've had on everyone."

"It's good to see you, too, Bastille. Are you taking good care of Celine?"

Bastille glanced at her and smiled.

"He knows his place," kidded Celine.

"So what's this I hear about Calamaari racers?" Shanna asked.

"We have one on board. It's way too fast for me."

"What? You don't like it?"

"I enjoyed the ride but it's not my style," he explained modestly. "This is my baby," he said as he patted the *Leviathan's* hull.

"Is it easy to fly?"

"It's not too bad but, unfortunately, my reflexes aren't up to the challenge. It's really something special."

"Maybe I can have a crack at her."

"Might as well. None of us are comfortable with her. She's a real speed demon, kind of like you."

Everyone laughed at his joke.

"How about a quick lesson? I'd love to take her for a spin."

"Come on. I'll show you."

"Be advised, everyone: we'll be at the portal soon," the co-pilot, Darien, announced over the intercom.

"Looks like we may have to save that ride for another time," said Bastille disappointedly. He departed up the stairs to the flight deck.

"Why don't we get you settled into your cabin?" offered Maya.

"That would be nice. I'd like to put Marina down for a nap."

Maya escorted Shanna and Marina to an empty cabin. Shanna sat on the bed and held Marina close to her.

Maya gazed at the two of them. "It's good to see you two reunited again," she remarked pleasantly. "It must have been hard on you."

"I couldn't bear to be without her any longer. It was tearing me up inside."

"What happened to Keira?"

"When we tried to return, she was…an avalanche nearly killed all of us. Rory and his wife rescued us during the ensuing snowstorm. We couldn't save her."

"That's so tragic. She was a good person."

Shanna bounced Marina on her knee.

Marina looked at her innocently. "Will we find Daddy?"

"I don't know, Honey," replied Shanna. "Her first words were 'dadda'."

"That's so sweet."

Shanna broke into tears and nestled Marina against her.

"It's alright, Shanna," said Maya compassionately.

Jack stood in the doorway of the cabin and watched sympathetically.

"What if we don't find Will?" Shanna asked.

"We'll find him. We found you, didn't we?"

"We believe he flew off toward Andros-3, a small, uninhabited planet," interrupted Jack. "It's located somewhere near the edge of the Calamaari territories."

"He's been out there alone for all this time?"

"Yes, he has. No one's been able to track him."

"I guess if you can't find him, neither can the Calamaari and the Weevil," Shanna said with a small sense of relief.

"That's one way to look at it."

"Maya or Shanna, please pick up," Celine's voice rang from the intercom

"I'll get it," volunteered Jack. "You ladies relax."

Jack went to the intercom. "Go ahead Celine. The girls are here with me."

"One of the man-o-wars has requested to join us. They're a little stir crazy and want some action."

"Of course. Anything else?"

"Yes, as a matter of fact. The portal isn't there."

"What do you mean 'it's not there'?"

"You heard me. It isn't there."

"Oh, shit!"

Shanna lowered her head dejectedly.

"How long is the trip without the use of the portal?" inquired Jack.

"During the trading days, it was about ten months in Earth time," answered Celine. "With this ship at full speed, seven."

"Shall we go for it anyway, Shanna?" Maya suggested enthusiastically.

"I'd be so grateful."

"I always wanted to see Orpheus-2," remarked Jack. "I've heard it's one hell of a trading facility."

"How about the Weevil and the Calamaari?" Shanna asked.

"I think we can handle them. Besides, they'll never expect to see *Leviathan* in their neighborhood."

"Then let's go," urged Maya.

"Okay, Celine. Set a course for Orpheus-2." Jack announced and smiled at Shanna.

"Thank you both. I missed Will so much."

"Did you ever think about coming back to find him?" asked Maya.

"Yes and no. I didn't know what to expect from everyone because of the way I left without saying anything."

"Don't worry about it. We all know it was a difficult decision."

**********

Will Saris, now twenty-one in Earth years, did pull-ups from a tree limb then dropped down to the ground. Months of intense training sculptured his physique. His chest was robust; his arms and legs were quite muscular; his hair long and tied in a bun on the back of his head. He wore a goatee and limited his dress to deerskin shorts and sandals. After his fool-hardy escapades on Orpheus-2, living in isolation on a primitive planet was the best thing for him. Here, he could hurt no one.

A drinking binge and the unexpected pregnancy of a friend and subsequent miscarriage filled him with guilt. He couldn't let that happen again.

Underneath camouflaged netting was the stolen Calamaari cruiser, the *Reaper*, partially covered on either side by vegetation. Hardly noticeable, it blended in well with the terrain.

The *Reaper*'s main cabin was decorated with furniture and a stereo, giving all the comforts of a regular residence. At the front of the quarters was the access to the pilots' cabin.

Will enjoyed his solitude on the uninhabited planet. For almost two years, the Weevil tried unsuccessfully to destroy him while the Calamaari tried to locate him with the intention of capturing him. Will was always ahead of them. His regular raids on Weevil supply ships with a Calamaari vessel left him in an advantageous situation. He hid within Calamaar's territorial limits and was protected by the truce from the Weevil. His attacks in a Calamaari ship complicated things for the Weevil who were reluctant to wage war against their formidable neighbors thus far.

When he finished his workout, Will entered the ship and turned up the stereo. Rock music filled the air as he folded laundry from a basket and pondered if this was all he had left to live for.

He sat down in a primitive chair, made from tree limbs and sipped from a container of water. A small monkey leaped onto his shoulder.

"Hello, George."

The monkey patted Will on the head and squealed.

A loud series of beeps rang over the intercom from inside the ship.

"Time to go for a ride," announced Will. "Duty calls."

The monkey jumped off his shoulder and raced inside the ship.

Will gazed at the painted images of the fire-breathing skull on the side of the ship, a present from his friends at the space station, and briefly reminisced. As much as he tried not to think of them, it hurt not seeing them for so long. He wondered what became of his wife, Shanna, and their daughter, Marina - how much she would have grown. More so, he feared that he would never see them again. The loss of his family left him bitter and driven to torment his enemies.

The monkey screeched from the hatch at him.

"Alright, I'm coming!" Will closed the hatch and entered the pilot's cabin.

"What shall we attack today, George?"

The monkey jumped up and down excitedly.

"I agree," answered Will, pretending to understand. "Let's try something different."

They strapped themselves into their respective seats and Will started the ship's engines. He eased the *Reaper* out from under the netting and accelerated through a long narrow valley. The ship departed from the opposite side of Andros-3 away from the view of Calamaar. This was one of Will's tactics to prevent being targeted by his enemies.

Will turned on the short-range sensors. The monitor showed the green dots and registered the signature of the ships as a Weevil supply ship and an escort cruiser. The two unsuspecting ships glided toward the location of a known Weevil portal.

The *Reaper* streaked through space toward the ships at top speed.

Will contacted the Weevil leader through a transmitter and monitor. "Hey, Polus, you ready to quit yet?" he taunted.

Polus' angry face appeared on the monitor. "Screw you, Saris," he shouted with help from the translator module attached to his rubbery neck.

"Oh, not again! When are you gonna' learn to watch that potty mouth of yours?"

Will toggled several switches and set up the armament control panel for firing. He sat back and directed the monkey, "Go ahead, George. Do your thing."

The monkey slapped the 'fire' button with his little hand and watched the monitor excitedly.

Four red bursts of energy darted from underneath the *Reaper* toward the supply ship. Soon enough, it exploded into a brief fireball. The monkey jumped up and down, clapping and squealing.

Will high-fived the monkey. "I see I trained you well, my friend."

The cruiser steered toward them and fired eight torpedoes. The bright red energy bursts darted at the *Reaper* but Will evaded them easily.

Will circled around and pursued the cruiser toward the portal. "What say we take care of this one, too, George?"

The monkey jumped up and down, clapping all the while.

Will set up the armament control panel again. The display on the panel indicated full charge on the weapons.

"Go ahead, George. Do it again."

The monkey slapped at the 'fire' button and danced on the seat with joy.

The cruiser nearly reached the portal but two of the torpedoes struck its tail section and it burst into a brief fireball then vanished.

"What do you say now, Polus?"

"You're going to pay one day."

The transmission ended, much to Will's amusement.

"Let's go home, George."

The *Reaper* turned around and headed back to Andros-3.

**********

Seven months later, the *Leviathan* and the man-o-war called the *Widow Maker* neared the end of their journey and entered the territory of the Confederation. Two man-o-wars from Orpheus-2 appeared and aggressively escorted the *Leviathan* to a dock on the outer deck of the station because of its size while the *Widow Maker* docked inside at one of the standard berths. Once docked, a long mobile jet way swung out to the hatch and secured to the side of the ship. The *Leviathan* immediately went into 'cloak' mode, becoming invisible.

Inside the Surveillance Control Center on the second floor of the station, General Arn Adolfo stood behind Severin, his security officer, as she contacted the *Leviathan* for identification.

The Control Center was a wide room with several monitors along the walls and a pair of super-computers to tally incoming data and control the stations functions.

Arn was short and chubby, dressed in a tan uniform with black boots. His balding head indicated that his age was more than fifty in Earth years.

Severin was tall with long dark hair tucked underneath her black officer's cap. She wore a tight black uniform with a high collar and stared with sharp piercing eyes. A sense of humor was something she never saw a need for. With her hardened expression, she appeared to be in her late twenties.

Maya, Jack and Shanna huddled behind Bastille and Celine in the pilots' cabin of the ship waiting for their first contact with the General of the Confederation. This was the first time that they heard of the group and were anxious to learn more.

"This is the *Leviathan* from the Yordic Empire," announced Bastille. "We're searching for a man named Will Saris."

Arn laughed hysterically.

"What's so funny?" asked Bastille, confused by the General's reaction.

"You came all the way out here to ask me that! Hell, we're all looking for Will," he replied. "He's been gone for quite a while."

"Any idea where?"

"He might be holed up on one of the small planets in the Calamaari territories in the next sector for all we know."

"No one's gone out to look for him?" queried Shanna disappointedly.

"Nope. We felt it was safer that way. He's got a chip on his shoulder and a broken heart. We thought it best to leave him be."

"I guess everyone hates me for this?" remarked Shanna gloomily.

"Everyone cares about you and Will," replied Maya sympathetically. "I doubt they would feel any other way." She put her arm around Shanna and hugged her.

"Mind if we stop in for supplies?" requested Bastille.

"That's what we're here for. Besides, I've always wanted to see the elusive *Leviathan*."

"Thank you, sir," replied Bastille.

The monitor went blank.

"Let's go out and see what else we can find out about Will," suggested Jack. "Maybe, if we can figure out what he was thinking, we might be able to plot where he's at."

"I'll stay here and monitor the communications channels," offered Celine. "Maybe Will can recognize our signature from where he's at."

"Thanks, Honey." Bastille kissed her cheek and left the pilots' cabin.

Everyone met at the hatch in the main quarters.

Twelve soldiers, dressed in tan uniforms like Arn, waited curiously in the mobile corridor as the invisible hatch opened, revealing the inside of the ship and the crew. The soldiers were amazed at the cloaking technology that the ship employed.

Bastille, Shanna, Jack and Maya were escorted from the ship to the Surveillance Control Center.

Arn and Severin stood up and greeted them with handshakes.

"Welcome to Orpheus-2," said Arn as he puffed on his cigar. "This is Severin, my security officer. She's the best in the business."

Severin nodded stoically at them.

"It's a pleasure to be here," replied Jack excitedly. "I can't tell you how much I've heard about the station and the Confederation from traders and travelers."

"Yes, well fortunately for us, we had some defectors from the Fleet or we'd be just a myth."

"You had defectors from the Fleet?" inquired Maya, surprised by the comment.

"I'm one of them," remarked Severin arrogantly.

"I see."

Severin noted the cynical tone in Maya's voice.

"Maya was once a commanding officer in the Fleet," Jack announced.

Severin studied her with a cold expression. "I can't say I respect the Fleet or any of its officers. They were a grave disappointment as was demonstrated by the results of the war."

"What do you mean by that?" demanded Shanna in defense of her friend.

"They had no intention of winning the war against the alien alliance. It was a game where innocent people were killed while they played like gods. They'll never succeed against anyone."

"Now, now, ladies," interrupted Arn, amused at their competitiveness.

"Obviously, you don't keep up on the latest reports of the war," Maya replied smartly.

"And why would I?"

"Because the Fleet has been disbanded for some time now. The alien alliance was defeated and the Weevil were left to fight alone against us."

"So I suppose you're a refugee from the Fleet," sniped Severin as she glared at Maya.

Maya kept her composure but fixed her gaze back at Severyn. "I'm no refugee, Severyn. I disbanded the Fleet."

Arn pushed Severin playfully as she was trumped by Maya's revelation.

"Perhaps we should carry on with this discussion at a later time. I'd like to hear more," Severin replied professionally.

Arn pointed to one of the large monitors. Severin, Bastille, Maya, Jack and Shanna huddled around it and watched.

"His ship appears randomly on our long-range sensors and our patrols claim he makes regular attacks on Weevil supply shipments," explained Arn. "We have tried many times to contact him but with no success."

"The range of our sensors only reaches to Sach-15, a large worthless rock of a planet," added Severin. "He's somewhere beyond it."

Arn pointed to a green spot on the monitor. "There he is. He's out hunting again."

Severin's transmitter beeped. "It's Severin. Go ahead" She listened for several seconds. "Thanks."

"Well?" asked Arn.

"It's him. He just took out a Weevil supply ship and a cruiser."

"So how often does he do this?" inquired Maya.

"At least once a week, maybe more - often outside the range of our sensors."

Maya activated her transmitter. "Celine, are you there?"

"Go ahead, Maya."

"Follow vector 7. See that ship?"

"Yeah."

"Track it. It could be Will."

"I'm on him," she replied.

Laneia, Shanna's long-time friend and Attradean Queen, entered the room, brimming with delight. "Shanna!" she shouted excitedly.

The sight of Laneia stunned Shanna. "Laneia!" She ran to her and threw her arms around her. "Laneia, how are you?"

"I'm fine. And you?"

"Under the circumstances, I'm doing well."

"Did you recover your daughter?"

"Yes I did. Now I have to find my husband."

"Oh, he's gonna be so happy to see you."

Severin looked surprised by Shanna's remark. "So this is the infamous Shanna who broke Will's heart," she remarked sarcastically.

"Yes, she is," answered Laneia. "She's also known as the Queen of Yord."

"I hope she's worth it. That man's gone through hell because of her."

Shanna looked shamefully down at the floor.

"It doesn't matter now," Laneia replied. "All we have to do is find Will and everything will be fine."

Shanna smiled and placed her hand briefly on Laneia's arm in appreciation of the support. "Thank you, Laneia. I feel really bad about how this had to play out."

"I understand. It's gonna' be okay, now."

They followed Arn from the room and down the stairs. A short ways down the wide corridor was the entrance to Arn's saloon.

Arn paused at the door and looked back at his guests. "While we're waiting, can I interest you all in a drink and a fight?"

"What do you mean 'a fight'?" asked Bastille curiously.

"Oh, you'll like this."

They entered the saloon and took seats at one of the round tables.

"We have the footage from Will's fight with the Calamaari prince. It was a dandy."

"Why the hell was he fighting a Calamaari prince?" Shanna demanded.

"It seemed they had a difference of opinion. Will's not one to let things go."

"You don't have to tell me."

"Hey Jeanie," shouted Arn. "Can you put Saris' fight on the screen and bring us a few drinks?"

Jeanie nodded and walked behind the bar. She operated the equipment under the bar until the large screen on the side wall illuminated and the arena appeared.

The crowd chanted Will's name. He entered the cage and scanned the crowd.

"I don't believe it," Shanna uttered in disbelief.

Maya's transmitter beeped. "Go ahead," she replied.

"I think I have his location," replied Celine. "There's a small planet called Andros-3. He did a few evasive maneuvers before disappearing in the planet's atmosphere. I'll try to contact him."

"No, don't do that!" exclaimed Arn.

Everyone was startled.

"Why not?" asked Maya.

"It'll give away his position to the Weevil and the Calamaari."

"Negative, Celine. We need to discuss how we'll pursue this."

"Roger."

Jeanie brought the drinks over and set them on the table.

Arn raised his glass for a toast.

"What is this?" asked Shanna.

"Rum – Orpheus style. Will enjoyed it very much."

"I can only imagine."

They raised their glasses in a toast.

"Here's to Will, the opening of the trade lanes and the truce with the Calamaari," announced Arn proudly.

Maya was surprised by his comment. "Will opened the trade lanes?" she asked.

"Yes he did. Will forged a truce with the Calamaari for at least seven striads. Come to think of it, we're approaching the end of that truce soon."

Shanna was riveted to the movie screen. She was appalled at the beating Will took from Goeth.

Arn noticed and was amused. "Don't worry, young lady. It gets better."

Shanna watched Goeth clothes-line Will and turned away. "I've seen enough," she said sadly.

They each sipped from their glass. All three women nearly gagged on the rum.

"What is this stuff?" Maya asked nauseously.

"I told you, it's rum," Arn answered innocently.

"It's way too strong."

"Yeah, Will found that out after about four glasses."

Maya and Shanna glanced at each other.

"I can't see Will drinking four glasses of this stuff," remarked Shanna disbelievingly.

"Yeah, he did," said Laneia.

"He'd never walk away."

Laneia shook her head sideways. "Nope, he didn't."

"He passed out?"

"Oh, yeah. He was out for nearly a week. Then he had to fight."

"Why would he do something as dumb as that?"

"Because you left him," replied Arn. "He was devastated."

"Leaving him was the hardest decision I'll ever have to make in my life. It wasn't his fault."

"Well, make sure you let him know when we find him. He thinks you're gone for good."

Shanna's face reddened.

"Are you alright?" Laneia asked.

"Yeah, but I feel really woozy."

"That's enough for you gals," said Arn. "Maybe it is a little too strong."

Maya's transmitter beeped again. "Go ahead, Celine."

"We've narrowed his location down significantly based on the trajectory of his ship and infra-red heat trails. He definitely hid his tracks well."

"Excellent! We're on the way."

"You're leaving so soon?" asked Arn disappointedly.

"I promise we'll be back," said Maya. "I want to check out this shopping mecca of yours."

"I've heard you have one hell of an arcade, too," added Jack.

"Sixth floor. It's state of the art. Nothing like it in the universe."

"I'll give it a good test. Thanks, General."

"My pleasure."

They left the saloon and returned to their ship.

Arn looked at the glasses with most of their contents. "Ah, what a waste," he muttered and chugged each one before coughing a few times. "Damn, that's good stuff."

**********

On board the *Leviathan*, six of them sat together in the main quarters.

Shanna stood up and leaned on the table with her hands. "I'd like to take your Calamaari ship down to Andros-3 and search the terrain."

"You've never flown it," replied Maya in a concerned tone. "I know you're anxious to find Will but that's just crazy."

"I learn fast. Besides, this is really important to me."

"Perhaps I can provide you with a few lessons," offered Bastille.

"Oh, Bastille, thank you so much!"

"I'll lead the ground patrol," volunteered Jack.

Sara entered with Marina at her side.

"Mommy," she shouted and ran to Shanna. Shanna knelt down and took her in her arms. "Hello, Sweetie."

"She can stay with my girls," offered Maya.

"I don't mind watching her if you like," volunteered Sara.

"She needs to see her father if he's down there."

Shanna left the quarters with Marina and Bastille. They descended the metal stairs to the cargo bay and entered the Calamaari ship. It was sleek and streamlined for speed with a shiny dark surface. Across the tail section were several Calamaari symbols identifying the ship.

Once inside the pilots' cabin, Shanna strapped Marina into the co-pilot's seat and studied the controls.

Bastille knelt down by her and explained each of the controls. Once Shanna felt comfortable, he wished her well and left.

"Marina, it's time to find your father."

"We're gonna find Daddy, mommy?" Marina asked excitedly.

Shanna fought to hold back the tears. "Yes, Sweetie, we're gonna' find Daddy."

The cargo bay door of the *Leviathan* opened. Shanna activated the smaller ship's systems and piloted the cruiser out of the bay.

Jack and Maya transported down to the surface and landed in a densely forested valley. The air was very humid and the temperature quite warm.

"Do you think he's here?" asked Jack nervously. He already felt uncomfortable with the climate.

"We studied the flight path and surmise that this is the most likely area he would have landed," replied Maya.

They spread out and searched for him.

After walking for an hour, Jack paused to wipe the sweat off his brow.

Maya sat down on a tree stump and sighed. "No wonder the Weevil never found Will. We can't either."

A long, gray snake hovered above Maya from the tree limb above. It stretched toward her from behind.

Jack scanned the area around them and listened for any sounds that might give them a hint.

Maya worried that, after all the excitement of finding Shanna, they would come up empty in their search for Will.

Jack turned toward Maya and quickly drew his pulse pistol when he saw the snake.

Maya, still unaware of the snake looked horrified. "Jack!"

Jack fired one shot and the snake's head exploded. The body quivered for several seconds and then hung motionless.

Maya leaped into Jack's arms, trembling.

"The old man's still got it," quipped Jack.

Maya regained her composure. "I knew there was a reason I keep you around. Thank you."

**********

Shanna navigated the cruiser slowly across the terrain at low altitude. The cruiser had the ability to glide at slow speeds and even hover for short periods of time.

She scanned the area over and over but saw nothing. "Come on, Will. Where are you?" she uttered frustratedly. She circled around and descended into the valley.

"Any luck, Shanna?" Jack asked over the transmitter.

"Not yet."

"He's got to be here. There's no place else he …"

Shanna hovered over a small clearing and noticed traces of color on a tree. She dropped down to treetop level and recognized several articles of clothing hanging from branches.

"Hold on, Jack. I think I see something. I'm changing the cameras to 'zoom'."

Shanna lowered the ship into the clearing and watched the monitors anxiously. She recognized a ship just like hers underneath the camouflaged netting, partially hidden by vegetation.

"I think I found him, Jack! I'm activating the homing signal so you'll find us."

Shanna toggled a switch on the panel above her.

"I have it," answered Jack. "We're not far. Shut down your signal for now. We don't want to attract any of our friends."

"Understood." Shanna shut down the ship's engines and unstrapped Marina.

"Come on, Honey! We're going to see Daddy."

"Daddy!" Marina exclaimed.

Shanna exited her ship with Marina and approached the camouflaged ship.

**********

Inside the Control Center at the Calamaari palace were a dozen technicians with Pinta and two of her personal guards, all with ashen leathery skin and gruesome, jagged teeth. Pinta studied the various screens on the central monitoring system and was elated when Shanna's cruiser landed on Andros-3.

"Notify our ships to stand by for attack. If Saris' ship tries to leave that planet, I want him destroyed!"

One of the guards bowed and departed the Control Center.

Pinta eyed the monitor and grew more confident that Will would soon reveal himself.

"What if he's not there?" asked one of the guards.

"Then we'll force him to come out from wherever he's hiding. Orpheus-2 could be the perfect bait."

"But our scouts say that there is some kind of super ship there. It could be the mythical *Leviathan*."

Pinta became annoyed with the guard. "Check the last scan, you fool! There is nothing bigger than a man-o-war on that station. Besides, if there was such a ship, it wouldn't be in our sector."

"But we know a ship arrived but there's no evidence that it ever left."

"What do you mean by that?"

"Our scouts report that the ship appeared to, uh, vanish."

Pinta glared at the guard and curled her claws into a fist. "Are you questioning my orders?"

"I'm sorry. I just… never mind."

"Then keep watch over the station until it does appear!"

The guard looked down fearfully at the ground.

Pinta shook her head in disgust and snarled. She left the Control Center.

**********

Shanna and Marina hid behind bushes near the hatch. Her heart raced as she prayed it was Will inside.

Rock music blared from inside the ship. Shanna took Marina by the hand and crept cautiously toward the hatch. She paused at the entrance. "Will, are you in here?"

The camouflaged netting hung down over the entrance, making it difficult to see inside.

Jack and Maya crept up next to her. Shanna glanced at them and returned her attention to the ship's hatch.

"It sounds like Will's kind of music," Jack remarked optimistically.

"Keep Marina for me, please, Maya. I'll go in first and make sure it's him."

"Of course."

"Be careful," warned Jack, "just in case it's a trap."

"One of us should go with you," Maya suggested.

"No, I need to do this alone."

She pushed the netting aside and stepped nervously through the hatch.

Inside the ship, Will hung upside down from a bar, bending repeatedly as part of his workout. He wore deerskin shorts and no shirt.

Shanna couldn't believe her eyes when she saw him. She gazed for several seconds and wondered if it was really him.

Will had developed into an incredibly muscular man. His finely sculptured body made her lust for him at once. She approached him from the side.

His eyes were closed and he sang the words to the song while bending upward.

Shanna admired the flexing muscles of his body and was overcome with incredible passion for him.

"This is my Will!" she thought excitedly. "My, has he grown."

Will suddenly sensed her thoughts and turned in her direction. He was startled to see her standing there. "Shanna?"

"Will!"

Shanna hugged him awkwardly and kissed him while he hung upside down.

Will tried to get down off the bar but Shanna clung so tightly that he couldn't move. Finally he pushed her away. "Please, let me down before I pass out."

Shanna waited anxiously as Will grabbed the bar with his hands and unhooked his legs. When she couldn't wait any longer, she put her hands on his waist and helped him down. It felt so good to touch him again. She sensed the magic again that they shared whenever they were close together. It all came back to her so vividly.

"Oh, Will!" Shanna kissed him like a starved animal.

Will was overcome with joy as he feasted his eyes upon her.

Her blond hair had grown to nearly hip length and her face reflected her maturity. She dressed much like Will once did, wearing a simple white blouse and loose fitting black pants with black boots.

Will eagerly embraced her. "Marina – did you find her?" he asked.

"Oh, yes. And now I've found you."

They hugged and kissed.

Shanna called out to the others, "He's here! He's here!"

Jack, Maya and Marina hurried inside the ship. They were thrilled at the sight of him.

"Daddy! Daddy!" shouted Marina excitedly.

Will saw Marina and instinctively took her in his arms. "Look at how she's grown."

Will cried as he hugged her. He pulled Shanna close to him and hugged her as well.

"To lose one's family is a burden that no man should bear."

"To choose between her husband and her child is a burden that no woman should bear," replied Shanna.

Marina touched Will's cheeks with her hands. "I missed you, Daddy."

"I missed you, too, Marina. I'm so glad you're here."

Will hugged Jack and Maya next.

Jack placed his arm around Maya and whispered, "Finally, everything is right."

"Yes, it is," replied Maya.

"So how did you find me?" Will asked. "I worked very hard to stay hidden all this time."

"It wasn't easy," answered Jack.

Will gazed at Marina again. "Oh, my little girl, how you've grown."

He ogled Shanna, still stunned by her appearance and squeezed her tightly against him. "I'll never let you go again."

"You'd better not," she replied.

"Wc all were so worried about the both of you," said Maya. "You're family to us."

"And it's good to be with you all again."

Will stepped outside and immediately noticed the second Calamaari ship. "How did she handle?"

"I liked the *Phantom* better," said Maya.

"It's got too much speed for me," added Jack.

Will awaited Shanna's response. She smiled coyly at him.

"I take it Shanna's already got dibs on it," Will quipped.

"Of course," she answered. I'll race you back to the station."

"You're on!"

Jack blocked the hatch before Shanna could leave. "Why don't we go back and let you spend some time together?" he suggested. "We'll wait for you on board *Leviathan*."

Shanna looked anxiously at Will. "What do you think?"

"I think it's a marvelous idea."

Jack pushed Maya toward the hatch. "Give us a holler when you're coming back."

"I sure will. Thanks, everyone."

As their friends departed, Will closed the hatch and eyed Shanna with a seductive grin.

Shanna folded her arms and gazed at him adoringly. "I can't believe we're standing here together."

"Look at you both," remarked Will. "How much you have changed."

Marina touched Will's cheek. "Daddy, I love you."

Will hugged Marina tightly and kissed her. "I love you too, Sweetie."

Shanna followed him to the couch and sat next with him. As Will played with Marina, Shanna suddenly grew somber.

Will noticed and became concerned. "What's wrong, Shanna?"

"There's some thing I have to tell you."

"What is it, Honey?"

"When I was away, I had some help finding Marina from a man. He was married but our searches took many days."

Shanna paused and studied the expression on his face. She dropped her head in shame. "I was lonely and I needed a companion," she continued dejectedly. Tears streamed down her cheek. "I… I made a mistake."

Will was stunned but calm.

"The worst part," she continued, "is that I thought about staying with his family and not coming back." Tears streamed down her cheeks. "I feel so terrible."

"Why would you even think that, Shanna?"

"Marina needs a father figure in her life and I didn't think you wanted to be that figure."

"I'm sorry if I led you to feel that way. I do want to be part of her life."

"Can you forgive me, Will?"

Will stared earnestly into her eyes. "Did you ever stop loving me, Shanna?"

"No. Even if I stayed there, I could never stop loving you."

She nestled her ear against his shoulder.

Now, Will looked down at the floor sadly. "I have something to confess as well."

Shanna became attentive and looked up at him.

"I was unfaithful to you as well. I was so upset and so afraid of being alone." Will wiped the tears from his eyes and nestled Marina against his other shoulder. "Can you forgive me?" he pleaded.

"We both screwed up big time. Can we start over and make things right?"

"Nothing would make me happier. I swear that, no matter what, I'll never betray you again."

"And I swear to you that I'll never leave you nor betray you again, either."

Shanna leaned forward and kissed Will.

Will's monkey, George, raced inside the ship and jumped on top of the couch. He clapped his hands excitedly as he watched them. Marina saw the monkey and clapped as well.

"Who's your friend?" inquired Shanna.

"This is my trainer, George. He convinced me that if I worked out everyday and looked sexy, you would come back to me."

Shanna stroked Will's chest with her hands. "If I knew you looked like this, I would have come back much sooner."

They laughed together.

"I think Marina needs a nap," she suggested.

"George will keep an eye on her for us."

Will went to the closet and brought out a blanket.

"It seems you went all out for your new residence," Shanna remarked as she admired the ship's decor.

"Not really. Tara, Vera and my friend, General Adolfo did it for me."

"Is there a story to Tara and Vera?"

"Not anymore."

"Good. Then you're all mine."

Will set Marina down on the blanket and kissed her. Shanna watched admiringly as Will tucked Marina under the blanket.

"George, keep an eye on her for me," Will ordered.

The monkey gazed at Marina adoringly and nestled down on the blanket. The two soon slept.

Will led Shanna into his cabin and closed the door.

**********

Jack paced back and forth on the *Leviathan.*

Bastille leaned against the wall next to Maya with an amused expression on his face.

Three men sat nearby at the bar. They noticed Jack's anxiety as well.

"It's been three days," complained Jack. "We can't plan anything until they return."

"Relax, Jack," Maya said sternly. "They've been apart for a long time."

"Maybe we should return to Arn's station. Will and Shanna have their own transportation."

"No, we'll wait for them."

"What about Will's friend, Arn?" one of the men called out. "I heard he's got some wicked rum."

"He's also got a video of a certain fight," mentioned Bastille.

"I'd love to see a good fight," the man replied.

"It's Will getting his ass whooped by a Calamaari prince," kidded Maya.

"No way! Will isn't that dumb."

The three men stared curiously at Jack.

"You don't know Will like I do," Jack reminded them. "He still hasn't learned street smarts yet?"

Jack's transmitter beeped. "I wonder who this could be," he said in mock surprise.

"This is Jack," he responded into the transmitter.

"Jack, it's Will. We're coming back."

"Two ships?"

"No, I'm leaving one here in case I need to return later."

"Alright, we'll see you soon."

Jack looked relieved. "They're on the way back."

Maya placed her arm around his waist. "Feel better now?"

"Yes, I do."

**********

Pinta watched the green object on the monitor depart Andros-3. "Now we'll put an end to the nuisance's reign"

She pressed another switch and the monitor zoomed in on the ship. It had only Calamaari markings on it.

"That's not him!" Pinta watched impatiently as only one ship left the planet. She shrieked angrily at a blood-curdling pitch. "Where the hell is he?"

"Maybe he's on board the ship," suggested the guard.

"No, he's too brazen to leave like that. Saris needs an audience whenever he does something."

"We should track the ship and see if it docks on board their mystery ship," suggested the second guard. "If it doesn't, then it will likely return to their station."

Pinta glared at the guard and then at the monitor. "Perhaps this time you have a point."

"Pinta, I think you should see this," said one technician urgently.

Pinta reluctantly approached him, annoyed by his interruption. "What is it?"

The technician slid his seat away from the monitor for her to see. The monitor showed twelve green shapes in the lower right quadrant.

The technician reached for the controls and pressed two buttons. Cameras from probes revealed Weevil battle cruisers in formation.

"Contact Polus now!" bellowed Pinta. "I want to know what his ships are doing in my territory."

The technician promptly hailed the Weevil leader via transmitter.

Both guards had concerned expressions as they waited for orders from Pinta.

"Keep staring and I'll rip those eyes out of your heads," she warned, "unless either of you have something of value to say."

"Do you really think we can trust the Weevil?" inquired one of them.

Pinta removed her pulse pistol from under her robe and pointed it at the guard. "Do you think I really trust you?" She pulled the trigger and fired an energy pulse into the guard's head. Brown matter sprayed across the monitor and the headless corpse fell to the ground.

The second guard was stunned by her actions. He kept his eyes focused on the ground.

The Communications Room grew quiet as the guard and technician were careful to avoid eye contact with her.

"Clean this up, now!" she ordered.

The guard removed the corpse from the room. Two more guards appeared with rags and wiped the blood and brain matter off the floor, wall and console.

Pinta returned to the first monitor and glared at the technician. Again he slid away from the monitor.

Polus' face appeared on the screen. "What is it, Pinta? I'm very busy."

"What are your ships doing in my sector?"

"Merely reconnaissance," he said slyly. "We tracked one of your cruisers from the human's space station to Andros-3 and wondered if this has anything to do with Saris."

"It appears to be a dead end. We hoped that his friends had found him for us."

"And you're sure he's not there?"

"Of course, I'm sure! We're making plans to draw him out and deal with him. Now get your ships out of my sector before I change my mind about this alliance."

Polus chuckled at her through his insect-like mouth. The transmission ended and the monitor went blank.

Pinta punched the monitor in a rage and shattered it. Drops of blood streamed from her clawed hand. She gnashed her teeth in a rage and stormed out of the Communications Room.

# II. Broken Truce

The *Leviathan* returned to Orpheus-2 in cloaked mode, still keeping its presence a secret.

Will and Shanna sat with Marina in the main quarters, surrounded by their friends. Shanna balanced Marina on her left knee and leaned against Will, who sat on her right. She nestled against him with his arm securely around her shoulders.

The main quarters was nearly the size of a large hall with a festive atmosphere. Thanks to several of the crew men, Caribbean music played over the state of the art sound system and lent to a relaxed environment.

Bastille escorted Arn and Severin down the stairs where they joined Will's group. Arn puffed on his traditional cigar that he was never without.

"This is one hell of a ship you have here, Will," declared Arn. "I've never seen anything like her."

"She has some amazing secrets," joked Will.

"Don't all women?"

Everyone laughed with the exception of Severin who remained disinterested as if absorbed in other thoughts.

"It's good to be back. I missed you all," said Will humbly.

"I thought it was my rum that drove you away," kidded Arn.

"No, I was afraid my problems would cause bigger problems. It was better that I left."

Shanna ran her hand along Will's chest and smiled seductively. "By your appearance, I think you handled your problems very well."

"I see some things never change," commented Jack playfully.

Everyone chuckled at Shanna's coy innocence.

"There are some things I need to discuss with all of you, if you don't mind," said Will on a more serious note. "I no longer want to make the decisions here. I've realized there will never be peace in the universe no matter what I do."

"But it's account of you that we're all here today," reminded Bastille.

"I have some personal things to settle with the Weevil and the Calamaari. Once that's done, I think I'd like to stay on my little world with my family and hopefully live happily ever after."

Shanna beamed proudly at Will over his announcement.

"There's always a price for freedom. You just don't walk away," replied Arn somberly. "Trust me, I tried."

"All of you are like family to me. I know you'll do the right thing to preserve peace. If you ever need me, you know I'll be there."

"Sounds like drinks are in order," suggested Bastille.

Everyone cheered and lined up at the bar along the rear wall. Two men took the bar tending responsibilities and served drinks.

Arn sat down across from Will. "There's something we should talk about while we have the opportunity."

"Of course, Arn. What is it?"

"The truce you set up for us with the Calamaari," he replied uneasily. "It's due to expire soon. I don't expect the Calamaari will be anxious to renew without some major concession."

Severin entered the main quarters through the hatch and joined them. She looked about the main quarters at the festive décor with little regard.

"Severin, this is a surprise," said Will pleasantly. "Arn says you have too many responsibilities to spend an evening with friends."

"That's hardly the case. I have priorities I must deal with."

"Speaking of priorities," remarked Arn, "Will and I just started to discuss the treaty and its termination."

"I've been studying the terms of the contract and made some inquiries," explained Severin. "It seems that the success of the truce hinged on the Calamaari Prince returning to his planet in a healthful state."

"Yes, that's about right," answered Will. "I will contact Earth and find out what Goeth's status is. Then I'll speak with Cintilla about the situation."

"I've already spoken with the facility on Earth that is handling Goeth's care."

Will was impressed by Severin's aggressive and ambitious nature.

Arn set his cigar down on the edge of a glass ashtray. "Yes, I almost forgot to tell you. Your friend Goeth is on his way here with a friend of your father's."

"Did they say if the treatment worked?" asked Will. "If not, our truce will be voided and the Calamaari will come with a vengeance."

"They told me that Goeth is just fine."

"I hope you two aren't thinking of beating the crap out of each other again," warned Shanna.

"No, no. Nothing like that. If Xerxes' people healed him, we can be assured of a lasting peace with the Calamaari. Then I can focus on a farewell present for Polus."

"They should be here in a pog or two."

"That's great news, Arn."

"Things have really turned around for us, haven't they, Will?" remarked Shanna.

"Yes they have. Now we have some things to discuss alone."

"I'd like that."

"Will you excuse us, Arn?"

"Of course. We'll talk later."

"Thanks for all your help, Severin."

Severin nodded in response.

Will escorted Shanna and Marina to their cabin.

"You don't like her much, do you, Sev?" asked Arn.

"Why do you say that?"

"Oh, it's not hard to see that you have feelings for Will."

"Doubtful. I do think it's wrong what she did to him."

"Maybe she had no choice."

"Perhaps. I wouldn't worry about it, sir." Severin got up and left the table.

Arn puffed on his cigar and chuckled.

**********

Pinta and the technician returned to the monitor and were surprised to see it clear. The guard at the door joined them.

"So where did that ship go?" demanded Pinta.

"It vanished while we watched the Weevil group on the other monitor."

"How could it just vanish?"

"I wonder if it's their mystery ship," mused the guard.

"There is no mystery ship! They must have returned to the space station. That's where we'll focus our attack."

"But, what if there is such a ship?"

"Then we'll find out just how powerful that ship is, and then we'll destroy it. Is that too much for you cowards?"

The guard looked away nervously.

**********

Inside the flight deck of the *Leviatha*n, Bastille ran a diagnostic test on the controls. Celine operated the sensors and positioned them toward Calamaar. She noticed a large fleet of ships amassing near the shipping lanes.

"It looks like the Calamaari are up to something, Bastille."

Bastille looked at the monitor uneasily. "I don't like the looks of that. Better see if Will or Jack is downstairs."

Celine left the pilots' cabin and hurried down the stairs.

Jack and Darien were in a heated discussion about the rules to a card game.

"Excuse me, boys," Celine said as she sat down between them.

"Something wrong, Celine?" asked Jack.

"A group of Calamaari ships have moved into attack formation near the shipping lanes."

Jack grew concerned. "I'll let Will know and see what he wants to do. Could you find Arn and Severin," he requested. "There's supposed to be a truce."

Celine left them and continued to Will's cabin.

Will and Shanna exited the cabin just as she arrived.

"Celine, I was just coming to see you. Everything alright?" asked Will.

"The Calamaari are up to something! You'd better come see this."

"It's probably nothing."

"No, I think this is something. They are in attack formation near the shipping lanes."

"That makes no sense."

They proceeded down the corridor to the main quarters.

"How long have they been there?" inquired Shanna.

"Not long."

Will activated one of the local control panels and waited as small green shapes formed at the edge of the screen. His face grew taut as he entered several digits into the computer.

"Something's wrong," uttered Will. He transmitted a signal to Calamaar and waited edgily. "They shouldn't be there."

The face of a Calamaari guard appeared on the monitor. "Who is this?" he demanded.

"It's Will Saris. I wish to speak with Cintilla."

"What do you want with her?"

"I wish to know why your ships are encroaching on the shipping lanes since we have a truce."

Pinta shoved the guard out of the way and appeared on the monitor.

"So you've lost your nerve, Saris! I didn't expect you to sneak off of Andros-3 like a thief in the night."

"Don't waste my time. Where's Cintilla?"

"Cintilla is unavailable from now on. I'm in charge and I personally don't like you."

Will muted the transmission. "Celine, tell Bastille to remain cloaked and get us out there in front of the Calamaari fleet in a hurry. Contact Arn and tell him the truce is off."

"What are you going to do?"

"Transport down to Andros-3. I have some business to tend to."

Celine returned to the pilots' cabin.

"I'm going, too," Shanna said firmly as if expecting resistance.

"Of course you are. I wouldn't have it any other way."

Will removed the mute from the transmission. "Why have you broken the truce, Pinta?"

"I haven't broken it yet, have I?"

Will laughed at her ignorance. "You aren't very smart, are you, Pinta?"

"Perhaps you are the one who isn't so smart. I suggest you turn yourself in at once or the consequences will be grave for your peers."

"Now Pinta, we both know it doesn't work that way. However, I'll play your little game for the sake of entertainment."

"Saris, you're a dead man! I'm tired of your games."

"And I am so tired of hearing that." Will replied wryly and terminated the transmission.

Shanna cracked a smile at him.

"What?" asked Will innocently.

"Some things will never change."

"No they won't. The universe is full of assholes like Pinta, Polus, Thorus, and the rest of the alliance of stupid creatures."

"What's the plan?"

"We're going to pay her a little visit. She wants me to come by, so I think I should accommodate her."

"Since we're going into battle, why don't we dress for the occasion, just like the good old days?" suggested Shanna.

"I think that's a very good idea."

**********

The *Leviathan* cruised toward Andros-3 in cloaked mode. Calamaari cruisers continued to amass near the shipping lanes, oblivious to its passage right in front of them.

Will instructed Bastille and Celine to stand by until the Calamaari came within range.

Three man-o-wars took a defensive position near Orpheus-2 as fifty Calamaari cruisers approached in a pyramid formation. *The Widow Maker* remained docked as her crew returned from the station.

Will and Shanna transported to the planet's surface and boarded the *Reaper*.

Celine and Bastille waited patiently at the *Leviathan's* controls for the alien fleet to draw close then opened fire with the ship's automated firing system. The man-o-wars, as if on cue, opened fire as well. After a short battle, thirty one cruisers were destroyed and seven crippled. The remaining twelve fled the area.

One of the man-o-wars sustained serious damage and returned to the station for repairs.

The other two man-o-wars destroyed the crippled ships one by one with a series of well placed torpedoes to the reactor core of each ship.

The *Leviathan* returned to 'cloaked' mode and waited for additional instructions from Will.

**********

Will and Shanna took their seats in the pilots' cabin of the *Reaper*. Will wore a sleeveless leather vest, black pants, and boots. The vest was open, half-way down his chest. Attached to his side was his sword and scabbard.

Shanna donned her black leather outfit with leather belts and knives strapped to her thighs. The black vest and tight pants accentuated her stunning figure. They each had a pulse pistol strapped to their waists.

Will gazed at Shanna until he caught her attention.

"What's wrong?" she asked suspiciously.

"I really missed you." He took her in his arms and kissed her.

"Wow!" said Shanna weakly. "That was awesome."

"Now, let's kick some Calamaari ass!"

Will powered up the ship's control systems while Shanna checked the armament system and inventory.

George rushed into the cabin and climbed onto Will's lap. Will scratched the monkey's head and set him on the floor.

"Why do you do that to the monkey?" asked Shanna curiously.

"For good luck."

"How about me?"

Will looked down at the monkey. "Sorry, George, she's got a point."

The monkey lowered its head dejectedly.

Shanna felt guilty and picked George up. She hugged him and set him on her shoulder. "You can be my good luck charm."

The monkey clapped its hands.

Will navigated the *Reaper* along the valley floor for a short distance and then darted up into the sky.

Shanna eyed Will and chuckled.

"What's that look for?" he asked curiously.

"I can't believe I was replaced by a monkey!"

"This isn't just any monkey. This is George."

The monkey affectionately nestled against her and she gently stroked his fur.

"I see you trained him to be a ladies' man, just like you."

"No way! George is his own man, I mean monkey."

Will watched twelve green shapes fleeing the battle area on the monitor.

Shanna also noticed and looked pleased. "They didn't leave much for us, did they?"

"Let's see if we can provide Pinta with the extra attention she deserves."

The *Reaper* raced after the twelve Calamaari cruisers.

"Aren't we at a disadvantage, numbers-wise?" inquired Shanna.

"That is our advantage – we are one of their cruisers."

Will entered several digits into the computer and transmitted. Pinta's angry face appeared on the monitor and startled him. "Damn, Pinta, you really ought to do something about those teeth of yours. You really scared me."

"I know where you are, Saris. You won't get away this time."

"Relax, Pinta. I'm coming in to drop off a little present from my friends on the man-o-wars. They appreciated the turkeys you sent us."

Pinta became enraged. Thick, white saliva drooled from her mouth as her face appeared to be pressed against the monitor. Will felt a brief instant of fear as he saw the hatred in her eyes. When she backed away from the monitor, Will regained his wit.

"Be patient, Pinta. We'll have our time together," he taunted as he terminated the transmission.

Shanna laughed hysterically at him. "Will, you are a mess!"

"Now wait until you see what I have planned for my Calamaari hottie," he joked.

"If she ever gets her claws on you, you are so screwed."

"Nah, she's not my type."

The *Reaper* closed on the twelve cruisers and soon passed between the ships. Will guided his cruiser into the rear of the formation as if he were one of them.

"I don't believe it!" exclaimed Shanna. "They have no idea we're here."

"That's the plan."

"This is almost too easy." Shanna reached over and stroked his cheek with her hand. "You amaze me."

"What's that for?" asked Will.

"I'm so happy that you included me in your plans. I didn't have to say anything to you about it."

"I've really changed a lot, Shanna. I think I'm a better person than I was before."

"You can say that again," she replied seductively.

Will's expression turned to one of disappointment. "No, I mean inside. I've matured."

"I think you've matured quite a bit, but so have I."

"I noticed. You have one hell of a figure and that long blond hair drives me wild."

"When I saw you that first time on Andros-3, I could hardly control myself."

"So, you think I'm sexy, huh?"

"Oh, incredibly."

"After we finish up here, I'll have to talk to Arn about a honeymoon suite."

Shanna unbuckled her belt and stood up. She took George off her shoulder and set him in the co-pilots' seat.

"What are you doing?"

Shanna climbed onto Will's lap and straddled him. "This will do just fine."

Will watched the monitor as Shanna kissed his neck. He felt his legs grow weak as he became hot for her.

Suddenly, Calaamar came into view and ruined the moment. Will reluctantly pushed Shanna away. "It's show time, Honey."

"Just wait until later. There's gonna' be fireworks on Orpheus-2 tonight," she said giddily as she got up and removed the monkey from her seat.

Will tilted his head back for a brief moment and sighed.

Shanna activated the short-range sensors and selected the monitor above the controls.

The Calamaari palace and fortress came into view. As they drew closer, large bay doors opened for the cruisers to enter. They formed a single line and eased inside the large bay, one by one. The *Reaper* dropped in behind the last cruiser.

"You know, Will, your girl is gonna' be waiting for you down there," teased Shanna.

"I know."

"What are you going to tell her when you see her?"

"I don't know. How about 'I'm sorry, Pinta, but things just aren't working out between us'?"

Shanna laughed, much to Will's delight. It felt so good to see her happy with him.

"I love your sense of humor," she remarked. "When did you get it?"

"I always had a sense of humor," he replied defensively.

"Not like this, you didn't."

Will brought the ship to a halt in the last berth of the bay. The outside cameras on his ship showed a large power supply enclosed at the end of the bay. He positioned the ship facing it.

"Program the armament control system for 'pairs' and a quantity of 'three'. Give me a lock on the power supply, the lift at the right corner of the bay and the tanks in the ceiling."

Shanna followed his instructions as Will scanned the structure.

"If I was going to guess, she's in the control center," he suggested. "Let's pay her a visit."

Shanna followed Will out of the ship. They drew their pulse pistols and crept along the wall behind the other cruisers.

Several Calamaari soldiers exited the ships and approached a hatch at the end of the bay. They chirped angrily back and forth at each other.

"Any idea what they're saying, Will?"

"No, but I think they're quite upset about the outcome of the battle."

They stayed close to the wall behind the ships and approached the hatch.

"Ready, Honey?" asked Will.

"Of course, I'm ready. Just like old times."

They ascended the stairs at the end of the hall and turned the corner. Ahead of them was the pilots' briefing room. It was filled with the angry pilots of the cruisers. Quickly, they ducked behind the wall.

They inched down the hall in the other direction and stopped in front of the Communications Center. Will glanced inside and saw four technicians in front of a series of monitors along the wall. They were staring at one of the monitors in particular.

Will glanced again and noticed that they were looking at the *Reaper* through a camera in the bay.

Will nodded to Shanna. They burst in through the door and drew their pulse pistols. Before the technicians could react, Will and Shanna fired several blasts of energy into them.

One of the wounded technicians reached for an alarm on the console. Shanna drew one of her knives form her thigh belt and fired it at the technicians hand, pinning it to the console. The blade of the knife passed through the clawed hand and into a small display. An electrical charge passed through the knife and into the technician. He moaned from the pain.

Will looked very annoyed over the sounds.

Shanna shrugged her shoulders at him and fired the pistol at the injured Calamaari's head.

The energy burst left a smoldering hole in his head. The confused expression on his face looked almost comical to Will.

Will fired a shot into the monitor that showed his ship and exited the room.

Shanna retrieved her knife and made sure the technicians were dead. Contented that they were, she followed after Will.

The sound of footsteps came from another hall. They ducked inside another room and waited for the Calamaari to pass.

As Will turned around, two pistols were pointed at their faces. It was a Calamaari Commander.

"Who are you?" he asked quietly.

"Does it matter?" replied Will.

The Commander's finger twitched on the trigger of the pistol by Shanna's face.

"He's Will Saris," blurted Shanna immediately.

Will glared at her.

"He was gonna' shoot me, not you, Will."

"Is this true?" asked the Commander.

"Yes, it is. What happened to Cintilla?"

"She isn't here anymore. That's all I can tell you."

"Is she dead?"

"Why do you care?"

"Because her son Goeth will want to know."

"Goeth lives?"

"Yes he does. He is traveling from a planet called Earth as we speak."

The Commander looked surprised. He seemed unsure of what to do.

"Look, we didn't come her to wage war with the Calamaari," explained Will. "We came here to take down Pinta."

"Not today. You must go now."

The commander lowered his pistols and backed away.

Shanna stared at the Commander and probed his thoughts.

Will peeked into the hallway. There was no sign of the pilots. "Come on, Shanna."

Shanna glanced back at the Commander. "Thank you."

He nodded and turned away.

Down another hall was a ramp up to the Command Center.

Ten Calamaari guards approached from the opposite direction. Will and Shanna ducked under the ramp. It was a tight squeeze but they managed to slide against the rear wall under the ramp.

Will was in the back and Shanna in front of him. He felt uneasy as the tight space and darkness bothered him. As Shanna peered out, she felt Will against her from behind. "Will, are you getting excited?" she whispered.

"Why the hell would you ask me that? I think I'm claustrophobic."

"It doesn't feel like it."

Will realized that despite his fears, it felt good to have physical contact with Shanna.

She slid out from under the ramp and helped Will to his feet. She had a sly grin on her face and glanced at him.

Will became annoyed and ascended the ramp. He paused at the top and focused his telepathy through the door at the entrance to the Command Center.

"I think she's in here," said Will. "She's not alone."

"I'll cover you from down here."

Will peeked through a diamond-shaped glass pane.

Shanna thought she heard a noise from around the corner and ducked into a dark office opposite the ramp. She warned Will telepathically and told him to stay still.

Two Calamaari guards approached him from behind.

"Don't move or you're dead," ordered one of them.

"No problem, boys," replied Will.

Shanna crept up behind one of them and held her pistol to the back of his head.

"Let's try this again. Don't you move or you're dead," she warned.

Will ducked as the other fired his pulse pistol at him. He flattened against the wall to evade the searing red burst of energy. Instinctively, he fired and struck the soldier in the neck, killing him instantly.

Will approached Shanna's captive and placed his pistol to the prisoner's face. He pressed an interpreting device on the alien's neck. "Do you want to live?"

"What do you want from me?" the Calamaari asked.

"Where's Cintilla?"

"I don't know."

Will raised his pistol to the alien's forehead. "Once more; where's Cintilla?"

"Pinta's taken over as leader and Cintilla was sent away. That's all I can tell you," answered the Calamaari nervously.

Pinta exited the Command Center with four guards.

"Well, Saris, I never expected you to surrender like this without a fight."

"Sorry, Pinta, but that's not why I'm here."

"It's time for you to die," she announced as she drew her pulse pistol.

Shanna aimed her pistol at Pinta's head. "Blink and you're dead."

"What have you done with Cintilla?" inquired Will.

"She is no longer in charge. In fact, she is banished someplace where she'll never interfere again."

"Correct me if I'm wrong, Pinta, but doesn't that make Goeth the next in line to succeed her?"

"Goeth is dead. You killed him, Saris, and that makes me the next in line to rule."

"Ah, but Goeth is not dead. He's returning soon and I'm sure he won't be happy with you."

The guards looked surprised. One asked, "Is this true, Pinta?"

Pinta became enraged. She rushed at Will, screaming like a banshee. Saliva dripped from her lower lip as she raised her claws to seize Will by the neck.

Shanna shoved her prisoner aside and retrieved one of her knives from the leather belt on her thigh. She fired the knife and struck Pinta in the shoulder. Pinta stumbled to the ground.

Shanna then fired her pistol at the four guards, forcing them to retreat inside the Command Center. They were lackluster about rejoining the battle and fled through a rear access in the control room.

Pinta fired a shot that glanced off Shanna's shoulder and struck the wall. She fell to the floor and clutched at her shoulder.

Will took aim with his pistol at Pinta's head but she kicked his legs out from under him and knocked him to the ground. She yanked the knife from her shoulder and raised it to strike Will.

At that moment, Shanna struggled to her feet and fired a shot at Pinta, searing her left ear off.

Instinctively, Pinta hurled the knife at Shanna. The knife embedded itself in Shanna's leg. Shanna fell to the ground in pain.

"Shanna!" cried Will.

Will fired a shot at Pinta and struck her arm near the shoulder. It hung, shredded and limp, by her side. She retreated up the ramp and paused at the Command Center door. "Your suffering has just begun, Saris!" She ducked inside the doorway.

Will fired again and struck her back side as the door closed behind her. He hurried to Shanna's aid while their prisoner stood by nervously.

"How bad is it?" he asked as he knelt by her side.

Shanna removed the knife from her thigh and placed it back in the belt.

"I'm okay. Let's get him back to the ship quickly for the inquisition."

"Turn around and walk," Will ordered the Calamaari.

Will placed one arm around Shanna's waist while keeping the pistol trained on the prisoner with the other hand. They escorted their prisoner back to the bay and onto their ship.

"What will you do with me?" asked the Calamaari.

"It depends on how cooperative you are."

Will opened the spare cabin door and shoved the Calamaari inside.

"You know she's letting you leave," the guard remarked. "It's part of her plan."

"I doubt it. She's licking her wounds right about now."

"You have no idea what she's done to you already."

"Do I look concerned?"

"You should be."

The Calamaari snarled and lunged at the door as it closed. Will pressed the red button on the door which locked it. The prisoner pounded relentlessly on it.

Will was pleased with the results and returned to the pilots' cabin.

"Light 'em up, Shanna."

George jumped up and down frantically.

"What's wrong with the monkey?" she asked.

"Oh, he likes to do the honors."

"Go ahead, George," said Shanna.

The monkey jumped on her lap and slapped the 'fire' button. Six fireballs of energy darted from the ship.

The first pair struck the power supply. The four sides blew out as the chemical composition exploded. Molten sodium splattered the walls and ships. Four nearby cruisers were damaged from the blast.

The second pair struck the lift for moving the cruisers into the hangar above. The resulting explosion took out six more cruisers.

The third pair struck the tanks mounted across the ceiling of the bay and knocked out a large section of the wall. The ceiling crumbled on five of the cruisers, leaving them heavily damaged.

The monkey high-fived the two of them excitedly. Shanna gave George a friendly hug and set him on the floor.

Will hurriedly piloted the ship toward the opening. "Boy, we're a hell of a team, aren't we?"

"Yes, we are," said Shanna proudly as she gazed at him admiringly.

Shanna programmed two more torpedoes and fired. The bursts of energy struck the bay doors and blew a gaping hole in them. Will guided the ship out of the bay and away from the palace. Soon after, the transmitter beeped, much to his delight.

"That must be Pinta,' quipped Shanna. "I'll bet she wants to kiss and make up."

Will pressed the 'receive' button and eyed the monitor.

Pinta's face appeared, looking more frightening than ever. She struggled to control her rage as she tried to speak.

"I should have killed you when I had the chance," she uttered.

"But you didn't. I'm sorry if I left such a mess but I was in a hurry."

"It seems I left a little present for you, Saris. Now we'll see how love can hurt!"

"Pinta, why would you say that?"

"I promise you, every day you'll see more of me in your life, no matter where you go."

Will was confused by her remarks. "Believe me, with a face like yours, I could never forget you."

Pinta glared defiantly at him. "And now for another surprise; we've signed a truce with the Weevil, Saris. I'm going to make your life a living hell."

Will was shocked by her revelation.

"I've never seen you at a loss for words before. What's wrong?" she asked mockingly. Pinta sat back and cackled at him.

"Well, since we made a mess of your fleet, Pinta, I guess you have no choice but to turn to the Weevil for help. I'd say that makes you – incompetent. You and Polus make a cute couple, just don't bear his offspring."

Pinta snarled and rammed the monitor three times with her head.

"I'll make sure I take you apart piece by piece while you live and I'll savor every piece of flesh as I swallow it. You'll beg for me to kill you."

Will terminated the transmission and looked down sullenly.

"What do you think, Will? Is she serious?"

"I hope she didn't hurt herself," he said somberly.

Shanna wasn't sure what to say until Will burst into laughter.

"Will, this is serious!"

"I know, but it's great! She is really pissed."

Will reached behind the seat for a first aid kit. He removed a bandage, a syringe and two small vials.

Shanna placed her leg up on Will's lap. She grimaced as he cleaned the wound off. He noticed a discoloration of the skin and became concerned.

"It looks like infection's setting in already. I don't like this."

"It'll be fine, Will. Don't worry so much."

Will looked unconvinced and gave her the first shot in her thigh.

"We'd better get this looked at by our medical girls when we get back."

"Come on, Will. It's only a knife wound."

Will set the cruiser on 'autopilot' and lifted Shanna in his arms.

"You are going to lie down and rest, my dear."

"But Will…"

Will took her into his cabin and set her on the bed. He kissed her forehead and then inspected her shoulder wound.

"Lucky for you, this one's just a flesh wound."

"Lucky! I think I dodged it pretty well, considering three of those guards were firing at me at one time."

"Yeah, but three years ago, you'd have dodged all of them."

"Shut up, Saris, before I kick your ass."

Will bandaged the wound and gave her the second injection.

"Did you happen to notice that most of the Calamaari we encountered weren't very enthusiastic about supporting Pinta?"

Will pondered briefly. "You have a point there. Get some rest while I fly us back."

Shanna reluctantly gave in and rested.

# Chapter Three

## Goeth's Return

The *Reaper* landed inside the *Leviathan's* large docking bay. The large doors closed and the pressure equalized inside. Air and coolant lines automatically extended to the ship from the platform and attached to ports on the ship's hull.

Jack and Maya waited by the hatch. Both of them were irate. As soon as the secondary power was turned on, Jack opened the hatch.

Will embraced Shanna as Jack and Maya stormed inside.

"What the hell were you two thinking?" Jack demanded.

"What's wrong, Jack," replied Will cluelessly. "Everything went well."

"Of course," chided Maya. "It always goes well, doesn't it?"

"Why are the two of you so upset?" asked Shanna.

"Because this was one of the stupidest acts I've ever seen either of you do," Jack chastised. "What did you think you were going to prove?"

"We spent so much time trying to find the two of you and you try and get yourselves killed like this!"

"Calm down, Maya."

"No, you calm down, Will. We've about had it with babysitting the two of you. Maybe one day when you both grow up, we'll talk."

Jack and Maya exited the ship.

"Wow!" remarked Will. "They're really steamed."

"Maybe we did push it a little bit."

As Will and Shanna exited the ship's hatch, Arn and Severin strutted toward them.

"You're boys on the man-o-wars did well, Arn," praised Will.

Arn shook Will's hand and passed him a cigar. "This is for the victory. Enjoy it because we have bigger problems looming."

"And that is?"

Arn deferred to Severin who stepped forward to speak. Will always found her attractive in a strange sort of way, but she was always so melancholic.

"The Weevil are amassing a large force in sector seven," she informed Will.

"How large?"

"Five battle groups."

Will pondered for a moment as he lit his cigar. "That means about three hundred fighters. We can handle them between the *Leviathan* and the man-o-wars." He calmly puffed on the cigar. "The battlestars could be a problem if they try to engage."

"That's not all. The Calamaari moved a large force in sector five. That leaves us in sector ten right in the middle."

"Oh," uttered Will uneasily. "Now we have a problem."

"How big is the Calamaari force?" inquired Shanna.

"About one hundred cruisers like yours."

"Can we handle all of them, Will?"

"Now I think we're pushing it."

"I say we go after the Calamaari first and do as much damage as possible," suggested Arn.

"No, that would leave the station defenseless," answered Severin.

"If all those ships attacked the station right now, we're done anyway."

"Then I'd better get busy," suggested Will.

"What do you want us do, Will?" Arn inquired.

Will paused and looked back. "How about joining us in an hour with some of that rum of yours?"

Arn and Severyn glanced at each other uneasily.

"Are you sure about this?"

"Of course, I am. Have I ever let you down?"

"Not yet."

"Then get the rum."

Will and Shanna returned to the *Reaper*.

Arn and Severyn were stymied as they wondered what Will was up to.

**********

Inside the *Reaper*, Shanna sat on the couch alone. The sound of soft music filled the main quarters.

Will entered from the pilot's cabin with a sly grin on his face. He removed his shirt and threw it on the floor.

Shanna gazed at him curiously. "What are you up to, Will Saris?"

Will sat down on the couch and gently kissed her neck, chin and lips.

Shanna eagerly unbuttoned her leather vest and pulled Will toward her. They kissed passionately until the song ended.

"I needed to feel you close to me," explained Will.

"Why do you cloak your thoughts from me? I had no idea."

"It's more spontaneous that way," he replied coyly.

Will slowly undressed Shanna and lay her across the couch. He noticed a rash on her thigh around the bandaged area.

"Shanna, we need to get this looked at."

"I'll be fine."

"Shanna."

"Stop it Will. I'll be fine."

They were interrupted by the beep of the transmitter.

"Alright, already," said Will disappointedly.

Will got off the couch and pressed the 'receive' button on the wall. "Go ahead. This is Will."

"Will, it's Arn. Your guest will be here shortly."

"Excellent. We'll be ready."

Will returned to the couch and sat next to Shanna. "I guess we have to get back to work, Honey. We'll talk about this later."

"What about our prisoner?"

"Oh, him. I think Goeth will help us extract information from him. I'm sure he'll want to know all about what happened to his mother."

"This isn't fair, Will. I mean this whole thing with the Weevil and the Calamaari. Why does it have to be us?"

"I guess fate dealt us a lousy hand."

"Let's take it to them hard," she said sternly. "The sooner we end this, the sooner we can have a normal life."

Shanna went into the cabin and donned a mid-length, black leather skirt with a matching tank top.

Will put his shirt back on and opened the hatch. When Shanna reappeared from the cabin, he smiled approvingly.

Arn peered inside the ship and held a bottle of his home-made rum in the air. "Knock, knock," he said politely.

"Come on in," replied Will nonchalantly.

Arn and Severin boarded the *Reaper*.

Arn handed the bottle to Shanna. "I suggest you take charge of the bottle, Honey. You heard what happened to Will last time."

"I'm taking charge of more than the bottle, Arn."

Shanna went to the bar and poured the rum into four glasses. She returned and handed one to each of them.

"Shanna, you're drinking, too?" asked Will.

She raised her glass in the air for a toast. "Yes, I am. What shall we toast to?"

"Extraordinary times call for extraordinary measures," he replied. "Death to Polus and Pinta."

Will, Arn, Shanna and Severyn tapped their glasses together.

"Death to Polus and Pinta," they chanted in unison.

Shanna chugged her shot first, followed by the others. They banged their glass on the table.

"We're taking the battle to them and we're doing it now," she declared.

Severin was impressed with Shanna's fire. "How do you propose to do so?"

Shanna glanced at Will.

"We had a truce and the Calamaari broke it," he answered callously. "They have a truce with the Weevil. I propose we break it."

"The two races are sworn enemies," replied Arn. "It's hard to believe they've united just to get you out of the way."

Will stood up and paced the floor. "What ulterior motive could either have for this unholy alliance?"

"Perhaps each is hoping to ambush the other," suggested Severin, "In a moment of weakness, of course."

"No, that's too obvious. There must be something else."

"Could there be another player out there?" Shanna asked Severin.

"Possibly."

"I say we board a Calamaari ship and coerce the information from the crew," suggested Arn. "Maybe apply some techniques of torture."

"We've already thought of that," replied Shanna.

A gray-haired, bearded man entered the ship accompanied by a Calamaari male.

"Excuse me, I'm looking for Will Saris," he said humbly.

The Calamaari politely pushed him aside and stepped toward Will. "Saris, you little runt!"

Will was thrilled to see the Calamaari prince. "Goethe! It's good to see you."

Will approached him and shook his clawed hand.

"I see you're walking. That's great."

"You kept your word and your people treated me very well."

"I knew they would. Come sit down."

Goeth sat down next to Arn, who fidgeted nervously.

The bearded man stood in front of Will and studied him.

"I don't believe we've met," said Will curiously.

The man shook Will's hand. "I am Tera's brother, Prax, which kind of makes me your uncle. I flew many missions with your father."

"Really!"

"Yes. I'm so sorry about their fates."

"Thank you. It was a shock the way it happened."

Prax placed a hand on Will's shoulder. "You look so much like your mother."

He glanced over at Shanna and beamed. "I see you've taken a liking to Tera's attire. It is a bit unique."

"It's a pleasure to meet you, Prax," she replied and shook his hand.

"Welcome aboard," said Will. "Please, sit down with us."

Prax sat down next to Shanna.

"Goeth, have you been in touch with your people yet?" asked Will anxiously.

"Not yet. I was hoping you'd return with me so my mother can thank you properly."

"Well, there's a little problem with that."

Goeth sensed the somberness in his tone and grew concerned.

"The truce has been broken," explained Will. "Pinta has taken over the Calamaari forces. She has led your people to believe that you were killed by me, thus making her the legitimate successor."

"That can't be! What of my mother?"

"I have no information. Worse, Pinta has joined forces with the Weevil."

"We must put a stop to this. My mother is in danger and my people are at risk."

"Do you have any idea why the Weevil and Calamaari would join forces? I hate to think that it's all account of me."

"There must be something far greater than you to forge such a vile alliance. I must return to Calamaar and find out."

"I have a better idea. Follow me."

Will led Goeth down the hall to the locked spare cabin. He pressed the red light and the door slid open. The Calamaari prisoner lunged out at him but Goeth stepped between them. He grabbed the prisoner by the shoulders and raised him off the ground. The two exchanged several words in their dialect before speaking in Will's language.

Goeth set the Calamaari down and placed a hand on his shoulder.

"This is Drun," explained Goeth. "He was close to my father in his younger days."

"I was hoping he could provide some answers for us," replied Will.

"We shall see."

They escorted Drun to the main quarters.

Arn, Severyn and Prax were stunned to see the second Calamaari with Will.

"I told you we had it covered," Shanna chided Arn.

"Well, I'll be." Arn poured another glass of rum and chugged it.

"My mother is imprisoned in a pit in the mining regions of Calamaar according to Drun," explained Goeth.

"How did all this come about?" inquired Will.

"Both races want you gone. You and your mystery ship are a big problem for everyone," added Drun.

"Will does have that effect on people," kidded Shanna.

It is believed that your people have a doomsday weapon as well and intend to annihilate both races with it."

"That's impossible!" exclaimed Will. "I would have known about it if there was."

"And you have a bigger problem, young lady," added Goeth.

"And that is…"

"Let me see your leg."

Shanna looked nervously at Will and stood up. She extended her leg and placed her foot on the chair. When she lifted her black mid-length skirt, there was a large green rash around a small square bandage.

Drun removed the bandage and inspected the wound. "You've been infected with Pinta's blood. It was on the knife she wounded you with."

"We have vaccines for this kind of stuff," she replied.

"Not for this you don't."

"What will happen to her?" asked Will uneasily.

"She will mutate until she resembles something of a Calamaari. It will be a painful transformation and, in your words, an ugly one."

"That's a lie!" cried Shanna.

"I wish it were," replied Goeth. "I'm sorry."

"How fast does this transformation take?" inquired Will somberly.

"It's hard to say. I'm not familiar with your species and I've never seen the end result."

"I don't believe any of this!" Shanna shouted and rushed away to their cabin.

"Do you have any suggestions, Goeth?" asked Will.

"No, and I've never seen the process reversed."

"Damn, this can't be happening!" Will stormed from the room, visibly upset.

**********

Shanna lay on the bed face down, sobbing like a child. She never imagined that something as simple as a knife wound could lead to circumstances so catastrophic.

Will entered the cabin and stood in front of her. "Let me see your leg."

"Leave me alone."

Will grabbed Shanna by her hips and rolled her over. The rash spread down to her knee and up to her hip.

"This can't be happening, Will. Please tell me it's not."

"The Calamaari don't have any reason to lie about this."

Shanna sat up on the edge of the bed. Her face was streaked with tears. "Do you remember what Pinta said about seeing more of her in your life every day?" she asked.

"She didn't mean anything by it."

"Damn it, Will. Can't you take anything seriously?"

"I'll think of something. Just give me some time."

"Maybe Jack and Maya were right."

"Well, guess what? Everyone's an expert after the fact," responded Will angrily. "We did what we thought was best at the time."

"What about the Calamaari and Weevil? What do we do about them?"

"We're between a rock and a hard place," Will answered sadly. "I don't think we can overcome these odds."

Shanna grew uneasy. She was used to Will's self-confidence and reassuring words. "Meaning what?" she asked.

"Meaning there might be only one way to save you, Marina and everyone else."

"You're scaring me!" she uttered tearfully.

"I'm scaring me. Both Polus and Pinta want me. Perhaps I can make a deal to turn myself over to them if they give you a cure."

Shanna slapped his face and glared at him. "You will do no such thing! You know neither of them can be trusted."

"Then we'll have to go to extraordinary means to stop them."

Shanna looked down at the floor sadly. After finally reuniting their family, fate is ready to destroy them once again.

"I'm sorry, Shanna. I didn't want it this way."

Shanna took the knives from the belt on each thigh and angrily threw them at the wall. Tears streamed down her cheeks.

"You always have an answer for every problem they throw at us! Think of something, Will!"

"I'm out of answers," replied Will dejectedly.

"Then I'll think of some. We're not giving up."

"Shanna, there's no place to run."

"Then, damn it, we're not going to run. Let's take them all down, once and for all."

**********

Arn and Severin waited patiently in the saloon on the space station. Arn puffed on his cigar while Severin carved in the wooden table with a knife.

"Don't do that to the furniture, Severin."

"We're trapped here like rats, General."

"I know, Dear."

Goeth and Drun entered the saloon with Jack and Maya. They pulled up chairs and sat at Arn's table.

"Any suggestions, Severyn?" asked Jack.

"We can't outgun all of them, even with the man-o-wars and *Leviathan.* I don't know what else we can do."

"If we only knew what pulled those two alien races together, then we could figure out a way to split them apart," said Arn pessimistically.

"What about abandoning the station and fleeing the sector?" suggested Maya.

"We'd have to take on either the Calamaari or the Weevil."

"Not if we made it back to Yord."

"Maya, no disrespect but you do realize the Weevil already tracked you to Yord once," reminded Severin.

Goeth and Drun silently took in the conversation.

"I know but if we could shut down their portal system, then we could cut off their reinforcements and their supplies."

"And you have a plan for that?"

"Not yet. We've been trying for some time to solve that."

"And what makes you such an expert on portals, Maya?" inquired Severin.

"For your information, Bastille is our expert on portals."

"And where is Bastille?"

"He's working on something very important."

Will and Shanna marched into the saloon and approached the table. Everyone became uncomfortably silent.

"Stop the pity party, everyone. I'm not dead," complained Shanna.

"Shanna gave me an idea," announced Will.

"It'd better be a good one," replied Arn as he puffed on his cigar.

"Before you go further," interjected Drun," I think you need to remember what I told you before, Will."

"And that is…"

"Your people have a weapon that is capable of annihilating an entire sector through black hole technology."

"I'm telling you, Drun, I don't know anything about this weapon."

"Well somebody does. This is the very reason for the union between the Calamaari and the Weevil."

"Perhaps Prax can help us with that," suggested Severin. "I'm sure he can contact Xerxes about this."

"Good idea," replied Will. "Goeth, I need you and Drun to board the Calamaari command ship. Once on board, find some loyalists to support you in taking over command. Can you do that?"

"I'm sure we can," replied Goeth. "I have many friends on that command ship.

"We got the impression that the guards and pilots aren't very supportive of Pinta," added Shanna.

"What do we hope to accomplish by doing so?" inquired Drun.

"You'll need to find what defenses we need to overcome on Calamaar so we can rescue your mother."

"Once I understand the circumstances, I will rescue her myself," Goeth declared.

"Your people need to know the truth. That'll never happen if you get killed."

"Then I will wait for further instructions once we have secured the ship."

"Arn, we need to meet with the commanders of the man-o-wars when I return."

"That can be arranged." Arn stood up and walked to the bar. He placed a call through his transmitter.

"Where is Prax, Maya?" asked Will. "Maybe he should be here, too."

"He's onboard the *Leviathan*."

Prax entered the saloon. "No, I'm not."

"Prax, I need you to contact Xerxes about a doomsday weapon that the aliens think we have. Then I need you to find out if his nano-plasma generator can help Shanna."

"Funny you should mention that. I have Xerxes' nano-machine on board my ship."

That's fantastic!" exclaimed Will. "But why do you have it?"

"Xerxes wanted that and several other critical technologies moved off of Earth. They've established a one world government that is taking control of everything. He felt that it would be better served with you."

"Why didn't he come with you?"

"He, uh, is missing."

"What?"

"No one knows when or where."

"Son of a bitch! I hope he's alright."

"Can we access the nanoplasma generator?" asked Shanna anxiously.

"It's gonna' take some time to set up and make operable," explained Prax. "I'll do my best for you."

"Why don't we move it into the space station?" suggested Arn. "I'll have my men set you up with whatever you need in the clinic."

"Works for me. Let's get moving!" Prax urged them and hurried out of the saloon.

"Severyn, get him whatever he needs," ordered Arn.

"Goeth, what do you need from me?" requested Will.

"A ship."

"Take the cruiser in the cargo bay of *Leviathan*."

Goeth and Drun paused at the door. "We won't fail, that I can assure you," Goeth stated confidently.

"None of us will fail. Good luck."

Goeth and Drun exited the saloon.

"Alright, everyone, we have work to do," announced Will.

"What do you need from us?" asked Arn.

"Keep your defenses on high alert. I'm going to create a little tension between our friends."

Will and Shanna left the saloon.

"Once we figure out what Will is doing, we'll be in touch, General," Maya assured.

"That's if Will knows what he's doing," replied Arn. "He's got a lot on his plate, especially with Shanna's injury. We have a lot at stake here as well."

As Maya and Jack left the saloon, Arn shook his head dejectedly and puffed on his cigar. "What a strange bunch."

**********

On board *Leviathan*, Shanna grabbed Will by the shoulder and spun him around to face her. "Do you want to tell me what we're doing and stop the games?"

"We're buying time," answered Will. "We have to hope that Prax can get the nanoplasma generator up and running before your condition gets worse."

"If we don't make it, then my condition really doesn't matter, does it?"

"You don't think we can pull this off?"

"Face it, Will, we're screwed again."

"Hey, you're the one who wants to go after them with a vengeance."

"To put an end to all this."

Will grew frustrated and toggled the intercom switch. "Celine. Bastille. Either of you on the flight deck?"

"We're both here," replied Celine. "We're running diagnostics on the ship's cloaking system."

"Forget about that. Get me back to Andros-3, pronto."

Jack and Maya boarded the ship. Jack grabbed Will by the arm and looked grimly at him. "Will, you have to stop doing this secret squirrel crap."

"You don't understand, Jack."

"Yes, I do. We've gone through hell while the two of you were gone. You owe us a little understanding."

"What's going on?" asked Maya.

Will glanced at Shanna and back to Maya. "I have to deliver something to Polus. I don't want him to feel forgotten."

"So where do we come in?" inquired Maya.

The transmitter beeped and distracted them.

"What now?" groaned Will. He approached the console and pressed the 'receive' button.

Arn's face appeared on the monitor. "Will we're taking fire from all over the place!"

"From who?"

"The Weevil. They must have come through a portal. Seems like the Calamaari are sitting back for now."

"I'll see what I can do."

Goeth and Drun barged in, looking distraught.

"We had to turn back. The cannon fire was too intense," said Goeth frustratedly.

"We going out there, all of us," ordered Will.

Goeth and Drun looked shocked.

"It's suicide out there!" exclaimed Goeth.

"Then stay here. I'm going."

Shanna followed Will out the quarters.

Goeth and Drun glanced at each other uneasily and reluctantly followed them.

**********

Weevil fighters scorched the space station with cannon fire and disabled many of its weapons. The man-o-wars spread out in an attempt to protect as much of the station as possible.

Will guided the cruiser from the external cargo bay of *Leviathan* and darted into space. He pressed the transmitter 'send' switch. "Bastille, it's Will. Drop your cover and join the battle."

"Understood, Will. We're going in without the cloak and we're going in hot."

"That's right. We'll be in touch."

The cruiser sped away from the battle and circled behind the Weevil forces. Will skillfully piloted the cruiser underneath and behind fighters, allowing Shanna time to target them.

The *Leviathan* opened fire with its automated system and immediately made an impact on the Weevil attack. Weevil fighters exploded left and right.

Will kept an eye on the long range sensors. He pinpointed where the portal was by the appearance of additional Weevil fighters.

As casualties mounted for the Weevil, their fighters focused on the man-o-wars and avoided *Leviathan's* deadly fire.

Will steered the cruiser away from the fray toward the Weevil portal. They took random cannon fire but drew little interest otherwise.

On the other side of the portal, Will studied the fighter formations and searched for the Weevil command carrier.

Goeth and Drun entered the pilots' cabin. Shanna was startled to see them. "What are you doing here?"

"Sorry, Shanna. We couldn't let you two do this alone."

"Thank you. We appreciate your help."

Will leaned back in his chair. "I knew I could count on you guys."

"So what's the plan?" inquired Goeth.

Will pointed to a large green shape on the long range sensor screen. "There's our destination – the command carrier."

"I see," Goeth remarked curiously.

"Shanna, let me know if we pick up anything on the short range sensors."

"Are you expecting something?"

"Yes, I am."

Will glanced back at Goeth. "Are there any turreted cannons on board the ship?"

"Two in the aft and one on top. They're discrete so you have to activate them."

Will eyed the armament panel but looked confused.

Goeth reached over him and toggled three switches in the 'up' position. "Drun, you take aft. I'll take the top."

"They aren't automated?" asked Will.

"No, too much weight if we installed a control system for auto-fire. We built these cruisers for speed, remember."

"My apologies. Shoot well, my friends," said Will. "Take Jack with you. He's a damn good shooter."

"Fly well," said Goeth as he and Drun departed the cabin.

Shanna noticed forty Calamaari fighters approaching from the rear on the short range sensor screen.

"Will, they just came out of nowhere!"

"Who are they?"

"Calamaari."

"Perfect."

"Huh!"

Will entered several digits into the console computer and pressed the transmitter 'send' switch.

Polus insect-like face appeared. "Well, Saris, I see you were thoughtful enough to say farewell before we eradicate you and your people."

"You know I don't believe in farewells. I did want you to know how impressed I am with your new friends."

"We came to an understanding that getting rid of you and your mystery ship is both our priority," boasted Polus.

Will targeted the control tower on the battle carrier as they approached.

Drun's voice rang from the intercom. "Shall we open fire?"

Will motioned to Shanna for them to wait. Shanna spoke softly into the intercom and relayed the message.

"I still don't understand why we couldn't be friends, Polus."

"Because I hate you, Saris and I hate all of your kind."

"I think you're jealous."

Will toggled the armament control panel to ‘pairs’ and ‘four’.

“Now why would I be jealous of you, a lowly human?”

“I think you and Pinta make a sweet couple but face it, she was mine first.”

“You are entertaining, but my forces are ready to destroy your space station.”

Will pressed the ‘fire’ switch. “Here comes the punch line, Polus. You’ve been set up. I’m leading a Calamaari assault unit toward you as we speak.”

Eight torpedoes streaked toward the command ship and created a line of explosions along the hull and control center.

Polus looked panicked on the screen and terminated the transmission.

Will depressed the intercom switch. “Fire, gents!” he announced over the intercom.

Shanna reset the armament control panel for more weapons fire.

Will maneuvered and evaded the Calamaari gun fire as the ship continued toward the battle carrier.

The Calamaari cruisers inadvertently riddled the battle carrier with stray cannon fire in a desperate attempt to strike Will’s ship.

Weevil fighters diverted away from the attack on the space station and returned to protect the command ship. They immediately raked the Calamaari cruisers with gunfire.

The cruisers then returned cannon fire at the Weevil. Cruisers and fighters exploded frequently, lighting up the sector with flashes of light.

Will guided his cruiser through the wave of attacking Weevil fighters and targeted several groups with torpedoes.

Goeth and Drun effectively thinned the waves of fighters with their cannon fire.

Shanna noticed numerous green spots on the short range sensor screen and grabbed Will’s arm. “Will, look at this!”

Will glanced at the screen once and then a second time. "What the hell! Where did they come from?"

Cannon fire peppered the cruiser from all directions.

Will frantically veered the ship in various directions, desperately looking for a way out of the trap.

One of the man-o-wars, *The Widow Maker*, glided into the melee with guns blazing in all directions.

The crippled Weevil command ship limped away and vanished through an unseen portal.

The man-o-war took heavy fire while inflicting severe casualties on the Weevil forces.

Will took advantage of the distraction and returned fire on the Weevil fighters around the man-o-war.

The Weevil fighters retreated and vanished through their invisible portal.

Will veered to a safe distance from the Calamaari forces and programmed the transmitter. He pressed the 'send' switch.

A Calamaari officer appeared on the monitor. He wore several colored stripes on his shoulder and a webbed plume on his head.

"Who am I speaking to?" asked Will.

"I am Zorick, the leader of the Calamaari forces. Do you wish to surrender before we destroy you?"

"Listen Zorick, I am not your enemy. Are you and your troops loyal to Cintilla or to Pinta?"

"Pinta is our queen. I obey her orders."

"How about Goeth? He is the next in line to the Calamaari throne should anything happen to Cintilla."

"Goeth is dead. Pinta has assured us of that."

Will glanced at Shanna. She nodded and left the cabin.

"Suppose I prove to you that Goeth is alive. Does that change anything?"

"Where is your proof?"

"Look, we did you a big favor and put a dent in the Weevil forces. We can finish them off together and live in peace."

"Pinta has instructed us that your people have access to a weapon that can destroy both the Calamaari and the Weevil. We have no choice but to destroy you and your forces."

"If there is such a weapon, I know nothing of it."

"And why should I believe you?"

"If someone had it, don't you think they'd have used it by now?" challenged Will.

Goeth and Drun entered the cabin. They looked surprised when they saw the Calamaari Commander on the monitor.

"Zorick!"

"Goeth! Pinta said you were dead."

"No, Pinta lied. I was injured and required treatment that only my friend, Saris, could obtain for me."

"Why would he do that for a Calamaari?" inquired Zorick.

"For peace. He and his people do not seek war with us. Their issues are with the Weevil."

"You cannot return to Calamaar. It's too dangerous."

"I understand. Do you know where my mother is being held?"

Zorick looked away uneasily from the monitor. "She is imprisoned in the mines at Rigor on Pinta's orders. I don't know how long she'll survive there."

"I must rescue her."

"I will speak to other commanders on this matter and we'll contact you."

"Thank you, Zorick."

"Be careful, Goeth. Pinta has many loyalists."

The monitor went blank.

Goeth and Drun stared at Will expectantly.

Will dejectedly placed his head in his hands. Shanna rubbed his shoulders and leaned against him.

"Drun and I have no choice but to go after Pinta," said Goeth sullenly.

"I understand. We will join you."

"This isn't your fight, Will."

Will looked up with anger in his eyes. "Yes, it is. I've had enough of Polus, Pinta and every other degenerate out there who wants nothing but war and death. I'll find a way to finish this once and for all."

"You can't change what is, Will. This is the way of the universe. It is one giant food chain."

"Then it's time to break that food chain."

Goeth and Drun looked skeptically at Will and departed from the cabin.

The cruiser returned to the station and docked away from *Leviathan* for once.

Will and Shanna stood by the hatch for a moment as Drun and Goeth waited for instructions.

"I need to assess the damage and speak with the other commanders," announced Will.

"We will join you," replied Goeth. "I cannot wait long, you understand."

Will put his arm around Shanna's shoulder and pulled her close to him. "We are both in a race against time, Goeth." He and Shanna departed the cruiser.

**********

A dozen people gathered in the saloon around Will, Shanna and Arn.

Goeth and Drun entered, accompanied by Maya and Jack.

Will stood and addressed the group. "As you know we have our hands full right now."

One of the commanders, a burly man with a pointed beard rose. "We sustained significant damage to our ships. I don't think we can survive another onslaught like today."

"I realize that. Who is the commander of the man-o-war that rescued us?"

A small woman with long black hair wearing a brown robe and a red sweatband stepped forward. A young boy about sixteen years old followed her.

"I am Malduna, the commander of the *Widow Maker*. This is my son, Victor."

"Thank you for saving our lives, Malduna."

"If only someone could have saved my husband's life."

"I'm sorry for your loss."

"Are you?" she asked bitterly.

The woman retreated to the rear of the saloon with the boy. She stared coldly at Will with a blank expression.

Will had a strange vibe from the woman and wondered what her story was.

"Why is it that the Calamaari didn't attack the station? They were out there," questioned Arn.

"Perhaps the word is out that Goeth is alive."

"It helped too," added Shanna, "that in their haste to pursue us, they appeared to be part of our attacking force."

"At least until we ran out of places to go," added Will. "Fortunately, the *Widow Maker* arrived and gave us an escape route."

"What are we going to do about this?" asked Severin.

"First, I am taking a team to find Goeth's mother, the real queen of Calamaar. Perhaps then we can put the Calamaari issue to rest."

"And what of the Weevil?"

"They aren't sure if they can trust the Calamaari yet, especially after our assault on the battle carrier."

"How bad was the damage to the station, Arn?" inquired Shanna.

"We lost over fifty percent of our cannons. I don't know how long it will take to make repairs."

"Then I want the man-o-wars and *Leviathan* in a defensive position around the station," ordered Will. "I'll make contact with Pinta and Polus. Perhaps, I can delay any further attacks."

"Is there any chance of rekindling the alliance with the Calamaari?" asked Severin.

"May I speak?" Goeth asked Will.

"Of course."

Goeth stepped in front of the group. "So long as Pinta is ruler, there will be no peace."

Drun joined him and addressed the group. "There is a fear that drove the Calamaari and the Weevil to unite against your people. That fear is a weapon that could annihilate all of us. That fear is so strong that they would put aside their hatred for each other to stop you."

"But there is no such weapon," replied Severin. "We've checked with all our contacts around the galaxy."

"Are you so sure of that?"

"We would know if such a weapon existed. I'm sure of it."

"Then you have much to learn, ma'am."

"Don't you have any information other than what we discussed, Goeth?" inquired Will. "If such a weapon does exist, we need to find out who has it and why."

"I can only tell you what I've heard."

"Then we have much to do."

**********

Zorick entered the Command Center with two lower-ranking officers. Pinta shouted at them for the failed attack on Will's cruiser until the beep of the transmitter on the console interrupted them. She approached the console and pressed the 'receive' switch.

Polus' angry face appeared with drool streaming from either side of his jaws. "We had a pact, Pinta, and you broke it!"

"What are you talking about? We did no such thing!"

"You joined Saris and attacked my battle carrier. And why didn't you attack the space station with us? We could have wiped them out."

"When we pursued Saris, we didn't want to intimidate the Weevil forces into thinking that we were turning on them," interjected Zorick. "We saw an opportunity and sent a limited contingent after Saris. Obviously, our cruisers approaching your command carrier from behind the battle was a very sensitive situation that needed consideration."

Pinta was pleased by Zorick's response. "Are you happy now, Polus?"

"For now. Next time I might not be so forgiving."

The transmission ended and the monitor went blank.

Pinta turned to Zorick and stared at him. Zorick returned the stare with cold, unflinching eyes and a confident smile.

"Is that all there was to your decision, Zorick?"

"Of course, Pinta. This is a very fragile alliance you have struck with the Weevil and, as you've just seen, it wouldn't take much to erupt into all-out war between us."

"Then you did well. Don't disappoint me."

"My decisions are based on tactics, not emotion."

Zorick led his officers out of the control room.

Pinta watched him suspiciously as the door closed behind him

# Chapter Four

# Unexpected Surprises

In a corner office of the clinic, Prax studied blueprints and notes at a desk.

Will entered the clinic and eyed the nanoplasma generator in one of the rear examination rooms. He recalled his experience with the device and how it repaired a number of life threatening injuries to his body. As he ran his hand over the complex instrumentation, he wondered if it could save Shanna.

Prax leaned back in his chair and looked through the door at Will. "Brings back memories, huh?" he called out to him.

"Sure does. If only it would do one more miracle, I'd be so grateful."

"I found something in Xerxes' notes that might help but I'll need a sample of Shanna's blood to work with."

"Prax, you mentioned that there were some other things Xerxes sent with you."

"Yeah, but I have no idea what they are. He arranged for quite a few crates, boxes and files to be placed on board my ship. You know him as well as I do. He was very secretive about his projects."

"Do you think he's still alive?"

"Honestly, no. The government on Earth has become more corrupt than it ever was. Something bad was happening there and he knew what it was."

"That's disappointing. My dad's friend, Dr. Smith, had high hopes for Earth with the technology Xerxes gave to him."

"Dr. Smith was a good man. I don't know what became of him over the years."

"You know, Prax, I am so tired of the fighting. I just want to live in peace with my family."

"If you can't live with the fighting, you can't live. That's the law of the jungle."

"But why am I always the focal point. Shanna and I had such a magical relationship and it's like fate is determined to take it away."

"Believe me, Will, I understand how you feel. We lost so many friends in the war with Pendragon, it was heart-breaking. Somehow, your father reached down each time and overcame his adversaries."

"This issue with Shanna is really tearing me up. I finally got her back and now this."

Prax patted Will on the shoulder. "Have faith, Will. That's all we can do."

**********

Shanna sat at a table on the observation deck with two young women, Tara and Vera. They talked about Will's spell of despair when she left him.

Will approached and was stunned to see the two women with Shanna. "Hello, ladies, it's been a while."

The women rushed at him and hugged him.

"Will, how have you been?" asked Vera excitedly.

"We never expected to see you again," remarked Tara.

"Shanna enjoyed the décor on the Reaper very much. I thought the *Leviathan* could use a little of the same."

"We're so happy to see you and Shanna together again," said Vera. "We hated to see you suffer like you did."

"Where are your sidekicks? Don't tell me you ditched them already."

"Hell, no!" exclaimed Tara. "They're on a job today."

"Sounds like you were a handful when I was gone," remarked Shanna.

"Yeah, that's why I had to leave."

"Well, we missed you, Will. All we had were the stories to keep us going," explained Vera. "You were a living legend."

"I must say, you look great since we last saw you," Tara commented.

"Yes, he does," replied Shanna proudly. "I couldn't believe how great he looks."

"Shanna and I have to go to the clinic and see Prax about something very important. We'll see you later."

Will took Shanna's hand and led her back to the clinic.

"Is the nano-generator up and running?" asked Shanna.

"Not yet. Prax found something in Xerxes' notes that might be helpful. He needs a sample of your blood for one of the tests he read about."

"What do you think?"

"It's too soon to tell. He's new to the technology so we have to be patient."

"Then we'll focus on the Weevil and the Calamaari."

"That's my girl."

They stepped onto an elevator and descended several floors.

"Look, Shanna, I don't want you to get your hopes up. This is still a long shot."

"I know, but at least there's a chance."

They stepped off the elevator and approached the clinic.

"Will, do you think Xerxes knew something about this doomsday weapon we keep hearing about?"

"I'm not sure. But if he did, how would the aliens know?"

"Think back to Rourke," suggested Shanna. "He made a deal with the aliens. Perhaps he knew something about Xerxes' research center and told them."

"I could ask Maya to look into it. She may know something about their militia history that could help solve this mystery."

Will and Shanna entered the empty clinic and approached Prax's office.

"We're here," announced Will.

Prax exited the office with a small kit. "Welcome to my world of weird science."

Shanna sat down in a chair and rested her arm on the table.

Will picked up one of four notebooks off a crate and flipped through the pages.

Prax prepared a syringe for the blood sample.

"Hey, Prax, do you know what a PBU-57 is?" Will asked curiously.

Prax inserted the syringe into Shanna's arm and removed a vial of blood. "No, why do you ask?"

"Because there's an entry here for a PBU-57 and a crate number. Perhaps this could be the weapon."

"Or a spare computer board," he replied stoically as he removed a second vial of blood.

"Maybe you're right. It sounds interesting, though."

"Look, Will, I'm going to focus all my attention right now on finding a cure for Shanna. If you want to know about the other stuff, that's on you."

"I'm sorry. It's just that if this mystery weapon really existed because of Xerxes, we'd be sitting on the sole reason right now for this whole war between us and the aliens."

"Perhaps we should leave it as a myth. Even if we had it, do we really want to know about it?"

"You have a point."

Prax removed a third vial from Shanna's arm and gave her a band-aid. "I'm going to try and implement a procedure from Xerxes notes on the nanoplasma generator. At the very least, I'm hoping that it will stop the spread of the Calamaari genes through Shanna's system."

"Let us know as soon as you find out something," requested Will. He helped Shanna to her feet.

"You know, Will, you remind me so much of your father."

"How close were the two of you?"

"My father, Xerxes, brought us all together, including your stepmother. We really grew close during our adventures against the Andoran alliance."

"Xerxes was your father?" inquired Will in a surprised tone.

"Yes, he was. When your dad and Tera first got together, he had no idea that Tera was my half sister. Your dad and Tera were 'interrupted' one night. That's how my dad found out about them."

"Wow! I can imagine what a surprise that must have been."

"Needless to say, all three were quite embarrassed."

"I'd love to hear more about them sometime."

"Looks like I'm not going anywhere for a while."

"I'll keep that in mind."

**********

The reaper was docked outside *Leviathan* at one of the station's regular docks. Repairs had been made by the station's personnel and the weapons system was recharged.

Will and Shanna sat together on a couch in the main cabin of the *Reaper*.

"We'll need Zorick's help to free Cintilla from the mine."

"So how do we make that happen?" asked Shanna.

Goeth and Drun entered through the hatch and stood before them.

"Like this," said Will as he pointed to the two Calamaari.

"We got your message," Goeth said.

"I want to coordinate a false attack on Calamaar with Zorick's help."

"Very good. I'll make it known that I am alive and coming to take the throne from Pinta."

"When we've rescued your mother from the mine and cleared the area, we'll blow it up."

"But why?" asked Shanna. "That makes no sense."

"Because Pinta will think we killed Cintilla to assure Goeth takes over the throne once Pinta's gone."

"Ah-hah," said Shanna slyly. "I see where you're going with this."

"The key is to get in there undetected," warned Goeth. "If they catch any of us, she will kill us."

"Let me ask you something, Goeth. Did your people ever deal with a human by the name of Rourke?"

Goeth pondered for a moment. "There was a man who met with my mother some time ago. He believed he had information that was very valuable."

"Did he reveal what he knew?"

"No. My mother didn't trust him and had him thrown out. Was this man important to you?"

"He killed several of my friends and led an insurrection to take over my kingdom."

"Your reputation precedes you in many parts of the universe. Friendship is hard to find."

"As you've seen, Goeth, I know how to earn friendship. I will never betray a friend either. We will rescue your mother."

Will took Goeth's clawed hand in his and the two shook politely.

Drun was impressed with the respect they had for each other.

Will extended his hand to Drun as well. "Drun, I believe I can trust you as I do Goeth. I consider you a friend as well."

Drun shook his hand. "I am honored."

"I'll contact *Leviathan* and see if she can support us for back up."

"One other question, Will," added Goeth. "Did you decorate the ship like this?"

"No, I had a little help from my friends here on Orpheus-2 while I was recovering from our fight."

"It's ...different."

Goeth and Drun chuckled at him in their strange manner. They left the *Reaper* and entered the other Calamaari cruiser.

Will used his wrist transmitter to contact Bastille on the *Leviathan.*

"This is Bastille. Go ahead, Will."

"We're going to try and rescue Queen Cintilla. Can you back us up?"

"Negatory. We're making repairs on the cloaking system and several coolant lines. Celine has the automated firing system down for repairs as well."

"Understood. Thanks, Bastille."

Will placed his hand on Shanna's. "Looks like we're on our own."

Jack leaned inside the cabin. "Oh, no you're not. Maya and I are coming, too."

"Welcome aboard, mates."

"I thought you'd have more appreciation for my shooting after our last excursion."

"Oh, I do, Jack. I've seen you shoot before, though, and. I'd expect nothing less."

"You sound like Maya."

"I'll handle the communications as usual," Maya volunteered.

"Thank you both," said Will appreciatively.

Jack patted him on the shoulder and left the cabin.

Will initiated the 'start' sequence and released the *Reaper* from its dock on Orpheus-2.

Once they left the station, Will contacted Goeth through the transmitter. Goeth's face appeared on the monitor.

"I will initiate contact with Zorick and discuss our intentions."

"We'll stand by," replied Will.

Will and Shanna waited patiently for several minutes. Finally Goeth's face reappeared.

"We're all set," he announced. "These mines are located north of the palace, quite a distance from it."

"How do we know where to find Cintilla?" inquired Will.

"You'll see a very tall tower with a rotating light on the top of it."

"We're on the way. Good luck."

"You, too, Will."

Will toggled the transmitter switch off and focused on the long range sensor screen. "Looks good so far. Why don't we take a break?" Will reached over and touched Shanna's thigh.

Shanna quickly pulled away and startled him. "Please, Will, don't touch me."

"What's wrong?" he asked.

"I'm ashamed of what's happening to me."

Will reached down and playfully slid her leather skirt up. He was appalled at how the green rash had changed into a leathery patch. He touched Shanna's cheek gently.

Shanna grew angry and her eyes glowed red like burning coals. She grabbed Will by the shoulders and stood up with him. She slammed him against the rear control panel and warned. "Please don't touch me again, Will."

"I'm sorry. I didn't realize you were so upset."

Shanna set him down and left the cabin.

Will's eyes welled up with tears as he realized she was becoming something else. He set the cruiser for 'auto-pilot' and recalled how different things used to be. When he first met Shanna, it was so much fun. There were no responsibilities. Parenthood hadn't entered the picture yet and they could do as they pleased. Now it appeared that fate finally caught up with them.

**********

Goeth and Drun watched the long-range sensor screen anxiously as they approached Calamaar. Suddenly, the transmitter beeped.

Drun acknowledged the incoming transmission and Zorick's face appeared on the monitor.

"Greetings, Drun. We are sending out a large part of our force to monitor a large Weevil buildup in sector thirteen. I will accompany them."

"Thank you, Zorick. We will attempt to minimize casualties."

"Regardless of what happens, you have my sworn allegiance."

"I appreciate that. Do you know how well defended the palace is?" inquired Goeth.

"I've consulted with many of our officers about the possibility that you live and that Pinta may be leading us to ruin. They are split in where their support would lie in the event of your return."

"So this won't be easy."

"No, I'm afraid not," answered Goeth pessimistically. "I fear that this split could present the Weevil with an opportunity to defeat us as well."

"Then our mission must be subtle to hide any evidence of a rift in our leadership."

The transmission ended.

Drun turned to Goeth. "Do you think we can pull this off?"

"If we create enough havoc, the remaining forces will have to focus on us. That should give Will a chance to rescue my mother."

"Then I will man the rear turret. Fly well, my friend."

"Shoot well."

The two Calamaari pressed their clawed hands together as a sign of friendship.

Drun left the cabin.

**********

Will met with Jack and Maya in the main quarters.

"Where's Shanna?" inquired Maya.

"She's not well. It's best to leave her be."

"Is she alright?"

"I don't know. Look, I need one of you to go down to the mine with me. The other will pilot the ship and take care of any resistance."

Shanna stepped into the main quarters from the hall. Her face was shaded in green and her eye brows enlarged.

Jack and Maya were shocked.

"I'm going with you," Shanna announced.

Will was at a loss for words.

"I'll cover you from up here," replied Jack. "Will the two of you be alright?"

"Let's just get this finished," she said coldly.

"I've got the controls," Maya replied uneasily.

Jack sat quietly, concerned for both Will and Shanna. He could see that she wasn't herself and wondered how unpredictable her behavior could become.

Will opened the weapons cabinet and removed four pulse pistols. He handed two to Shanna and stowed two under his belt. He removed a large coil of rope and slung it over his shoulder.

"Are you ready, Shanna?"

"Of course. Let's go."

The two stepped on the platform and waited.

Jack reluctantly operated the local transporter controls. "Good luck, you two. Come back safe."

Neither acknowledged him. He pressed the "sequence initiate" button and turned away.

The red light blinked and turned green. Both Will and Shanna vanished from the platform.

Jack returned to the pilots' cabin and sat in the adjacent seat to Maya. He prepared the armament control panel for 'single' fire and 'six'.

"Talk to me, Jack," said Maya uneasily.

"I don't like this at all."

"Neither do I. We don't have much choice, do we?"

Jack switched the scanners to 'local' control and to 'surface scan'. He noticed several military vehicles at various points around the tower.

"What can we do?" he asked despondently.

Maya hesitated for a moment then replied, "Lock on the vehicles nearest the mine entrance but don't fire."

Maya quickly activated the 'communications' mode and selected 'channel monitor'.

The computer beeped several times and finally stopped. Several coordinates appeared on the small monitor.

Maya pressed another button for 'download data'. The information vanished and noises could be heard from the speakers. She pressed another button and the voices were translated. "Sounds like Goeth started his attack."

"I see three cruisers emerging from a hangar in the side of the mountain. Let's see what happens."

The three ships sped away toward the palace.

"That's our cue, "replied Jack. He initiated the armament control panel and methodically took out the military vehicles with torpedo fire.

**********

Will and Shanna waited behind rocks as the vehicles exploded one after another.

Calamaari troops scattered in different directions, seeking shelter.

"Just like old times. Let's kick some alien ass," said Will half-heartedly.

Shanna didn't reply. He grew more dejected by her coldness toward him.

The two raced toward the tower and fired randomly at soldiers. When they reached the tower entrance, Shanna entered first.

A stun grenade exploded nearby and floored Will. He lay on the ground with stars in his eyes. He tried to focus but couldn't. Will expected Shanna to come to his aid but she continued ahead, unconcerned by his condition.

Five soldiers stood around him. One raised his weapon and aimed at Will's head.

Shanna dropped down from three stories up on the tower and landed on the soldier, killing him instantly. She drew her knives and methodically cut down the remaining four soldiers in a whirlwind attack.

Shanna stowed the bloody knives and lifted Will over her shoulders. She carried him across the camp as if he were weightless. Will's head began to clear and he realized Shanna now had the strength of a Calamaari. Her facial features changed again and she took on more of a resemblance to them.

Will wondered if her loyalty to him would change as she mutated. Shanna set him down at the mine's entrance and glared at him. "You question my loyalty, Will?"

"No, Shanna. I just fear how far these changes will go."

When Will stood up, Shanna clothes-lined him. He lay on the ground unconscious.

Shanna took the coil of rope from Will and tossed it over her shoulder. She entered the mine with a knife in each hand. Her pulse pistols remained stowed in her belt.

Three soldiers rushed toward the mine entrance through dim evening light. Shanna fell to the ground and lay prone until the soldiers reached her. She leaped up and kicked one in the throat while slicing the throats of the other two. They fell to the ground dead. The Calamaari mutation enhanced her fighting skills significantly and left her feeling little if any emotion for her victims.

Shanna continued through the tunnel until she came to a small shack with a light in the window. Inside the shack, she spotted two soldiers. As if on instinct, she leaped through the window and broke the light. Before the soldiers could react, she left both with their throats cut and their guts slit open.

Behind the shack were several pits. Each pit had a scaffold built over it with rigging devices mounted over each one.

Shanna inspected the pits. She noticed that all were lit except for the last one. This pit had no rigging device and appeared abandoned.

Shanna tied the rope to the scaffold and retrieved a lantern from the wall nearby. She climbed down the rope into the pit.

When she reached the bottom, she found three more shafts extending horizontally in different directions. She tossed a rock into each of the shafts and listened.

From one direction, she heard something move in the darkness. She held the lantern up and approached the source of the sound.

"Cintilla, is that you?" She called out. There was no reply.

Shanna paused at the edge of another pit, much shallower but wider than the others. She held the lantern up and saw something move in the shadows at the far side.

"Cintilla, is that you?" Still there was no reply.

Shanna leaped down into the pit. She approached the figure and recognized the decrepit Calamaari as Cintilla.

Cintilla looked feeble and emaciated. She had a broken leg and a dislocated shoulder. The lantern light hurt her eyes and she turned away.

Shanna set the lantern against the far wall and approached her.

"Who are you?" asked Cintilla weakly.

"I am Shanna, Will's spouse."

"Why are you here?"

"I've come to rescue you."

Shanna lifted her and carried her toward the lantern. She raised Cintilla up and pushed her from the pit. She then passed the lantern to Cintilla and stepped back. She rushed at the wall and leaped up. With ease, she grabbed the ledge at the top of the pit and pulled herself out.

Cintilla motioned for Shanna to stay back. "What do you want with me?" she asked defensively.

"Your son is distracting the palace forces so we can rescue you. We have to leave now."

"My son?"

"Yes. Goeth is alive and well."

Shanna lifted Cintilla and took her to the wall of the main pit where the rope hung.

Cintilla studied Shanna and noted her condition. "Who did this to you?"

"Pinta."

"She will pay for what she's done."

"And I will see to it that she does," promised Shanna.

Shanna tied the rope around Cintilla's waist and scurried to the top. She carefully pulled Cintilla from the pit and set her down gently.

"Why would you help us? We have always hated your race."

"Will taught me to see the good in everyone."

Shanna drew her pulse pistol and turned instinctively. She fired four shots and killed three approaching soldiers. After stowing the pistol, she lifted Cintilla and hurried to the mine's entrance.

Shanna emerged from the mine with Cintilla and set her down next to Will.

Cintilla was surprised to see Will unconscious. "Is he alright?"

"Yes. It was for his own good."

Shanna pressed the transmitter on her wrist. "Maya, are you there?"

"Go ahead, Shanna."

"Two coming up, now."

"Did you find Cintilla?"

"I said 'two coming up now'."

Shanna pressed the transmitter again and turned it off.

"Tell them to follow the plan," ordered Shanna. She then raced off into the night.

Cintilla and Will were transported onto the cruiser.

Jack was stunned to see only the two of them on the platform. "What happened?"

"Shanna said to follow the plan," replied Cintilla.

Jack helped Will to his feet. "Are you alright?"

"Ask me tomorrow," Will uttered nauseously.

Jack frowned and returned to the pilots' cabin.

Will rubbed his neck and waited for the cobwebs to clear from his head.

"Isn't this ironic?" she asked Will.

"What happened down there?"

"Shanna remained on the ground to take care of things."

"We have to help her!"

"No, we don't. Stick to the plan, Will."

Jack returned to the main quarters and approached them.

"You didn't destroy the mine, Jack, did you?"

"We're following the plan."

"But, Shanna's down there!"

"We know."

Maya emerged from the rear corridor with three wooden splints.

Jack retrieved several utensils from a first aid cabinet and set them down next to Cintilla. He inspected her leg and began to set it using the splints.

Maya hugged Will tightly. "It'll be alright."

Will couldn't speak and walked away from them in tears.

Maya retreated to the corner of the chamber and broke down in tears.

"I still don't understand your race," Cintilla remarked.

"Sometimes I don't either," confessed Jack.

He helped her into a chair and attempted to make her comfortable while he tended to her shoulder.

"I'll check on you later," said Maya. "I'll be at the controls if you need me."

Maya left them and went to the pilots' cabin.

As soon as she was seated, she glanced at the short-range sensor screen and noticed twenty green dots approaching them. The sensor alarm annunciated over the ship and alerted Jack.

Maya toggled the intercom on and shouted, "Jack, man the turret! We have lots of company."

Jack finished wrapping Cintilla's arm to her shoulder when he heard Maya's call. "Here we go again," he groaned.

Jack left the main quarters through the hall and climbed the ladder to the turret.

Cintilla activated the local monitor and watched the approaching cruisers. She placed her good hand on the switch to transmit but then balked. She knew it was too dangerous to contact anyone.

Maya veered away from the approaching fleet but saw a large red dot on the screen. She transmitted an SOS and waited.

"Come in, *Reape*r, this is *The Widow Maker*. Do you read us?" a voice rang from the speaker.

"Hell, yeah!" exclaimed Maya. "Boy, are we glad to see you."

"We'll handle them. Return to base."

"Understood. Thank you."

Maya watched with relief as the pursuing cruisers dispersed rather than engage the man-o-war.

**********

The *Reaper* docked On Orpheus-2, followed soon after by Goeth's cruiser.

Jack and Maya helped Cintilla off the ship and waited at the jet way.

Goeth and Drun anxiously exited their cruiser and rushed to Cintilla with remarkable speed for the large creatures that they were.

After a brief reunion, Goeth asked, "Where are Will and Shanna?"

Maya turned away sadly.

"Shanna's …gone," replied Jack. "Will's on board. I don't think he's taking this all too well."

"Shanna is alive and well. I believe she is making her way to the palace for Pinta," explained Cintilla.

"Are you sure about that?" asked Jack.

"Yes, I am. She left the mine before you destroyed it."

"I'd best let Will know."

# Chapter Five

## Chaos and Confusion

Will lay in bed in his cabin and sobbed.

Jack entered and pulled up a chair. He watched Will silently for several moments.

Will rolled over and sat up. "What?"

"I think you have to get it together."

"Why?"

"Because a lot of people are counting on you."

"Who's Shanna counting on, huh?" shouted Will angrily.

Jack stared at him sympathetically. "You. She's counting on you and you're failing her right now."

Will stood up and pounded the wall with his fist. "What the hell am I supposed to do?"

Jack shook his head in disbelief. "We've come so far, Will, and you've learned so little."

Will paced the room several times. He turned a chair around backwards and sat facing Jack.

Jack maintained a motionless expression.

"What do you expect me to do, Jack? Help me out here, will you?"

"I expect you to set your priorities and address each one individually. I expect you to discuss the difficult ones with your friends. We have never let you down. I expect you to keep on fighting no matter how dismal things look. Anything else?"

Will leaned his head down on the back of the chair and sobbed again.

Jack stood up and walked to the cabin door. He paused and looked back. "Call me when you've found your spine." He stepped out into the hall and walked away.

Will went to the door and leaned into the hallway. "Wait, Jack."

"You want something?"

"Yeah. Let's go see Prax first."

"It's still a little early for a cure, if that's what you're hoping for."

"No. I need to know something else."

The two men left the *Reaper* and walked through the space station.

**********

Inside the station, Malduna looked both ways before leaving the stairwell. She proceeded cautiously down the hall to the front door of the clinic and slowly opened it.

The clinic was empty and the door to Prax's office was closed. She noticed the light under the door and knew someone was inside.

Malduna slipped inside the clinic and quietly closed the door. She crept about and checked each of the rooms. When she tried the last door, it was locked. She took out a small leather bundle from under her robe and removed two thin strips of metal. Within seconds, she picked the lock on the door and opened it.

Hurriedly, she searched three boxes. The first two were filled with historical documents. The third held a collection of notebooks with titles on the spine. The one titled PBU-57 caught her attention. She retrieved the notebook and eagerly opened it.

Will and Jack approached the clinic door and paused.

"Look, Jack, this problem with Shanna is really hard for me. I don't want to lose her and it may already be too late."

"Did you notice anything strange about her other than her physical features?"

"Yeah, she was as strong as an ox. She manhandled me twice and knocked me out."

"So maybe she thinks she can do more for us from down there. If she has that kind of strength, she's not worried about tangling with a few Calamaari."

"I hope you're right."

They entered the clinic and approached Prax's door. Will tapped on the door and entered.

Jack noticed the farthest door down the aisle was ajar. He approached the door and peered inside.

Malduna leafed through one of four notebooks.

"Looking for something in particular?" he asked.

Malduna was startled and dropped the book. "Uh, no. I was curious what kind of things the research center was into."

"Wouldn't it be easier to ask Prax?"

"I'm a stranger on this station. No one would give me the time of day."

"Try again, Malduna."

"Alright, I… I wondered if there was information on the technology used on *Leviathan.* I'd love to upgrade *The Widow Maker*."

"You do realize that Xerxes had nothing to do with the construction of *Leviathan*, don't you?"

Malduna nervously retreated toward the door. "I'm sorry, I didn't know that." She brushed past Jack and hurried to the clinic door.

"Wait a minute, Malduna."

Malduna paused but didn't look back.

"Why have you made it a point to watch our backs?"

"Is that a problem?"

"No. It's just hard to understand why you risked *The Widow Maker* without any support more than once."

Malduna turned around. "It seemed like the right thing to do, at the time."

"Why do I find that hard to believe?"

"Perhaps I wanted my ship to be part of your success. It was an opportunity to fit in."

Jack grinned. "Now that, at least, is somewhat believable."

Malduna forced a smile and closed the clinic door behind her.

Inside his office, Prax studied several notes while a flask warmed over the small flame of a burner. An electronic microscope was next to him and several slides were stacked in a wooden rack in front of him. Six small vials of various colored fluids surrounded the slides.

Will sat across from him as Prax slid his chair away from the desk and folded his arms.

"You understand what I'm going through with Shanna, don't you, Prax?"

"Of course, I do. I've seen your father go through similar problems."

Jack paused at the door and eavesdropped.

"How did he handle it?"

"He kept a lot inside him," answered Prax. "There was so much heartache in his life but he channeled it into fighting his enemies."

"What was the worst thing he had to face?"

"That's hard to say. He lost so many friends. His relationship with his first love, Penny, was tragic in so many ways. When he was finally able to walk away with Tera, most of their friends were gone."

"So I need to ride this out to the end."

"I'm afraid so, Will. And there is the possibility that you'll lose many of your friends as well. Life is short."

"Well, it's not inspiring but it does help to know that I'm not the only one to deal with such grief."

Jack stepped in and leaned comfortably against the wall. "Hello, Prax."

"Hello, Jack."

"Did you know you had a visitor in the locked room?"

"No, I didn't. Who was it?"

"Malduna."

"What? Why would she be down here?"

"I'm not sure. Her story didn't add up either."

"So, Prax, what have you found so far?" inquired Will.

"Dr. Smith worked with Xerxes on a process to halt mutations of humans from alien interaction."

"Did they have any success?" asked Will.

"Apparently so. They believed that if they could stop a mutation, then there had to be a way to reverse it as well."

"That's encouraging."

"Now, I need to replicate the serum from Shanna's blood and the chemical compounds named in Xerxes' notes."

"So this is doable?" Jack asked anxiously.

"It sure looks like it. Just a matter of time."

Jack patted Will on the back. "See that, buddy."

Will still looked despondent and became teary-eyed.

"How soon before this serum is ready?" asked Jack.

"I may have the first stage serum by tomorrow morning. Xerxes' notes are pretty detailed."

Jack took Will by the arm and ushered him to the door. "Come on, Will. We have work to do."

"We'll see you tomorrow, Prax."

"Have faith, Will. I won't let you down."

"By the way, Prax," added Jack, "do you know anything about the weapon used in the Andoran war?"

"Dark Horizon. I remember it well."

"Could there be another weapon like this in someone's hands?"

"The Archaenians were forced to develop the weapon for the Andoran leader. Once they were freed of his control, they vowed never to make another weapon again."

"Interesting."

Jack and Will left Prax's office and closed the door.

"I think you need a drink," suggested Jack. "It'll settle your nerves."

"I won't argue that."

They proceeded to the saloon.

"Jack, what happened to us?"

"What do you mean?"

"Everything was going fine until Rourke and his mercenaries interfered. The war might be over if they hadn't interfered."

"I know. Sometimes I think about it as well."

When they entered Arn's saloon, they found Goeth and Cintilla seated at one of the tables. They conversed in their native tongue until Will and Jack approached.

Cintilla stood with help from Goeth. "I want to thank you and your people for what you've done for us," she said sincerely.

"I only wish it didn't come at the expense of Shanna," added Goeth.

"Thank you for your thoughts," replied Will.

"Why don't the two of you have a seat," suggested Goeth. "My mother would like to discuss something with you."

Jack and Will sat at the table.

"All is not what it seems," said Goeth somberly.

"There is a traitor among you," warned Cintilla. "I believe it is a female."

"That's impossible," replied Jack. "No one among us would sell us out."

"Goeth told me of your interest in a man named Rourke. He came to me and offered to turn you over and provide me with sensitive information about a doomsday weapon."

"But Rourke is dead. I saw him die," answered Will.

"There was a woman with him as well. She did not partake in the meeting but she did come to the palace with him."

"It sounds like one of his mercenaries," suggested Jack.

"So, how does anyone know that this doomsday weapon really exists?" inquired Will. "I don't have any knowledge of it and no one else seems to either."

"It was already used once to annihilate a barbaric alliance led by Pendragon."

"This sounds like the Dark Horizon weapon Prax mentioned," remarked Jack.

"How can I find Shanna?" asked Will eagerly.

"She will likely make her way through the Valley of Serpents to reach the palace," answered Cintilla.

"The Valley of Serpents - that doesn't sound very enlightening."

"I don't think you give her enough credit, Will. She is very capable."

"And she's alone!" uttered Will. "If Prax can replicate the serum, how do I find her to administer it?"

"I will help you," offered Goeth.

"But what about Pinta?"

"If Shanna doesn't kill her, I will," vowed Cintilla.

"And if I get to her first, I will, too."

"You have some capable support within her ranks. Zorick is very loyal to us and will do what he can to oust her from power."

"We need to be there to make this happen. Nothing changes so long as we're sitting around this tin can of a station." Will departed the saloon alone.

"I'm really concerned about him," said Jack.

"There are many things at work here. Will must focus or he will be destroyed," warned Cintilla.

"And the rest of us as well," added Goeth.

Jack fiddled nervously as he considered their concerns. "I'll talk to him."

"Please do," requested Cintilla. "Let him know that we must work together to overcome these issues."

"I will. I'll also talk to Prax and see if we can find out anything else about the previous use of the weapon."

Jack stood and left the saloon.

"We can trust him, mother," Goeth said. "Will has true friends."

"And what of us?"

"We are counted among them."

"It does seem so."

**********

Maya sat at a table in the center of the main quarters of the *Leviathan*. She watched her girls play with Marina and recalled how she and Will once played together as children.

Will paused at the door and looked in.

Maya pointed to a chair and ordered him to sit.

"Will, we have to talk."

Will sat uncomfortably and stared sadly at Marina.

Marina came to him with arms extended. "Daddy," she blurted. "Where's mommy?"

Will picked her up and hugged her tightly. Tears streamed down his cheeks.

"When Shanna was gone, you had to continue on with the battle. Now, it's her turn to continue on with the battle."

"But look what's happened, Maya? She's mutating into who knows what and she's in danger. Worse yet, I can't do a damn thing about it!"

"Yes, you can. What would she want you to do?"

"I don't know."

"Then you'd better find out – fast."

"I can't. I'm a mess right now. Help me."

Maya reached out and placed a hand on the back of his head. She rubbed it gently. "Think of this as a puzzle. Do you have all the pieces?"

"What do you mean?"

"Just what I said. Do you have all the pieces?"

Will rested his head against Marina's. She noticed the tears in his eyes. "Daddy, why are you crying?"

Will turned away from Maya and Marina.

"Alright, Will, I'll help you. First you have to get a grip."

Will took a few moments but regained his composure. "Thanks, Maya. I really do need someone to help me through this."

"What did Prax say about the serum?"

"Maybe tomorrow it'll be ready. It won't reverse the mutation but it will stop it from getting worse."

"That's a start. When the serum's ready, then we'll go to Calamaar, but not until then."

"But what if Shanna doesn't recognize me or if I don't know her?"

"We'll deal with that later. Next, we have to figure out what's going on with this doomsday weapon. Any ideas?"

"I'm hoping the answer is in Xerxes' notes. Maybe he designed it for all we know. There was something strange, though."

"Try me."

When Jack and I went to see Prax, Jack caught Malduna in the locked room. She was browsing through one of Xerxes' notebooks."

Maya became concerned. "How did she get in?"

"The lock wasn't damaged. She must have picked it."

"Then we need to discuss the security of the room's contents with Severin."

"Jack is with her now."

"Did Malduna say why?"

"Not really. Can you check your sources for a background on her? I have a feeling that something about her isn't right."

"I'll see what I can do. Have you spoken to Bastille?"

"Not in a while."

"Well, he's been dying to discuss his latest discovery with you."

"Oh, really!"

"Yes. He's broken the Weevil portal system down to a lattice type network. He's plotting all the points with the help of several probes he's launched through one of their portals."

"But what can we do with that kind of information?"

"It's another piece of the puzzle. Save it for later."

"I'll talk to him about it and see what he thinks."

"You'd better before you do anything else."

Will stood up and set Marina on the floor. "Could you watch her for a bit? I'm going to see what was in Xerxes' notes that interested Malduna so much."

Maya hugged Will and gazed proudly at him. "That's more like it."

Will lowered his head and stared at the ground humbly. "I'm going to give it my best. There isn't a lot left inside me, though."

"There's enough to make a difference. Now get going and keep believing."

"Thanks, Maya." Will departed the main quarters.

Maya watched him despondently. "If only I could believe things will get better."

**********

Prax exited the clinic carrying a satchel and a small box. He locked the door and walked down the long corridor.

Two shadows hid around the corner at the near end of the corridor. They watched as he disappeared from sight.

He ascended the stairs to the main deck and paused outside of Arn's saloon.

Arn and Severin approached from the opposite direction.

"Have you seen Will around, General?" asked Prax.

"No, we haven't. We just stopped by for an evening drink and to discuss some of our options. Would you care to join us?"

"I'd love to."

Severin took note of the satchel and box under Prax's arm. "Are you protecting something valuable, Prax?"

"Since you are the security officer, perhaps you might be of some assistance to me."

Arn smiled at her and replied, "She's all yours."

"I guess you heard about the break in at the clinic."

"One of my officers just informed me. I've dispatched two guards to watch over the clinic. I've also increased surveillance over all critical areas of the station."

Prax placed the satchel and box on the table. Before he could speak, a young waitress named Heidi stopped at the table.

"Can I get you something to drink?"

"I thought you'd never ask," quipped Arn. "I'll have the usual."

"A cold beer would be nice," added Prax.

Severin pondered but refrained from answering.

"Come on, Severin. Let me buy you a beer," urged Prax.

"Thank you but I'm on duty."

"When aren't you on duty?"

"One beer won't ruin your day, Sev. Let the man buy you a beer?" Arn insisted.

"Alright, I'll have a beer as well."

Heidi left them and disappeared behind the bar.

Prax opened the satchel and set two notebooks in front of Severin. "I think you'll find these interesting."

She flipped through the pages of the first notebook.

Heidi returned and set the cold beers and a glass of rum on the table.

"Do you remember an Andoran leader named Pendragon?" Prax inquired.

Arn became uneasy and quickly sipped from his glass.

Severin placed both hands on her beer and stared at her glass.

"I see this is a touchy subject," remarked Prax. "Jack and I just had a brief discussion on this and it got me thinking."

Arn took another healthy swig of his rum and took a deep breath. "I remember Pendragon's assault on us with his alliance of murderers."

"We had countless casualties and two other stations the size of Orpheus-2 were destroyed," added Severin.

"I lost most of my fleet to those bastards," complained Arn as he chugged the remainder of his drink.

Prax sipped his beer and flipped open the second notebook. "These are Xerxes' notes. It appears that the weapon we once knew as Dark Horizon was perfected by Dr. Smith's people."

"Another drink, Heidi!" shouted Arn. "And how far did they get with the development of said weapon?"

As Severin read, her eyes widened. She looked up at them in utter surprise. "They developed two of the weapons!"

Arn stood up and placed both hands on the table. "Tell me they aren't on my station, Prax."

Heidi returned with two glasses of rum. She set them on the table in front of Arn. "It looks like you'll need the other, General. It's on me."

Arn chugged one glass and handed it to her. "Thanks, Heidi. I may need a whole bottle before tonight's over."

Heidi returned to the bar.

"I don't know that for sure," answered Prax.

"Let's keep it that way, no matter what."

"I understand."

Severin continued to browse through the notes.

"Now, what's inside that little box of yours?" inquired Arn.

Cintilla hobbled into the room with the aid of crutches. She was followed by Goeth.

"In a moment. Our friends may be interested in this," replied Prax.

"Put the notebooks away, now," ordered Arn. Not a word about our Horizon problem."

Severin took both notebooks and slid them into Prax's satchel.

Cintilla and Goeth stopped at the table.

"Please join us," said Arn politely.

The two Calamaari sat down on chairs near the table.

"We need to speak with Will but he doesn't seem to be around," said Goeth.

"Anything we can help with?" asked Arn.

Prax slid it to the middle of the table and opened it. A small vial with green fluid rested on velvet lining inside the box.

"Perhaps…" Cintilla paused and eyed the vial curiously.

Cintilla took the vial from the box and studied it. "This appears to be quite important. What is it?"

"This is the serum that will stop Shanna's mutation," answered Prax. "I believe it can be modified to reverse the process but I need more time for that."

Cintilla and Goeth glanced at each other and then at Prax.

"I will take it to her," offered Cintilla. "I owe her for rescuing me from the mine."

Prax became uneasy about her offer.

Goeth rested his large clawed hand on Prax's hand. "We would not betray Will. If you give him the vial, he will go down to Calamaar alone and search for Shanna. She is not herself which could bode poorly for Will."

"Pinta cannot know that Shanna is there," remarked Cintilla. "She would place all her forces on alert and Shanna would be in grave danger."

"And we'd lose any opportunity to overthrow her," added Goeth.

Goeth helped Cintilla to her feet. He removed a small container from his belt and placed the vial inside it. "You have my word; Shanna will receive it."

"It sounds to me like you are leaving us."

"Yes, General," answered Goeth. "Maybe it's better that Will doesn't know."

Arn stood up. "Then the best of luck to you."

Severin also stood respectfully. "Is there anything we can do?"

"Just make sure Will stays away from Calamaar until he hears from us."

"I assure you, we will," answered Arn.

Goeth and Cintilla left the saloon.

**********

Will descended the stairs from the far end of the corridor and approached the clinic. The door was ajar and the sounds of papers being tossed on the floor could be heard. He opened the door and peered inside.

The clinic was dark except for the back room. A ray of light shined from under the door.

Will approached the door and placed his hand on the knob. As he turned the knob, he felt a stinging sensation on the back of his head and then blackness.

**********

More than half of the dozen tables were filled by soldiers and their female friends. Each table had at least two pitchers of beer.

The men were rowdy as they discussed the earlier battle and how many Weevil fighters stormed the station and the man-o-wars.

Bastille and Celine entered Arn's saloon.

Arn, Severin and Prax remained at the table in discussion. Arn noticed the two of them and promptly invited them over.

"Hello everyone," said Bastille cheerfully. "We have some news I've been dying to share but I can't quite seem to find you all of late."

Bastille and Celine took seats at the table.

"My apologies, Bastille. We've had our hands full over the Weevil and Calamaari issue."

"Bastille found out something very important about the Weevil portal system," boasted Celine.

Severin grew attentive while Prax and Arn waited passively for their explanation.

"Please tell me you know how to shut it down," urged Severin.

"We're very close," Bastille answered. "I've sent probes into a vacant sector and they identified a very tiny portal."

"That's nothing new," complained Severin disappointedly. "We all know the portal will open when a ship approaches and the Weevil will storm through again."

"There are a bunch of those tiny portals around the sector. What good does knowing the location of one do?" complained Arn.

Bastille eyed Arn's glass of rum. "Might I trouble you for a glass of that famous rum of yours, General?"

"Of course. And you, Celine?"

"I'll try some as well."

"Heidi!" shouted Arn. "Three more rums."

Heidi waved to him and lined up three glasses on the bar.

"I sense you have more to tell, Bastille," he continued.

"Yes, I do. Two of the probes made it through the second tier portal."

Heidi hurried to the table with the glasses of rum and set them down.

Bastille and Celine raised their glasses.

"A toast," declared Bastille. "We've taken a big step to stopping the Weevil."

Prax and Severin glanced at each other impatiently but hoisted their glasses of beer in the air.

"This had better be good, Bastille," warned Arn as he hoisted his glass. "I'm not very good with suspense."

They tapped glasses and sipped the contents.

"And now for the good news," Bastille continued. "The Weevil portal system is a lattice network that must be balanced at all times."

"How far does this network extend?" inquired Severin.

"It appears to go all the way back to their planet," answered Celine.

"So, if we were to introduce a weapon that could destabilize this network, we could collapse the entire system," Bastille announced proudly.

"What kind of weapon are we talking about?" inquired Severin uneasily.

"I'm glad you asked. I believe we can use the *Leviathan's* power source as a weapon to reverse the polarity of the network and as a result, overload the Weevil's own power source, thus destroying it."

"How soon can we do this?" asked Arn anxiously.

"As soon as I develope the amplifier for the signal strength. I need to generate a strong enough signal aimed at four of the lattice's critical nodes to lock onto them from the ship."

"That sounds risky, even for the *Leviathan*," remarked Prax. "She'll be swarmed on by Weevil fighters as soon as she leaves the station."

"We could use a quick strike on the third portal back. That would allow us the element of surprise."

"The man-o-wars are still undergoing repairs. They won't be available for some time yet."

"If we're quick enough, we can initiate a system overload and return through the portal before they summon reinforcements," added Celine.

"Have you forgotten about the Calamaari?" reminded Severin. "We should run this by Will, especially since Goeth and Cintilla are on their way back to Calamaar."

"Where is Will?" asked Bastille. "I've been trying to locate him for quite some time."

Arn pressed a button on the silver watch-like transmitter he wore on his wrist. "See if you can contact Saris and send him to the saloon," he instructed a member of the security team. "It's important."

Arn pressed the transmitter button again and turned it off. "My men will find him and send him up."

"There's something about this plan of yours that concerns me," Severin commented. "If we shut down the portal system, the Weevil forces on this side are stuck here."

"Well, yeah, that's true," replied Bastille

"They already outnumber us. Isn't that a problem?"

"That's definitely something to consider unless we find a way to draw them back through the portal," replied Bastille, uncertain of how to execute that part of the plan.

"I believe we should refrain from attacking the portal until we have a handle on their immediate fleet," announced Severin.

"Perhaps you're right," relented Arn. "When the time is right, that may be the answer to the Weevil."

"I have no problem with that," replied Severin. "In the mean time, I'll figure out a way to draw them back."

"I see why Arn holds you in such high regard," Prax complimented her.

"She is worth her weight in gold," said Arn proudly. "And she's the best looking officer I've ever seen.

"Alright boys, you've obviously had too much to drink," she replied. "I have to go now."

Prax looked disappointedly at her.

"Would you walk me, Prax?" she requested. "There are some things I need to discuss with you about these notebooks."

"Of course I would." Prax anxiously chugged his beer.

The two of them left the saloon.

"I hope he doesn't have ideas of taking away my security officer," fretted Arn. "There's no one like her."

"Sometimes you have to let nature take its course," remarked Celine. "On that note, we must go, too. Thank you for your hospitality."

"But what about Will?" asked Arn. "He'll be here soon."

"Bastille can stay with you. I need my beauty sleep."

"It would be inconsiderate to leave the General with a full drink in his hand. I'd be happy to stay and drink with him."

"That works for me," replied Arn.

Celine chuckled at the two men. She finished her glass of rum and left the saloon.

**********

Prax and Severin walked along the outer corridor of the station until they came to a glass corridor. Prax carried the empty box that held the vial of serum under his arm. Severin held the satchel with the notebooks. They paused to admire the stars through the thick glass wall.

The view outside displayed the man-o-wars docked along the port side along with several freighters. Beyond the ships, a beautiful view of the galaxy could be seen.

"So, how is it that a woman of your stature and beauty has stayed single for so long?" inquired Prax curiously.

"Someone has to take responsibility for what happens around here."

"Isn't that Arn's job?"

"Arn is the muscle. I'm the spine and the brain."

"And the beauty."

"Are you hitting on me?"

"Of course not. I'm almost old enough to be your father."

"Good. Now I feel as though I can be truthful with you."

"About…"

Severin's transmitter beeped, interrupting the conversation. Her transmitter was a small device that stowed in a pocket in her belt. "This is Severin." She looked uneasily at Prax. "Is he alive?"

Prax waited anxiously for Severin's response.

"We're on the way," she replied and stowed the transmitter.

"Will is hurt badly. We have to get down to the clinic."

They hurried down the hall to the elevator.

"The clinic? What's he doing there?"

The elevator door slid open and they entered.

"It seems that someone else was in there before Will. The back room was ransacked. My men found Will unconscious when they arrived."

The elevator door slid open. Severin blocked the doors with her leg and grabbed Prax's arm before he could exit. "I'd like to finish our conversation later. It's important."

"I'd be happy to."

They hurried to the clinic and found six of Arn's soldiers inside. Four medics emerged from the back room and carried Will into the patient area on a stretcher.

Will was unconscious with blood smeared on his head and neck.

Severin and Prax entered the rear room. There were files and papers thrown all around the room.

"Someone was very interested in the contents of those boxes," she remarked as she read the titles of the upended boxes on the floor."

Prax tapped her on the shoulder. She looked up curiously.

"They were." He pointed to the satchel and then to one of the boxes. "The notebooks I gave you were in that box."

Arn burst into the clinic. "What the hell's going on?"

"It appears someone wanted Prax's notebooks and Will walked in on them," answered Severin.

"Who would know anything about those notebooks or what's in them?"

"Jack caught Malduna in this room earlier," Prax responded. "She had to pick the lock to get in here."

"He also mentioned that she was looking through one of the notebooks," mentioned Severin.

"Find Malduna and bring her in for questioning," Arn ordered one of the soldiers. The sergeant promptly left the clinic.

"Get Jack and Maya. I want to know what they know about Malduna," ordered Severin. Two more soldiers left the clinic to comply with her wishes.

"Whoever did this won't get far," declared Arn.

"That's only part of the problem," replied Severin. "We have a weapon, a portal system, two arch enemies who are allied and a spy within our station. Something big is going on and we have to stop it before it's too late."

"But if Malduna is on her ship, can we still bring her back?" asked Prax.

"Only if the ship is still docked."

"Then we have to hope Will recognized his attacker," replied Arn. "Otherwise we have no grounds to hold her."

Severin's transmitter beeped. She anxiously answered it. "I see." She turned off the transmitter.

"What is it?"

"Malduna is back on board *The Widow Maker*."

"And?"

"They just departed from the station."

"Order them back here!" bellowed Arn.

Jack and Maya were escorted into the clinic by two soldiers and the sergeant.

"What's going on, General?" demanded Jack.

"Will was attacked by someone, possibly Malduna and/or members of her crew. We believe they were looking for notebooks with details about a weapon."

"Is this the weapon that our alien friends are worried about?" asked Maya.

"Let's stop the conversation right there," commanded Arn. "This needs to be discussed in a secure area."

"I'll see what I can do about *The Widow Maker*," Severin informed Arn and left the clinic.

Arn entered the patient area and questioned one of the medics. "How is he?"

"Severe head trauma and possible broken ribs. Those are the worst of his injuries."

"How did this happen?" inquired Arn.

"I'd say he was struck repeatedly from behind and possibly attacked by more than one person."

"Damn it! This is my station and I want them captured now!"

The remaining soldiers fled the clinic.

Arn looked tired and frustrated.

"Maybe a good night's sleep and then we'll discuss our course of action in the morning," suggested Jack. "You're in no shape to make decisions tonight."

"Alright," he answered reluctantly and departed the clinic.

Maya glanced at Jack then stared at Will. "I'm worried, Jack."

"I know."

"Will he be alright?" Maya asked the medic.

"I believe he'll survive but he really took a beating. There could be permanent damage."

"Thank you."

Maya and Jack left the clinic in silence.

**********

Mountains loomed eerily in the night sky with only starlight casting a dim glow over the landscape.

In the distance, the lights from a Calamaari convoy approached along the lone highway that split the valley.

Shanna crawled along a ledge overlooking the Valley of Serpents. Sweat beaded on her ashen forehead from the warm, humid air. She eyed the convoy with vengeance flowing through her veins. Her body continued to mutate and she knew that, no matter what, Pinta was going to pay for doing this to her.

Shanna slithered along the side of the mountain until she reached the narrowest part of the valley. She scanned the trees around her and found one in particular that would serve her purpose. It was an old, rotten tree that grew diagonally from the mountainside. Much of the soil was eroded by recent rains and the roots were exposed, clinging desperately to the mossy soil. A hissing sound startled Shanna. She immediately retreated from the source of the sound.

A long lizard resembling a Komodo dragon emerged from the trees and stalked her. Another crept behind her and then a third. She calculated her chances of reaching the tree before the lizards. When a fourth lizard appeared, Shanna fled to the tree and scampered to the upper limbs. She reached up and grasped the limb of another tree for support while balancing herself on the rotten branch.

The lizards climbed onto the tree and inched toward her. Long tongues lashed out at her whenever the creatures hissed. They snapped at her, baring rows of sharp teeth.

Shanna rocked the limb and agitated the lizards. They clung tightly to the tree with their claws latching onto the bark.

The convoy was nearly beneath her now. She leaped frantically until many of the roots lost their support and broke away from the ground. The tree creaked and bent lower each time Shanna's weight came down on the limb.

The nearest lizard lunged at her as the last remaining root broke free. Shanna curled up onto the limb of the other tree.

The old tree tumbled down the mountainside. The lizards hissed wildly as they rolled with it until they were bashed to death. The tree and the lizard carcasses came to rest in the middle of the road. Shanna sneered at them with delight.

The convoy of seven trucks was forced to stop in front of the fallen tree. Calamaari soldiers exited the trucks and formed a line on either side of the vehicles with their pulse rifles drawn.

Their vehicles were built with traction devices down the middle of the frame like an inverted half-track which only allowed for engine and fuel to be mounted underneath the vehicle on the outer sections of the vehicles. As a result, they could be targeted easily and the volatile gas that fueled them could be ignited by gunfire.

Six soldiers attempted to move the fallen tree from the road. Three others stood by the carcasses on the other side of the tree with their weapons pointed into the trees.

Shanna felt the mossy ground for small rocks. When she collected a handful, she drew closer to the three soldiers. She lobbed two rocks into the trees on the other side of the road.

The unsuspecting soldiers immediately focused on the sounds and nervously fired their weapons. When the first soldier turned back in her direction, she hurled a stone and struck him in the face. He fell to the ground in pain. The two soldiers near him, unsure of what happened, rushed to his aid.

The remaining soldiers dropped the tree in a panic and retreated to the trucks. Their comrades shouted angrily and urged them to quickly get the tree out of the way.

Shanna saw her opportunity and drew her knives. She rushed at the two soldiers and barreled into them. They were knocked to the ground, stunned by the impact. One of the soldiers cried out for help. Shanna pounded his face and rendered him unconscious.

She quickly slit the throats of the others and retrieved their weapons. Before they noticed her, she disappeared into the trees.

Two soldiers fired randomly at the trees in a panic until the leader grabbed them both from behind.

The firing ceased and only the sound of the trucks' engines could be heard. Their fear was evident and Shanna knew she had them at a disadvantage.

She took a position in the trees looking down at the soldiers. She picked off six of them, one at a time with one of the rifles, then moved to a different location. The light from the red energy pulses gave away each position as she fired.

Shanna eyed the front of the convoy and the soldiers that attempted to move the fallen tree. Four more pulses of energy from her rifle and the soldiers were dead.

The driver of the lead truck frantically drove the vehicle into the tree and tried to ram through it. The lizard carcasses on the back side blocked his progress.

Shanna took aim at the fuel tank and fired two more pulses. The tank exploded and the truck was quickly engulfed in flames.

Again Shanna moved to another location where she could see the tail of the convoy. The soldiers near the burning truck fired frantically into the trees and swore in Calamaari that they would kill their assailants.

Shanna took aim at the fuel tank on the last truck and fired two pulses at it. The truck exploded and burned like the first. The soldiers massed together toward the middle of the convoy in a panic.

As the flames illuminated the night, Shanna noticed the trees along the roadside shaking violently. Lizards emerged from the trees and attacked the soldiers. She listened to the firing of shots until there were no more and the lizards vanished as quickly as they appeared.

Additional explosions rocked the ground as the fires spread to the other trucks. Flames lapped at the sky from the flaming trucks and dark smoke blotted out the stars.

Shanna continued along the mountainside in the direction of the palace.

**********

Inside her crystal palace, Pinta paced like a rabid animal. A senior Calamaari officer stood before her. Two soldiers nervously stood at attention behind him.

"How can you let an enemy vessel get so close to us and destroy that outpost?"

"Most of our forces are focused on the Weevil. We had no reason to expect an attack in Rigor of all places."

Another soldier entered the room and saluted her by tapping his chest and bowing.

"What is it?" she shouted at him.

"The convoy has been attacked."

"By whom?" she screamed.

"We received a radio message that they were pinned down and under attack. The message stopped and we haven't made contact since."

"I don't care who or what you take but get to that mine and find my sister before someone else does," ordered Pinta. "If you don't, I will kill you myself."

The soldier hurried out of the room.

"And as for you, how could anyone know Cintilla was at that mine?"

"I don't know," replied the officer sheepishly.

"Wrong answer!" exclaimed Pinta as she slashed his throat with her long clawed hand. The officer slumped to the ground, clutching desperately at his torn throat.

One of the soldiers behind him thought quickly and requested, "May I speak?"

"You'd better have something useful to say or you'll join him," she warned.

"If it's true that Goeth is alive, then he may have allies among us. If he wants to claim the throne, then he needs both you and Cintilla out of the way."

Pinta pondered for a moment. "That would make sense but what if they rescued her? That won't bode well for us if our people learned that both of them are alive."

"I don't see how they could have gotten through our troops to her at the base. Someone would have called for help," he suggested.

"Find out what happened to that convoy and then find me Cintilla's corpse. Do you understand?"

"Yes, Pinta," replied the soldier and hurriedly exited the room.

**********

Polus picked at a plate of chunks of pink meat with his lobster like claws.

A Weevil officer entered his throne room and stood before him.

"This had better be good," he warned. "I don't like interruptions when I'm eating."

"Polus, something strange is happening on Calamaar. I thought you should know about it."

Polus glared at the officer and set his plate aside. He stood up and extended a mechanical arm to the officer's shoulder. He gripped it tightly until the officer's legs buckled.

"What is so strange that you find important enough to vex me?"

"There was a large explosion in the mining region of Calamaar. Later, we targeted a convoy heading toward the region. It appears the convoy was attacked and destroyed."

"So what?" replied Polus sarcastically as he tightened his grip on the officer's shoulder until brown blood seeped from the wound.

"A much larger convoy just left the palace and is headed for the mining region. Perhaps Pinta has a revolution on her hands."

Polus released his grip on the officer's shoulder. "Then Calamaar could be in a vulnerable state right now. Monitor that convoy and let me know what happens."

"Yes, Polus." The officer turned and left the throne room.

"Perhaps I don't need this truce after all," he uttered to himself and laughed sadistically. He grabbed a pile of meat from the plate and shoved it into his insect-like mouth.

**********

Goeth, Cintilla and Drun transported down to the mining region on Calamaar from their cruiser. They didn't have much time before the Calamaari command would send troops to investigate their idle vessel so they moved quickly.

The base and mining facility were reduced to still smoldering rubble. In the distance, a plume of smoke from the convoy's wreckage muddied the early morning sky.

"It seems that Shanna's been busy," remarked Cintilla.

"We'd best find her quickly," commented Goeth. "We don't want her to attract too much attention."

"Why not let her take care of Pinta for us?" inquired Drun. "That would save us a lot of trouble."

"If the Weevil suspect a revolt, they might use that opportunity to strike at Calamaar," explained Goeth. "Perhaps someone has already conspired with them to supply the doomsday weapon we've heard about."

"Then why the alliance?" asked Cintilla.

"It's a distraction to provide the traitor with the opportunity to locate and steal the weapon. Will's people are naïve about the situation. It is much more serious than they know."

"Then we must make haste."

The three Calamaari left the camp and pursued Shanna.

**********

Shanna hiked through the rough mountainous terrain through the daylight hours. As evening approached, she spotted the second convoy several miles away. The vehicles camped at the entrance to the valley, reluctant to enter under the darkness of night.

Shanna's arms grew more muscular and her locks of blonde hair receded. Her breasts were non-existent and her chest widened.

"They never learn, do they?" she muttered to herself. She checked all three rifles and turned off the safeties. She placed two of them at thirty foot intervals against trees and the third was strapped around her shoulder.

Shanna broke into a run and continued parallel to the road. She reached the convoy in the middle of the night and descended along the side of the road.

She studied the encampment and saw many more soldiers camped about than she expected. There were several guards posted with large scale weapons designed to take out a larger area than the pulse rifles could.

The vehicles were parked in two rows down the middle of the road.

Shanna scouted them and decided it was too risky. She continued past the convoy toward the palace.

After another day of travel, she finally reached the palace. It was a beautiful, crystal palace surrounded by high walls of granite and reached many stories upward.

Near the top was the flight deck for the cruisers. The outside walls were stained with soot and marred from the explosions set off by Shanna and Will earlier.

Shanna crept around the palace property until she reached the main gate. Ten men manned a checkpoint before the gate. An armored vehicle with two cannons mounted on top blocked the front of the gate.

Inside the walls were a number of support buildings and a large courtyard.

Shanna retreated up the road and waited for an unsuspecting vehicle to approach the palace. As evening approached, so did a lone vehicle with three civilian Calamaari in it.

The soldiers became attentive to the vehicle. The cannons mounted in the rear of the jeep targeted it as the civilians stepped out. They became engaged in a heated discussion with the leader of the security detail.

Shanna saw her opportunity and crept along the wall behind the jeep.

The sound of the mechanical latch unlocking the gate brought about everyone's attention. The gate slid apart in two sections and disappeared into the walls.

Another armored jeep emerged followed by a military transport. They stopped next to the civilian vehicle. A high ranking Calamaari officer stepped out of the transport and met the civilians. They greeted each other and the officer motioned for the troops to allow them admittance.

Shanna saw her opportunity and slid underneath the transport. She wedged herself between the fuel tank and the transmission. Fortunately, the transmission on the transport was still cool and she could hold on to it.

The officer returned to the transport and drove inside the palace grounds followed by the civilian vehicle. The jeeps remained outside the gate.

The two vehicles parked outside one of the support buildings. Shanna lowered herself on the ground and watched the legs of the officer and the civilians leave the vehicles and enter the building.

Shanna hid behind a row of trash dumpsters and waited for nightfall.

When darkness set in, Shanna moved stealthily across the grounds to the palace. She scaled the wall using drain pipes and balcony railings for footing.

After ascending six floors, she climbed onto the balcony of a dark office. The only visible light inside was a solid red one on an alarm panel.

She gripped the handle and forced the door open. The broken pieces of the handle and lock shattered and fell across the floor.

The solid red light blinked steadily. Shanna knew she triggered an alarm and guards would be there soon to investigate. She left the room and hurried down the hall in search of a stairwell. She turned the corner at the end and found the stairwell.

Several guards raced down the hall from the other direction and entered the room. Shanna hurried up the stairs to the ninth floor and left the stairwell.

An officer stood outside one of the offices and fumbled with the key code to the lock. Just as he opened the door, Shanna rushed up on him from behind. She shoved him inside the room and bull-dogged him to the ground.

The officer tried to fight back but she had position on him and rendered him unconscious with a shot to the back of the head. She hurried to the door and closed it.

**********

On the eleventh floor, Pinta addressed a group of officers about their declining discipline. One of the officers attempted to explain the issue but further enraged her. She stared the officer down for several seconds and appeared to relent. When she turned away, the officer took a deep breath and relaxed. Pinta then spun around and gripped his throat until she ripped it out. The surprised officer fell to the floor, gasping desperately for air until he died.

The other officers were aghast of her extreme actions.

"This is a perfect example of what happens when you let down your guard," explained Pinta arrogantly. "Don't fail me again."

When Pinta exited the briefing room, the officers expressed their rage against her.

"We've got to do something!" exclaimed one officer. "She's insane."

"Don't let her hear you talk like that," replied another.

**********

Shanna waited patiently for the officer to regain consciousness. When he did, she applied pressure to his neck and head, threatening to snap his head off his shoulders.

"What do you want, mutant?" the officer blurted raspily.

"Watch your mouth," she warned as she loosened her hold on him. "Where's Pinta?"

"What do you want with her?"

"I owe her for something she gave me."

"You!" he gasped. "You are Saris' mate!"

"Why does that matter?"

"Is it true that Goeth lives?"

"Yes, it is," replied Shanna. "Now where is Pinta?"

"Please, I am not your enemy."

"Prove it."

"I will help you find Pinta," the officer agreed. "You must know that Zorick has plans to overthrow Pinta and you could jeopardize those plans."

"You see what Pinta has done to me. I will personally take her apart, piece by piece."

"It won't be so easy."

"And why is that?"

"You left her with a useless arm last time."

"Why does that create a problem for me?"

"Because she had it removed. It's been replaced with a mechanical arm that is much stronger than any Calamaari."

"That's a chance I'll have to take."

Shanna got off of the officer and allowed him to stand. "If you cross me, I will kill you, too."

"You need not fear me."

Shanna stepped back and allowed the officer access to the door.

"You will pretend to be my prisoner. That will allow me access to Pinta's location. Then it's your game."

"Very well."

The officer drew his pistol and escorted Shanna into the hall and to the elevator. They rode to the eleventh floor where Pinta waited to step on.

The door opened and the officer nudged Shanna forward.

Pinta was startled to see Shanna. "What is this?"

"She must have broken into the palace. I caught her on the sixth floor."

"Oh, this is wonderful. If only Saris was here with you. Or is he?"

"This is personal. You and I have unfinished business."

The group of officers appeared from the briefing room. They, too, were surprised to see a mutant prisoner.

"Take her to the laboratory. I'm sure we can take her apart and study her physiology. Then I'll eat her."

The officer stepped back. "I don't think so, Pinta."

Shanna took a fighting stance with Pinta.

"Arrest them both," ordered Pinta.

"Stand down," replied the officer to the others.

Shanna noticed the mechanical arm underneath Pinta's robe and positioned herself away from it.

"Come on, mutant. Do you fear me?" Pinta taunted her.

Shanna lowered her head and lunged at Pinta. She drove her into the wall, ramming her shoulder into Pinta's midsection.

Pinta struck at Shanna's back repeatedly but could do no harm from that position.

The officers from the briefing room dispersed for fear of reprisal if Pinta survived.

The remaining officer was angry at their cowardice. "Why do you flee when you have a chance to be rid of this evil tyrant?"

The officers ignored him and fled down the stairwell.

Shanna locked her arm around Pinta's mechanical arm and twisted. Pinta grimaced in pain and shoved her clawed hand into Shanna's face. Shanna twisted harder and Pinta screamed. Shanna head-butted her and twisted again, exerting all her might on the mechanical arm.

Pinta cried out obscenities at Shanna as her eyes bulged from the pain. The mechanical arm tore out of Pinta's shoulder socket.

Shanna held the arm up triumphantly and tossed it aside. Pinta rushed at her and shoved her claws toward Shanna's eyes. The two spun around as Shanna gripped her wrist, pushing the claws aside.

Shanna head butted her again and wrestled her to the ground. She pressed the elevator button and the doors opened.

Pinta tried to get free but Shanna yanked her to her knees and shoved her forward on her face. Pinta's head rested inside the elevator and the doors began to close.

Pulse fire filled the hall as seven guards approached. They fired and struck the officer with several shots. He shoved Shanna into the elevator before the doors closed as he collapsed and died.

Pinta pulled away from the elevator just in time to avoid the doors. She was rattled and bleeding badly.

The guards lifted her up and took her for medical attention.

Shanna got off the elevator on the sixth floor. The hall was empty and the office door where she came in was closed. She hurried to the door and kicked it open. Two guards stood by the open door to the balcony and were startled by her entry.

Shanna raced forward and shoved them over the railing. The three of them hurdled toward the ground. Shanna desperately pulled the two guards together beneath her and waited for the impact when they hit the ground.

Upon impact, her organs shook so badly that she vomited on the dead guards and urinated uncontrollably. Her head hurt so badly that she had little balance.

Pulse blasts from the balcony above sent pieces of dirt and rock spraying around her.

Shanna staggered to her feet and climbed into an armored jeep. She started it and attempted to drive.

The gate was closed and a line of soldiers formed in front of it. They fired at the jeep, hoping for a lucky shot at her.

Shanna turned around and drove away from the gate. She tried to collect her thoughts and find a way out of the palace.

The jeep struck the corner of a building and flipped over. Shanna was thrown from the vehicle. She lay helplessly on the ground until she saw a sewer drain. Desperately she crawled to it and forced her large frame through the slot and under the street.

Her instincts told her to keep moving no matter what. The sound of voices and red flashes of light from pulse blasts sent her into a panic.

As she leaned forward, she felt weightlessness and realized she was falling. She no longer cared if she died and waited to collide with something solid.

After what seemed an eternity, she splashed into an underground river and floated down stream. She couldn't decide if she was really lucky or really cursed.

Shanna drifted along, dazed and confused, for hours until she bumped against large rocks. She climbed onto one of the rocks and collapsed.

Daylight arrived and immersed the rocks at the entrance to the small cave.

Shanna's eyes stung and her body ached. She squinted as she scanned her surroundings and tried to gather her senses.

When she stood up, everything swirled around her. She fell into the water and waited for several moments. Slowly, she regained her senses and when she could stand, she left the cave and entered the forest.

She hiked through the trees and rocks until she recognized the entrance to the valley.

The road nearby had tracks from the vehicles that camped there earlier.

Shanna felt renewed confidence and continued into the valley. She didn't kill Pinta but she did get some measure of revenge. Now, Pinta would be looking over her shoulder and know that no matter where she is, she's vulnerable.

Nightfall arrived and Shanna perched on a ledge overlooking the road. She could see lights from the convoy at the mining site. Her body healed and the pain she felt earlier had subsided. She traveled along the ridge at the top of the valley until she was within visual range of the mine.

She found the first rifle she left strategically along the ledge after her attack on the first convoy.

A large green snake slithered along the rocks above her. It was nearly twenty feet long with loose scales on its skin, an indication that it was beginning to shed. It hovered above her and prepared to strike.

Shanna crouched over the ledge and eyed the convoy. Suddenly, she sensed the snake and leaped sideways. She immediately tossed the rifle to the ground and drew both knives.

The snake struck at her and she again side-stepped its head. Instinctively, she leaped on its back and drove both of her daggers into its head. The snake shuddered and shook frantically until both of them tumbled down the mountainside.

Shanna crashed onto the side of the road and lay unconscious while the snake caught up on tree limbs above her.

The snake desperately tried to free itself from the limbs until the limb snapped. The snake tumbled down on Shanna and lay dead.

Shanna stirred and slowly regained consciousness. She felt the weight of the snake across her back and struggled to free herself. After several attempts, she managed to wriggle free of it.

She retrieved her knives from the snake's head and staggered to the side of the road.

When she felt strong enough to continue, she crawled part of the way up the mountainside. Using tree branches and roots, rocks and shrubs, she pulled herself up until she reached the ledge. She lay across the rock's flat surface, spent from the climb and her injuries. She became dizzy and passed out from fatigue.

She lay in a deep sleep, exhausted, and dreamed for hours. Memories stimulated her thoughts and brought back some of her Firengian feelings. She recalled the day she met Will and how much it seemed like a fairy tale – her fairy tale. She had her knight in shining armor until fate struck.

When she became pregnant with Marina, things changed. They were targeted by enemies all over the galaxy. There was no peace for them. Friends died and sacrifices had to be made.

Shanna dreamed that Will arrived to rescue her. Then, he saw her mutated shape and fled from her. Shanna cried out for him to return but he disappeared. She called to him again but now she couldn't speak. She felt as if she were suffocating.

She gasped and realized she was suffocating. She awoke to find herself in the mouth of another snake, being devoured slowly. Without the will to fight, she could only hope to die quickly.

Goeth followed the ledge and discovered one of Shanna's rifles propped against the tree. Cintilla and Drun followed a short distance behind.

"She was here," Goeth said with certainty in his voice.

From the next ledge down, Shanna sensed that someone was above her on the upper ledge. She tried to focus and recognized blurry shapes

"Help me," blurted Shanna. "Someone please help me."

Goeth motioned for Cintilla and Drun to halt and be silent. They listened carefully and heard Shanna's feeble call. When they saw Shanna below them in the snake's mouth, they were horrified.

"Wait here," Goeth ordered Cintilla. "It's too risky for you."

Goeth and Drun scurried down the slope to the lower ledge.

The snake gulped and Shanna slid further into its mouth up to her shoulders. Tears streamed across her face as she prayed death would take her soon. Her eyes displayed the horror that she felt over her fate.

Another snake appeared and raised its head above her. Its tongue slithered in and out, followed by sharp hissing. Two beady black eyes stared at her like the devil waiting to claim her soul. It poised to battle for Shanna's body with the first snake.

Shanna felt the last breath leave her lungs and saw death come for her. An evil sinister voice filled her head, "You won't escape me." Then she blacked out.

Goeth grabbed the snake's head and savagely gutted its throat with his dagger.

Drun fired several shots at the second snake. Pieces of flesh splattered the area as red pulses of energy shredded its head. Finally the second snake was dead and, except for an occasional quiver, lay motionless on the ground.

Goeth gripped Shanna around her shoulders and tugged desperately while Drun sliced the snake open. After much effort, they freed Shanna from its vice-like grip and set her down on the ground.

Shanna was barely alive but the sight of her cold eyes and white leathery skin covered with slime mortified Goeth and Drun.

"We have to do this," said Goeth. "We owe it to her for saving my mother."

"If we must," replied Drun.

They reluctantly lifted Shanna and dragged her up to the ridge.

Cintilla watched nervously as they set Shanna down on the ground. She bent over Shanna and examined her. "We can't give her the serum in this condition. It's too risky."

Goeth looked at Shanna with pity.

"You've taken a liking to the humans," commented Drun. "I am surprised."

"They are not all the same. I respect this group."

"As do I but how far can we trust them?"

"I trust Will and Shanna completely. The others – well, we'll see."

The convoy stopped in the road by the wreckage from the previous convoy. They saw the flashes of gunfire on the ridge above when Drun shot the snake. The soldiers quickly exited the truck and formed a line.

Drun saw the formation of shooters. "Get down, quickly!"

Goeth helped Cintilla to the ground behind a boulder. Shanna was screened from the gunfire by an old tree stump.

Energy pulses sprayed all around them. Trees and rocks shattered around them.

"We've got to move fast!" exclaimed Drun. "Cover me."

Drun picked up Shanna's body and scurried through the trees to higher ground. Goeth laid down a line of gunfire from behind a large tree. When the soldiers concentrated their gunfire on him, he dove between two trees and laid flat on the ground.

Four soldiers crept behind Cintilla and placed the muzzle of their rifles against her head. Goeth ducked into the bushes before they could spot him.

Cintilla made no effort to resist but stared at them with disappointment.

"Cintilla! We weren't expecting to see you here," said the leader of the group.

"And whom did you expect?" she replied.

"We thought we'd find Saris and his gang."

"So what do we do now since you have likely allied yourself to my mutinous sister?"

"We were told that you had a fatal accident. Pinta claims that she is the next in line to rule since you and Goeth were gone."

"All lies. Goeth is alive and well as am I."

"Then we serve you. What do you require of us?"

"I must return to Saris' people until I am in a position to retake my throne."

"But why not now?" the leader asked.

"If the Weevil find out that there is a rift in the Calamaari leadership, they will see it as an opportunity to destroy us. Things must appear normal."

"But they are not. One convoy has been destroyed on the way to the mines and another was under siege. We suspect that Saris has landed with a large contingent to overthrow Pinta."

"You fools! Don't tell me you heard that from Pinta."

"It was she who sent us capture or destroy whoever was responsible for the assaults on the convoys."

Another soldier inquired, "How is it that you trust Saris and his people?"

"He has earned my trust."

"But they have the doomsday weapon! They will decimate us when the time is right."

"That's precisely why I need to stay close to Saris' people. If they really have such a weapon, I will find it and destroy it."

Goeth stood up and lowered his weapon. He stepped out into the open.

Goeth!" exclaimed one of the soldiers.

Drun appeared from the trees with Shanna's prone body over his shoulders. He drew his pistol and aimed it at the lead soldier's head.

"It's alright," replied Cintilla and motioned for them to stand down.

Drun lowered Shanna onto the ground and eyed the soldiers carefully.

The forest grew silent.

The leader stepped forward and extended a clawed hand to Goeth in friendship. "I am Riven, son of Zorick. I have heard many courageous stories of you. We were told that you were dead."

Goeth shook hands with Riven. "As you can see, I am alive and well. The human, Will Saris, is responsible for that."

"What are your orders?" asked Riven.

"Return to Pinta and tell her that we were killed with the other rebels in the valley. She must not know that we are here."

"I will make sure that she gets that message."

"I also need you to be ready when I return. Your father is already aware of the situation. We need this transition to be quick and quiet or the Weevil will surely take advantage and launch a major assault on Calamaar."

"We will be ready."

The soldiers dispersed down the mountainside and returned to their vehicles.

**********

The ruins at the mine were eerily silent. The corpses were devoured by the large carnivorous denizens of the valley leaving only scant remains.

A small stream flowed past the entrance to the mining site from the forest and ended at a large pond on the other side of the camp.

Goeth set Shanna on the ground next to the stream. Cintilla knelt next to her. She cupped her clawed hands in the water and poured it across Shanna's forehead.

Drun scavenged the area for torn clothing from the corpses' remains. He returned and soaked the rags in the stream.

Each of them took a piece of garment and wiped the snake's residue from Shanna's body.

Shanna shuddered and awoke in a frantic state.

Goeth held her arms firmly. "You're safe now, Shanna. You're with friends." He thought about his words and felt strange. When he looked up at Cintilla and Drun, they seemed touched by his compassion.

Shanna burst into tears and breathed irregularly.

Cintilla placed her hands on Shanna's temples and concentrated.

Goeth and Drun wondered what she was doing.

Shanna's body relaxed and her breathing became normal.

"Give her the serum," directed Cintilla.

"Are you sure?" Goeth asked uneasily.

"Yes, do it quickly."

Drun raised Shanna up and tilted her head back gently.

Goeth removed the vial from his belt and poured the contents onto Shanna's lips. She sipped the liquid instinctively until it was gone. Drun laid her flat again and she slept. He eyed Goethe curiously.

"You need to realize that Will and Shanna could be the key to our survival if the doomsday weapon really exists," explained Goethe. " They have proven their friendship to me and I will prove mine to them," declared Goeth.

"It seems there is much about the human race we don't know," added Cintilla. "Shanna risked her life to rescue me. After all that's happened, I never expected that."

"I wouldn't be so quick to praise them," remarked Drun cynically. "They are much like us in many ways including treachery and distrust."

"And because of that we will learn to build friendship upon this," replied Cintilla. "I admit I was resentful against all humans and considered them weak. Now I see that the Calamaari are no different."

"We all have our strengths and weaknesses," explained Goeth. "How we control our weaknesses is determined by our strengths."

"You have learned well, my son. Better than I. You will make a good ruler of your people."

"Thank you mother. If it weren't for Will, we might all be dead."

"I will stand watch," offered Drun.

"Mother, you must rest," advised Goeth.

Cintilla touched Goeth's arm affectionately with her clawed hand. She closed her eyes and slept.

# Chapter Six

## Puzzle Pieces

Severin entered the clinic and approached Will. She watched him breathe peacefully for several minutes and wondered if there could have been something special between them if he wasn't married to Shanna. They both were committed to their responsibilities and both were stubborn in their beliefs.

Prax stepped out of his office and was surprised to see her standing there. "Severin, how long have you been here?"

"Not long. How is he?"

"No good. There's been zero improvement and I'm really getting worried now."

Severin noticed the equipment that monitored Will's brain activity and vitals. "His vitals are weak and brain activity is minimal. We need to do something soon."

"The doctors spent hours with him today and made no progress," said Prax sullenly as he gazed at Will's face. "He is so much like his father; it's almost as if he was still here."

"I take it you flew with him in the Andoran war."

"We did. His dad had the heart of a lion."

"And so does Will," she affirmed. "Prax, we have to talk."

"Yes, we do. I may be closer to the second stage of Shanna's serum than I thought."

"No, I'm talking about the PBU-57."

"I can't tell you anything more than I told the others," replied Prax. "I don't know anything about it."

"No, I think it's me who can tell you a few things I read in the notebooks."

"Such as…"

"Apparently Xerxes was coerced by the government on Earth to make an improved version of an alien weapon that's designed to create a black hole of immense size."

"Does it say if he developed it?"

"His notes are very cryptic," explained Severin. "It sounds like it didn't work but at the same time it did."

"That makes no sense."

"Not until he mentioned that a single element is the difference."

"An element?"

"Yes. He also lists a series of numbers as well. I think they might be identification numbers for crates that were shipped."

"Look, Severin, I know this is important to you but I owe it to Will to take care of Shanna first."

"It won't matter if we are slaughtered by the Weevil or the Calamaari. Think about that."

"Alright, I'll do this but only for you," said Prax reluctantly.

Severin smiled appreciatively.

The two of them left the clinic.

**********

Arn stood in front of the monitor and barked into the mike. "I don't give a hoot. Get her on, now!"

A young man glared back at Arn. "You don't speak to us in that tone. I don't care who you are."

Arn puffed on his cigar and leaned closer. "You remember that, sonny boy, while your ass is getting incinerated 'cause in about one minute, we're going to blast that tin can you call a ship into smithereens."

Another man pushed his way in front of the monitor. "Now hold on. What's this all about?"

"I want to speak with Malduna, now."

"Stand by. I'll inform her." The man smacked the younger fellow in the head and whispered threateningly in his ear.

"Militia assholes!" grumbled Arn. "Got no respect for authority."

Malduna appeared on the monitor. She wore a black sari and a small turban. "You wish to speak with me, General."

"Yes, I do. We've had an unfortunate incident occur and we'd like to question you."

"Why would you think I am involved in this incident?"

"You were discovered in a secure room in the clinic with documents considered a potential threat to the well-being of the station," he informed her. "You and your ship conveniently departed the premise, which doesn't bode well for you."

"When would you like to conduct your inquisition?"

"So you would return for an inquisition?"

"I have nothing to hide."

"Then we'll plan for tomorrow. I'll assemble my staff to question you and the evidence we have."

"I will be there. Several of my men will accompany me as well to procure rations and supplies. We have a long journey ahead of us."

"Thank you for your cooperation, Malduna. Hopefully we can put this to rest."

The transmission ended and Arn threw the cigar at the trashcan. Ashes scattered across the floor as the butt bounced off the lip of the can and fell harmlessly to the ceramic tile floor.

Arn paced back and forth in a snit. "I know I'm being played and I can't do a damn thing about it!" He stormed out of the Communications Room and slammed the door behind him.

**********

Prax opened the cargo bay door at the outer hull of his ship. "Are you sure you want to do this now?" he asked Severin hesitantly.

"Look, we have nothing but questions so far. We have to start getting answers."

Prax unlocked a small lockbox on the wall and removed a binder. "This is a log of everything Xerxes placed on board." He then took a remote control from the box and turned on the power. The cargo bay illuminated seven aisles of crates and boxes.

Severin took the log from him and scanned several pages as they walked slowly down the first aisle of crates.

"Some of the entries make no sense to me whatsoever," remarked Prax.

"These items must have been important for him to go through so much trouble."

Severin paused in front of a crate shaped like a large coffin. She glanced at the log and then at the designation on the crate. "Let's check this one."

Prax pressed a button on the remote control unit. A robotic forklift came to life and rolled toward them. The lift had a bright light at the top and operated silently.

At Prax's control, the forklift removed the crate from the rack. Prax guided it outside his ship onto the space station's dock. He set the crate down along side the ship and shut down the forklift.

They locked eyes for an instant. Each sensed the attraction between them. Prax felt awkward due to their age difference. She was seventeen years younger than he was at twenty-six in Earth years.

Severin had never been close to anyone before. She always wished that Will could have been the one but here was Prax, a road warrior like Will and his father before him. Prax was more sentimental than Will and she wondered if that's what was missing in her life. She was all business and no fun.

Severin took over the roll of security officer at nineteen when she abandoned the Space Fleet. One year out of the academy and she knew they were as much to blame for the war as the aliens.

Prax took a crowbar from a small tool box on the side of the forklift and pried the top off the crate. He flipped the cover off with disregard and it crashed to the deck behind the crate. Inside was a large coffin with a recorder mounted on the cover. Prax froze at the sight of the coffin.

Severin feared it could be Prax' father, Xerxes. She placed her hand on Prax's shoulder to show her support. His eyes welled up as he fell to his knees.

He reached unsteadily to the recorder and pressed his finger against the display.

The recorder acknowledged his print and beeped. Xerxes' voice played back to him.

"Prax, if you have reached Will, you are among friends. You have the key to the future of mankind. They will help you to do what is right. I will always be with you my son."

Prax sobbed. Severin placed a hand on his shoulder. "I'm sorry, Prax."

The coffin vibrated and hummed. They were startled and backed away.

"Did you hear that, Severin?"

"I sure did."

Severin approached the coffin and reached out to touch it. Suddenly the latches sprang open. She shrieked and backed away.

They glanced at each other and then at the coffin. It opened slowly by a mechanized device.

"What the hell is going on here?" Prax uttered.

They crept closer and looked inside the coffin. What they found wasn't Xerxes' body but an electro-mechanical device that took up the whole inside of the coffin.

"I don't believe it!" exclaimed Prax.

"Could it be the doomsday weapon?"

"What else could it be?"

Prax studied the device and found identification markings on a two-stage tank in the middle of the device – PBU-57A.

"We've got to let Arn know right away," exclaimed Prax anxiously.

"I'll take care of it," replied Severin. She turned away from him and spoke into her transmitter.

Prax ran his fingers across the device in awe.

Severin returned and pressed the screen on top of the coffin's lid. It automatically closed and sealed. "We've got to get this to a secured area."

"What happens if word gets out that we really do have the weapon?"

"That could be a big problem. I'll make arrangements to get it out of here ASAP. You secure the ship and meet me back here."

Prax returned the forklift inside the ship.

Three men entered the bay. Each had long hair and beards. They were dressed casually in jeans and t-shirts. One of them climbed inside the space station's transport cart and drove behind them. The men approached Severin with grim expressions.

"Can I help you, gentlemen?" she asked sternly.

"You need something moved?" said the taller of the men.

"This coffin goes to deck three. It needs to be quarantined until further notice."

"Of course."

Severin noticed that none of them wore identification badges. "Hey, wait a minute!" she shouted.

One of the men drew a pistol and fired at her. A pulse of energy left a burning hole in her right shoulder and knocked her into the hull of Prax's ship. She lay motionless on the deck.

The men operated the transport cart and loaded the coffin on the back. They hopped on it and quickly drove away from the dock.

Prax emerged from inside the ship and closed the hatch. As he turned, he saw Severin on the deck unconscious and rushed to her aid.

Prax tried to wake her but to no avail. He called Arn on the transmitter and informed him of the missing coffin and the attack on Severin.

Four medics promptly arrived in a cart and administered first aid to Severin's shoulder. They placed her on the cart and returned to the clinic.

Prax lowered his head sadly and opened the hatch to his ship. He returned to the cargo bay inside.

Across the aisle were the notebooks he gave to Severin earlier. Prax opened the first one and read more about the PBU-57. At the bottom of the page was a reference to page thirty three of the second notebook. He opened the other notebook curiously and scanned through several pages. At the top of page thirty-three was an entry from Xerxes.

"By itself, the PBU-57A, although very effective, is limited to a small range. The missing element that the Andorans had access to is called Crylum and was imported from Calamaar during the early stages of the alien alliance's formation."

Prax sighed with relief. "So this isn't the end all weapon everyone feared it was." He read on. "A second prototype, the PBU-57B, is stored at location C6X64M. This has been modified to accept 0.6 kilograms of finely ground Crylum with 0.4 kilograms of C-76, also finely ground. They must be thoroughly blended together using an air-fired centrifuge. If the two ingredients aren't completely blended together, the resulting compound will be volatile and extremely dangerous."

Prax proceeded down one of the aisles. On the bottom rack at the very rear of the bay, he found it – C6X64M.

"We've got them now," he shouted. "They took the wrong friggin'weapon!"

Prax continued to read the notes.

**********

Arn waited at the clinic as the medics arrived with Severin. The cart stopped in the hall and the four men carried her in. They laid her gently on a bed across from Will and promptly operated on her damaged shoulder.

Severin awakened and reached for Arn. He came to her side and took her hand. "Who did this, Sev?"

"They didn't have badges. I tried to..." she uttered and passed out.

"Please, General, not now," urged one of the medics.

Arn backed away and turned to Will. "Son, I could really use your help. Where are you?"

Will's hand twitched and startled Arn. He pulled up a chair and sat close to Will.

"Will, can you hear me?" whispered Arn.

Will's hand twitched again. Two of his fingers raised in the air briefly.

"Will, you've become like a son to me. I never thought I'd admit that to you. If you get through this, I'll make you proud."

Will's hand went limp and there was no further activity.

Arn turned his attention to Severin and the medics. "Is she gonna' be alright?"

"She's lost a lot of blood," replied one of the medics. "I think we've stabilized her for now. The next six hours will be critical."

"I'm posting four sentries in here with them at all times. I want to know immediately if there is any improvement in either Severin or Will. Understand?"

"Yes, sir."

Arn left the clinic and pondered as he walked down the hall. "Where's Prax? He should have been with her."

Arn pressed the alarm mounted on the wall by the elevator. He picked up the page and announced, "The station is in lockdown until further notice. This is General Adolfo. I repeat; the station is in lockdown."

Arn met a dozen soldiers as they stepped off the elevator. "You four; get to the clinic and stay there. Severin and Will could be targets of an assassin."

The four soldiers nearest him hurried down the hall to the clinic.

"The rest of you come with me."

The remaining eight soldiers escorted him to the elevator.

**********

In the pilots' cabin of the *Leviathan*, Jack and Bastille studied the long range monitor. Bastille pointed out several locations in various sectors.

"So those bastards creep into a sector and dump off their probes that set up the next grid in their portal system?"

"That's right," answered Bastille. "The recent attack by the Weevil was a distraction while they planted more of these probes."

"Now we have to figure out how to use it against them."

"Suppose we did get our hands on this doomsday weapon that the aliens are so afraid of. We could enter into their system and launch the weapon. Then we turn around and destroy the probes on our way out. If this weapon is anything like the Andoran weapon Dark Horizon, everything in their grid system will be obliterated all the way back to their planet."

"Bastille, if that's possible, then you're a genius, my friend" Jack remarked. "I'll inform Arn and Severin that we may have a plan if they find the weapon."

"Wait a minute, Jack. I think we'll need to map out where all of the probes are in this sector before we try anything of the sort."

"Can you do it?"

"Of course but it'll take time and I'm sure the Weevil don't want us snooping around their probes either."

"Then get on it, man!"

Maya entered the cabin, looking somber.

Jack almost collides with her and pauses. "What's wrong, Honey?"

"Malduna. I did some research on Rourke and sent out some queries."

"And?"

"She is Rourke's wife. They led the rebel takeover on Earth until the *Leviathan* arrived and drove them out."

"Then she's out for revenge for quite a few reasons."

"Uh-huh. She wants to take care of Will, Shanna and the *Leviathan* personally."

"We'd better get a hold of Arn now. If she's on board, they need to take her onto custody and fast."

"She's here for the inquiry – voluntarily."

"What? I don't like this at all."

The two of them hurried out of the pilot's cabin.

"Nothing is simple anymore," uttered Bastille to himself.

Celine emerged from a panel in the floor. "Hi there, stranger."

"Just in time, my desert flower."

"I heard what happened."

"Yeah, every time we think we have an edge, we're two steps behind."

"I've been working on the cloaking system for several hours and I think we have a problem."

"Great. More bad news," complained Bastille.

"The circuitry is slowly degrading. The composite material in every system's circuit boards isn't compatible with the power source of the *Leviathan*."

"That explains why we're having all these recurring problems with the control and the cloaking systems."

Celine climbs out of the compartment and sits next to him. "What are you thinking?"

"I'm thinking that we may have to send our gal out with a bang when the time comes."

"Like the *Phantom*?"

"Maybe bigger," he remarked.

**********

Prax pulled out a small case off the rack and set it down on the floor. He unlatched the locks and opened it.

Inside was a device that resembled a blender with a computerized control system beneath it. Mounted on top was a block with several probes extending into the cylindrical tank.

He glanced back at the notebook for additional instructions.

The hatch opened and startled him. Arn barged in with his fat cigar tilted out the right side of his mouth as usual, followed by his escort of soldiers. "Prax, you have some explaining to do."

"Yes, I do. How is Severin?"

"We won't know for sure for a few hours. What was in the coffin that Severin mentioned?"

"The doomsday weapon."

"Well, it's been stolen. My men are searching the ship but so far there's no sign of it."

"That's great!"

"What do you mean 'great'?"

"It's not the doomsday weapon after all."

One of Arn's officers entered the room. He approached Arn secretively and whispers in his ear.

"Very well," replied Arn. "Find Malduna and take her into custody."

The officer nodded and departed.

"Malduna's men were seen on the security camera bringing in a large crate. A short while later, they left with one."

"They left one, huh?" Prax pondered aloud.

Arn noticed the device in front of Prax. "And what is that?"

"This is an emulator. It will replicate a clone of Shanna's original blood type. Once complete, this serum will overtake the alien genes that have rooted themselves in her body."

"How the hell does it do that?"

"Nanotechnology. Xerxes really knew his stuff."

So what does that have to do with the doomsday weapon? Come on, boy!" exclaimed Arn. "We're on the edge of Armageddon here."

"It's simple. They both need Crylum to function."

"What in the world is Crylum?"

"It's a raw element found on Calamaar. Once we have about a kilogram of it, we can complete the emulator and the doomsday weapon, too."

"What got stolen then?" asked Arn with a confused expression on his face.

"That's the first prototype. It's effective in a small range only. We have the latest version in our possession. I told you it was simple."

"Simple, my ass! How are we going to get this stuff from Calamaar without getting our butts blown off?"

"I got us this far, General. You'll have to figure out the rest for yourself."

"Does the prototype use black hole technology like the Andoran weapon?" asked Arn curiously.

"Not at all. The compound, when activated and ignited by a laser to 4000 degrees, releases a deadly ray that disintegrates anything metal or flesh in its blast radius."

"Then I should let our intruders get away with the first prototype?"

"Yes and no. If we make it too easy, they'll know something's up."

"Man, I need a drink. Bring your book of tricks and come on."

"I thought you'd never ask."

Prax secured the ship and they returned to the saloon. The two men entered the bar where Prax laid the notebooks on the table.

Jack and Maya entered shortly after and pulled up seats next to them.

"We always know where to find you, General," kidded Jack.

"Unfortunately it comes with the job."

"Where's Severin, General?" inquired Maya. "I have some information she'll be interested in."

"She was assaulted on the dock at Prax's ship a little while ago."

"Is she alright?"

"We'll see. Next few hours are crucial."

"We know for sure that Malduna is behind this."

"So do I," replied Arn. "How do I prove it?"

"You don't. We know who she is."

"Jeanie, I need a drink!"

"Yes,sir," she shouted from behind the bar.

"Give it to me," he relented.

"Malduna's husband, Rourke, ran a large operation on Earth," explained Jack. "They had control of most of the world until the *Leviathan* arrived to stop their insurrection."

"So she wants your ship?"

"Yes but there's more," replied Maya.

"Jeanie, make that a double!" Arn ordered. "Alright, I'm listening."

"Rourke launched a takeover of Will and Shanna's kingdom," explained Maya. "They murdered several of their friends before we were able to stop them."

"And…"

"Will and Shanna killed Rourke."

"So the bitch wants revenge against Will for her husband and her empire."

"You get the picture," remarked Jack.

Jeanie arrived with six glasses of rum.

Arn looked puzzled. "Why six?" he asked.

"You look like you'll need six glasses, sir"

"If Jeanie was thirty years older, I'd marry her in a heartbeat," joked Arn.

"The General is like my father," said Jeanie coyly. "He looks out for me." She returned to the bar.

"If we get our hands on Malduna, she's got to be put down," declared Maya. "She is dangerous and likely suicidal."

Arn chugged two glasses of the rum. "Alright, now I have some news for you."

Jack and Maya gave him their undivided attention.

"They escaped with the weapon."

Jack and Maya were stunned.

"It's alright," said Prax calmly. "It's not a doomsday weapon after all."

"They tried to pull a switcheroo on us with a couple of crates, and then left with the prototype."

Where are they now?" inquired Maya.

"They got away."

"What about the remaining crate?" asked Prax. "We never resolved that issue."

"They delivered it to the security deck on level three."

"Anyone check it, yet?" asked Jack uneasily.

"They quarantined the crates. Probably just some junk inside to distract us."

Maya leaned on the bar with both hands. "Or a bomb, General! We have to get to that crate now!"

Jeanie approached them but Arn held his hand up to her. "Sorry, Jeanie. Something just came up."

The four of them hurried out of the saloon and took the elevator to level three.

Five soldiers guarded the entrance to deck three. When Arn emerged from the elevator, they saluted and stepped back.

"Where is the crate that was quarantined a short while ago?"

"Follow me, sir," replied one of the soldiers.

They entered the large bay and approached a wooden crate the size of a coffin.

Several other soldiers joined them from the opposite end of the bay.

"Open it," ordered Arn.

The soldiers used bayonets to pry the top off the crates.

When they removed the lid, they were horrified to see an explosive device with a timer on a computerized screen. The timer indicated one minute and twenty seconds.

"Jesus H. Christ!" bellowed Arn. "We're screwed."

Jack and Prax knelt over it and studied the device. "Cutters, quick!"

One of the soldiers retrieved cutting pliers from a workbench. "Pliers, sir."

Jack took the pliers and paused over the device. "We're gonna' have to cut more than one wire. I've never seen anything like this."

Jack reached inside and raised a wire bundle. Prax grabbed Jack's arm and took the bundle.

"Allow me," Prax said confidently. He reached inside to a clamp and slowly turned the key on it. Once it loosened, he slid it to the right. He then gripped a coupling and slid it apart from the casing.

"You know what you're doing?" asked Jack nervously.

"Sure do. The wires are just a distraction."

"You only have a minute," warned Arn.

"Not a problem." Prax reached into the casing and unscrewed a small component resembling a spark plug. He tossed it up in the air to Jack.

Jack grabbed it and stared at it. "What is it?"

"The igniter. That's what drives the firing train into the bomb's body and detonates the contents."

Arn watched the screen uneasily. "Is it supposed to keep counting down like that?"

"It's harmless," said Prax calmly. "We've disengaged the laser."

Jack looked inside and followed two wires. He stepped around the other side of the crate and peered at the underside of the bomb assembly. The two wires entered a black box. The box was mounted to a small gearbox attached to the rear of the drive train. "How much time on the timer?" he asked.

"Oh, about ten seconds," answered Prax.

Jack reached in and yanked both wires from the device. He held them up between his fingers as the timer expired. Sparks flew off the ends of the two wires.

Prax suddenly looked ill. "I…I thought I disabled it."

"You did. This is an alternate detonator."

Prax felt ill and rushed into the hall. His face was ashen.

Jack came out and patted him on the shoulder. "Don't feel bad. We got it."

"Enough games! Everything's going to hell around here and we're no closer to a solution than before," chastised Arn.

"We need to do something now," added Maya. "Where are Malduna and the *Widowmaker*?"

"I'm waiting for word back from my Communications Officer now," answered Arn. "Prax, what's this Crylum crap?"

"It's a mineral found on Calamaar. We need it for Shanna's cure and for the PBU-57B."

"Then we need to get to Calamaar and find some. How much do you need?"

"One kilogram should suffice."

"We're going to Calamaar," announced Maya. "Give us a description of what we're looking for and where to find it."

"But you could jeopardize Goeth's mission," warned Prax.

"Then contact Goeth and have him get the mineral for us! My space station was nearly blown up and a potential doomsday weapon was stolen from right under our noses. It's time to play hard ball with this bitch," bellowed Arn.

"Understood. We're out of here, General," replied Maya. She and Jack quickly departed the room.

"Prax, do whatever you've gotta' do for Will and Severin. I need their expertise badly."

"Right away, General."

"I'll be down to see them shortly."

Prax left the area.

Arn puffed on his cigar and muttered under his breath.

**********

Prax instructed the medics to move Severin into the tube-shaped nano-plasma generator and programmed the controls for scan. Once the medics closed the cover on the glass tank, the power supply hummed loudly. The glass became tinted gray for a moment. Information scrolled rapidly on the display monitor

The medics waited anxiously to see the results of the strange machine.

Prax eyed the information and pressed several buttons on the keypad next to the monitor. At the console, a pipe-shaped tube filled with a pink solution. The solution warmed to body temperature as was indicated by the console monitor. The glass cleared and Severin was again visible.

Prax was amused by the looks on the medics as they gazed at Severin as if they were frozen.

A long needle appeared from the rear of the glass tank and penetrated Severin's neck. The small tube on the console emptied its contents through a flexible tube that passed through the rear of the tank and into the needle. When the last of the plasma was inserted into her body, the needle retracted.

Prax pressed several buttons and another scan was done by the device. A new set of information appeared on the display. He was pleased with the results and turned off the machine.

"Return her to her bed," he ordered. "She'll be fine."

"That's it?" inquired one of the medics curiously.

"That's it," replied Prax. "The scan shows that she's healing."

Arn burst through the door with a concerned look as the medics moved Severin. "Did you use that nano thing on her?" he asked worriedly.

"Sure did. She's gonna' be fine, General."

The medics gently set Severin in the bed and covered her.

"How about Will?"

"I don't know if that's a good idea. He's had this done before."

"So?"

"So, the body can only take a limited amount of the plasma. Theoretically, too much plasma can lead to complications."

"Like?"

"I don't know. No one's done it before."

"Do it now."

"But, General…"

"We have to do this. I love Will like a son and if you can heal Severin, I know you can heal Will."

"Yes, General," Prax answered nervously. The medics lifted Will from the bed and carried him to the nano-plasma generator. After setting him inside the tank, they closed the cover.

Prax reluctantly programmed the device and initiated the scan. Information scrolled across the display monitor. As he read it, he frowned and pressed three more buttons. He slid a lever down and watched as an indicator changed from thirty percent to ten percent. When he reached ten percent, he pressed another button and initiated the plasma process.

"You didn't hesitate while pressing those buttons, did you?" remarked Arn.

"We don't have any choice," said Prax somberly. "He's dying."

Arn nearly choked on his cigar over Prax's revelation.

They watched anxiously as the small tube filled with pink plasma. The plasma warmed to body temperature inside the generator and was injected into Will's neck just like with Severin.

The needle retracted and another scan was performed. Will suddenly lurched and shuddered violently. The machine alarmed until Prax acknowledged it.

"He's having a heart attack!" shouted Prax.

The medics pulled over a crash cart with a heart defibulator on it. Prax opened the cover on the tank and stepped back. One of the medics slapped two paddles from the defibulator onto Will's chest and stood clear. They shocked him but to no avail.

The medic attached smaller pads to Will's temples and connected them to a machine on the cart. "Hit him again!" shouted the medic. Will's body shook as another charge zapped him.

The monitor on the crash cart showed a faint heartbeat and low blood pressure. The heartbeat grew stronger and the blood pressure rose to an acceptable level.

The medics removed the paddles from Will and backed away from the glass tank.

Prax closed the cover and initiated another scan. He watched the monitor nervously as the information scrolled.

"Well?" asked Arn.

"He'll be okay for now."

"What the hell does that mean?"

"He's suffered damage to forty percent of his heart. It's irreparable."

"Holy shit!" Arn exclaimed as the cigar fell from his mouth to the floor. He leaned his head on Will's chest and gripped both of Will's hands tightly. "I'm so sorry, Will. I'm so sorry," he sobbed.

Prax placed a hand on Arn's shoulder. "Come on, General. Let the medics get him into bed."

"It's my fault his heart is ruined."

"No it isn't. If we didn't do this, he would have died."

Arn didn't feel any better about it.

The medics set Will in bed and hooked up a monitor to track his heart and blood pressure.

Prax escorted Arn out of the clinic and into the hall. "General, let's go have a drink and wait for them to awaken."

"I can't drink right now. I've lost control of everything."

"No you haven't. Let's at least go someplace where we can talk."

"My office - now."

The two men walked slowly down the hall. Both were trembling from their experience in the clinic. They reached the elevator and waited quietly.

When the doors opened, Jack and Maya barged out and nearly knocked the two over.

"Excuse us, General," said Maya respectfully. "We tried to contact Goeth but with no success."

"I see. Join us in my office. We have some things to discuss."

"I think Bastille should be there as well," suggested Jack. "He has some important information that's critical to our next move against the Weevil."

"Very well. Summon him immediately."

**********

Severin lay asleep in the clinic and dreamed of what her life might be like if she didn't join the fleet. She imagined having a family and living a normal life on Yord or Earth or any other planet that hosted human life.

Suddenly, she felt as if someone else was in her dreams. "Who's there?" she thought.

"It's Will. Can I come in?"

"Will! How are you in my dreams?"

"I'm in your thoughts and you are in mine right now."

"How…how is that?"

"The nanogenerator not only heals but it helps to develop mental capabilities as well. You always had the ability to be telepathic but didn't know how."

"How much of my dream did you see?"

"Not much. Just enough to know that you want what every other woman wants – to be human."

"I always took pride in my military responsibilities until recently. Now I realize that I have nothing to show for it."

"You have friends, Severin. You have a father of sorts in the General."

"I know but there's something missing."

"There's always something missing. That's what keeps us going – the search for fulfillment."

"You are very wise for a smart ass."

"If I was wise, we wouldn't be in this mess."

"So what do we do about it?"

"Let's get up and get this party started. We have Weevil ass to kick!"

"Now you're talking my language, Will."

Severin opened her eyes and sat up in bed. She waited anxiously for Will to move.

Will's eyes opened but he struggled to sit up. When he finally made it to an upright position, the monitor alarmed.

"What the hell is going on?" he complained.

Two medics rushed into the room. One of the men placed his arms around Will and held him down on his back. The other acknowledged the alarm and prepared a sedative for him.

"What's that for?" inquired Will.

"It's to settle you down. Your heart was damaged during the plasma regeneration process."

The medic injected the clear solution into Will's arm. The wave patterns on the monitor stabilized and the second medic released his hold on Will.

"You cannot leave this bed," ordered the first medic. "You could go into heart failure."

Severin watched despondently.

"And you, ma'am," he chastised, "don't leave until we do a complete evaluation on you."

"And when is that?" she inquired irritably.

"Tomorrow morning. The doctor won't be back until then."

The two medics left the room.

"Any more bright ideas, Will?"

Will sat up slowly while he watched the monitor. He removed the IV from his arm and turned off the monitor. "That'll take care of them," he remarked and removed the monitor's probes from his chest.

Severin stood up slowly and regained her balance.

"How do you feel?" asked Will.

"Not bad, considering," she answered. "Just a little sore."

Will stood up but held onto the bed tightly for support.

"Are you sure this is a good idea, Will?"

"We don't have time to lay around and heal. If we don't do something soon, it won't matter much, will it?"

Severin's head drooped as she looked sadly at the floor.

Will reached for his clothes on the table next to the bed. He tossed off the gown and dressed.

Severin watched subtly and longed to feel a man's body next to hers.

Will touched her cheek gently. "Don't torture yourself over what can't be."

"But what if it were, Will?"

"Severin, it isn't. I care about you very much but you, of all people, understand our predicament."

Severin reluctantly took her uniform from another table and tossed her gown on the floor. "Your turn, Will. You tell me what's real."

Severin stood naked in front of him and gazed into his eyes. She dressed slowly and ensured that he saw every deliberate motion as she donned each article of clothing.

Will broke into a sweat and turned away. "You are heartless, Severin."

"Not anymore. I know I can't have you but don't tell me you never thought about having me."

"There will always be a place in my heart for you. You are like a sister to me."

"You aren't helping me, Will. A sister?"

"Alright, maybe a cousin."

"Second cousin?" she teased.

"Maybe just a real close friend."

Severin hugged him. "I can live with that."

Will stepped aside and pointed to the door. "After you, ma'am."

"Smartass," replied Severin. She grinned at him and approached the doorway to Prax's office.

Inside the office, the medics played cards. Will and Severin inched quietly past the door.

When Will opened the door to the hall, the four guards stood attentively and glared at him.

"Going somewhere?" asked the sergeant.

"Yeah, we have a war to win,' replied Will. "Where's the General?"

"His office. We'll escort you."

"No, we'll be fine."

"We have orders."

"Then stay behind us."

Severin followed Will into the hall and kept an arm around his waist for support.

The sergeant glanced at his three men. They understood and followed Will and Severin.

**********

Arn sat behind a large oak desk and puffed nervously on his cigar.

Across from him sat Prax, Jack, Maya, Bastille and Celine.

"It looks like we're going to Calamaar, General," said Maya stoically.

"You'll need a distraction for this." Arn glanced at Bastille. "Is the *Leviathan* ready?"

"There's something we need to discuss about the *Leviathan*, General."

"Don't tell me she's still out of service, Bastille?"

"No, sir, at least not now she isn't."

"Meaning?"

"The ship's circuitry is degrading as a result of emissions of energy given off by the power source. We can only repair so much at this point."

Arn stood up and placed both hands on the table. "You've got to be kidding me!"

Will and Severin entered the office and startled everyone. Arn's cigar fell from his mouth again as he stood in awe. "Severin! Will!"

"You're making a habit of losing that cigar, General," teased Will.

Arn raced from behind the desk and hugged the two of them. "You two are like manna from heaven."

"I'm sure you were lost without the best security officer in the galaxy," remarked Will.

Arn gazed at the two of them in admiration. "If you only knew how glad I am to see the two of you." Arn sat down behind his desk and picked up his cigar.

"We have some serious issues," Bastille informed Will.

"Yes but we need to make sure Will stays calm", warned Severin. "His heart is in a delicate condition."

"Sit your ass down, Will," ordered Arn. "I'm not taking any chances on losing you."

"We are going to Calamaar to get the Crylum," Maya informed Will.

"Take ten of my men," offered Arn.

"No, that's too risky. Besides we don't want to give the wrong impression, do we?" Jack joked. "They'll think it's an invasion."

"Bastille will cover us in *Leviathan*," added Maya.

"*Leviathan's* days may be numbered," replied Celine somberly.

"Is that true, Bastille?"

"Unfortunately that's the case. Now we understand why the cloaking system kept failing."

"And the PBU-57, Prax. Any success?"

Malduna stole the prototype. It's small scale compared to the B model when it's armed with the Crylum."

"We need to know where she's at and when she offloads the weapon. I suspect we'll tie her to the Weevil."

"I'll find that bitch. That's a promise," replied Severin sternly. "And when I do…"

"Easy, Severin," advised Arn. "Let cooler heads prevail."

"You of all people, General, should be hungry for revenge."

"Oh, I am, but this is a delicate situation. That's why I need you and Will both with your 'A' game."

"Bastille understands the structure of the Weevil's portal system," Celine informed Will.

"That's right, Will," affirmed Bastille.

"Explain."

"In simple terms, their portal system is based on the positioning of probes that balance it. Their raids appear to be more of a distraction while they lay out these probes."

"So, without the probes, they can't open a portal?" inquired Will.

"That's right."

"So we could disable their access to our sectors by destroying a few probes?"

"I highly recommend that we don't do that until we are ready to deliver a well-placed weapon into the heart of the Weevil Empire."

Will chuckled. "I like where this is going, Bastille."

"I've already detailed what probes are critical to the overall structure of the portal system."

"I'll want a copy of those details, if you don't mind," interjected Severin.

"Of course."

"Prax, you and I have preparations to make for Shanna."

"You have my support, Will."

"Then let's get this party rolling. Good luck everyone."

Severin and Prax left the office first.

"We were so worried, Will," said Maya. "You're not superman, you know."

"I couldn't imagine fighting this war without you," said Jack somberly. "You are the heart and soul of our group."

"Thank you both. Can I ask you one favor?"

"Anything," answered Jack.

"If you find Shanna, please bring her back. Tell her I need her."

Maya took Will's hands in hers. "We'll make sure. Now you take it easy."

"I'll be fine."

Maya and Jack left the office.

Arn held the cigar in his hand and gazed at Will proudly.

"So, General, I'm like a son to you, huh?" Will reminded him.

"Yes you are. You and Severin are my children."

"I fear that what must come will not be very pleasant," Will pondered aloud. "To destroy the Weevil, some will be sacrificed as have sacrificed before in the war with the Andorans."

"War is an ugly thing, Will. If only we and other species were smart enough to accept each other for what we are."

"The Calamaari can be reasoned with. That is the only hope we have. The Weevil cannot nor will they ever be reasonable. They know only one thing – destruction."

"Then God help us all if we fail," uttered Arn somberly.

# Chapter 7

## A Gathering of Forces

The winds picked up to almost gale intensity on Calamaar as a raging storm swept into the valley. Goeth and Drun carried Shanna into the mine for shelter. Cintilla hobbled behind them. She scanned the trees cautiously for soldiers or assassins.

Once inside, they set Shanna down inside the guard shack. Drun gathered planks of wood and started a fire. Goeth stood watch by the mine shaft entrance.

Cintilla sat next to Shanna and pondered the fate of her kingdom. She wondered if she would gain her revenge against Pinta for her treachery.

Shanna shuddered and convulsed. She broke into a sweat and heaved violently. Cintilla tried to calm her but Shanna became unstable.

Drun dropped the planks and rushed to assist Cintilla. They held Shanna down forcefully until the seizure passed.

"Is this to be expected?" asked Drun.

"I don't know. I've never seen a human go through this before."

"How can we help her if we don't know what to do?"

"Make the fire, Drun. We'll know when the time comes."

"But how much longer can we afford to wait?" inquired Drun impatiently. "We have our own plans to execute."

"And we will, when the time is right."

**********

On board the *Leviathan*, Jack and Maya waited anxiously on the transport platform. They were armed with pulse rifles and grenades. Jack donned a leather backpack as well for the Crylum. The main quarters were filled briefly with a bright flash and the platform was empty.

Jack and Maya appeared a short distance from the entrance to the mine shaft. They rushed through the torrential rain and gusting winds toward the mine shaft.

Goethe saw both figures rushing through the darkness toward him. He hid behind a reel of cable and waited. When Jack and Maya entered, Goeth leaped out at them from behind. He gripped Maya in a headlock and caught Jack by the throat with his free arm.

"We come in peace," pleaded Jack.

Goeth recognized his voice and loosened his hold. "Jack?"

"Goeth?"

"Yes."

Goeth released the two of them and stepped back. "What are you doing here?"

Maya and Jack each rubbed their necks and breathed a sigh of relief.

"We need to find a small quantity of Crylum. I was told it's abundant in the mines here."

"Why would you want that?"

"For an emulator. It's a device that will clone a sample of Shanna's original blood."

"Come with me," instructed Goeth. He glanced at them suspiciously.

They followed Goeth back to the shack.

"Drun," shouted Goeth. "I need your help."

Drun exited the shack and was surprised to see them.

"I need you to take my watch while we speak."

"I will." Drun glances at them curiously as he passed.

"Come inside," he ordered.

Jack and Maya followed him into the shack.

Cintilla knelt over Shanna with her hands on Shanna's head. She appeared to be praying.

Jack and Maya were stunned by how much Shanna mutated.

"Is she alright?" asked Maya.

Cintilla looked up at them and removed her hands from Shanna. "She lives but she is in a bad place."

"Can we do anything?" asked Jack.

"You must take her back with you but she needs to be confined. Until she stabilizes mentally, she is dangerous."

"Cintilla was calming her thoughts," explained Goeth. "Shanna has been through things that neither man nor Calamaari could ever imagine."

"Shanna's tough. She'll pull through this," assured Maya.

Goeth and Cintilla looked at her in disbelief.

"You don't know her like we do," said Jack uneasily.

"When we found her, she was nearly ingested by a large snake," explained Goethe. "Drun and I were fortunate to slay the snake and retrieve her. How strong can one be especially while dealing with a complete mutation?"

Maya burst into tears and turned to Jack. He nestled her against him for support.

"Shanna has been to the palace and encountered Pinta," continued Cintilla. "She inflicted significant injury to Pinta but was forced to flee before she could end her life."

"We can never repay you for saving her and for your compassion."

"Yes, you can," answered Goeth. "Tell us about the weapon and why you need the Crylum."

Cintilla glanced at Goeth and then at Jack.

"We found the weapons," explained Jack somberly. "There was a prototype that's been stolen and then the real weapon."

"So you lied to us," said Goeth threateningly.

"No. We just discovered the weapons. The leader of the *Widow Maker*, Malduna, stole the prototype as soon as we discovered it among a shipment of items from Earth."

"What will she do with it?" inquired Goeth.

"I suspect she'll attempt to sell it to the Weevil for something of value."

"Like what?"

"Like our worlds. A complete planet or two under her rule. That's what psychos usually crave."

"And why the Crylum?"

"We found a device that should be able to cure Shanna. It requires Crylum to function."

"And that's all you want it for."

Jack glanced at Maya then answered, "Yes and no. The real weapon requires Crylum to be functional as well."

"And you'll use it to destroy the Calamaari!" shouted Cintilla.

"No. The Calamaari are capable of living in peace with others. The Weevil cannot."

"And how can we be assured of this?" asked Cintilla.

"We will do whatever it takes to make you comfortable. If you prefer to be at the station until we disperse it, then we'll accommodate you."

"We trust Will and Shanna. Can we trust you?"

"You have my word," promised Jack.

"And mine," added Maya.

"I will make sure they keep their word," said Shanna gruffly. She sat up and glared at them with swollen eyes.

"Lay down, Shanna." Cintilla ordered. She placed her hands on Shanna's head and closed her eyes. After several moments, Cintilla removed her hands.

"You will show Shanna how the Crylum will be used," explained Cintilla. "She will ensure that you use it for the right reasons."

"How is that possible?" asked Maya.

"Mind control. It should keep her calm for a while."

"But why burden her with this responsibility?"

"Shanna's mutation has granted her incredible strength. She is an important part of your people and has become one of us as well. She will do what is right for both of us."

"If you deceive us, Shanna will know," explained Goeth. "She'll take the appropriate action. We are taking a serious risk in trusting, not just you, but your people, too."

"We accept those terms. Is Shanna stable enough to return with us?"

Cintilla clutched Shanna's shoulder and whispered into her ear. Shanna collapsed into Cintilla's arms unconscious."

"So you'll help us?" inquired Maya uneasily.

"Goeth will obtain the Crylum for you."

Cintilla nodded to Goeth and he left the shack.

"We thank you for your help, Cintilla. I know it's hard to trust another species like this."

"I fear that the Weevil will attack my people if they suspect the Calamaari leadership is in disarray," Cintilla said somberly. "We need to work quickly."

"One of our people discovered how the Weevil portal system operates. We believe that once we locate the probes they placed in this sector, we can stop them."

"With the weapon?"

"Perhaps," answered Jack. "If it does what they say it does, we could exterminate the Weevil completely using their portal system against them."

"We've tried a number of times to reach a peaceful agreement but they refuse," said Maya. "We found a history of the worlds they conquered and it's immense."

"So we would exterminate the species?" asked Cintilla.

"I hope not, unless we have no other option."

"You must leave as soon as possible. Shanna will only be subdued for a short while."

"Thank you for your help, Cintilla," replied Maya. "Perhaps we will speak again under better circumstances."

Goeth returned with the backpack full of Crylum. It appeared as chunks of white talc. He handed the backpack to Jack who nearly fell over from the weight.

"It is time," announced Cintilla. "You must leave now."

Goeth lifted Shanna over his shoulder and opened the door. He waited for Jack and Maya to exit first.

"I wish you well," called out Cintilla.

"And you, too," answered Jack.

They left the shack.

As they walked to the mine entrance, Goeth inquired, "How is Will?"

"He is recovering from a vicious assault by Malduna and her henchmen. I don't think he'll be the same though."

"Tell Will that our friendship stands strong in these trying times."

"Gladly. He speaks highly of you," remarked Jack.

They reached the mine's entrance and Drun stepped into the open.

Goeth set Shanna down on the ground in an open area in front of the mine's entrance. "It is up to you, now."

"I see you have what you came for," commented Drun. "I trust you because Goeth trusts you. He has taught me to look for the good in all species. Don't prove him wrong."

"We won't," promised Maya."

Jack removed a remote device from his shirt pocket and pressed a button.

The three of them disappeared in a flash of light.

Goeth glanced at Drun uneasily and returned to the shack.

**********

Arn, Severin and Prax watched Will from the table as he paced the saloon.

"Will you sit your ass down!" ordered Arn irritably.

"We're going out to find those probes," Will announced determinedly.

"Are you crazy?"

Severin glanced at her transmitter. She placed it by her lips and whispered into it.

"They are the key to any counter-attack we can mount against the Weevil," continued Will.

Severin stowed the transmitter and stared coldly at them.

"Something you want to share?" inquired Arn.

"The *Widow Maker* is headed toward Weevil territory," she replied. "I say we go after the probes and the *Widow Maker*."

"That's what I'm talking about!" exclaimed Will.

"Then I'm going too," added Prax.

"No," replied Severin. "You have to be here when they return with the Crylum. Shanna's counting on you as well."

"But I…"

"You know it's the right thing to do, Prax," assured Severin. "We'll be fine."

Prax expression showed his frustration as he left the saloon.

"He cares about you both," commented Arn. "He's a good man."

"We don't have time to let our emotions get in the way," Severin responded callously as she glanced at Will.

"She's right," added Will. "All these distractions are buying time for the Weevil."

Arn stood up and puffed again on his cigar. He walked around the table and placed his hands on the shoulders of Will and Severin. "I always trusted the two of you and you've never let me down. I won't change now."

"We won't let you down," assured Will.

"Let me know what you need from me and I'll be there for you."

Will glanced at Severin and back at Arn. "Just get your defenses back up ASAP and be prepared for anything. We'll be in touch."

Arn shook Will's hand and then uncharacteristically hugged Severin. A tear formed in her eye and she left the saloon.

Will nodded to Arn in an understanding gesture and followed her.

Arn looked up at the ceiling and groaned.

Jeanie approached him and watched pitifully.

Arn noticed and chuckled. "Yeah, I need one, Jeanie," he said sarcastically. "In fact, make it a double."

She smiled and returned to the bar.

**********

Will and Severin approached the *Reaper* with a sense of urgency. Severin's transmitter beeped.

They paused as she pressed a button on the device and read the display. She looked up at Will uneasily.

"Well?" he asked anxiously.

"The *Leviathan* just returned."

"And …?"

"Shanna's on board."

"We have to see her first," said Will with determination in his voice.

Severin grabbed his arm and stared into his eyes. "You know she doesn't look like your Shanna."

"I know, but it's still her. She'll need my support."

"Very well. They're in dock five."

They left dock three and hurried over to dock five.

**********

Will and Severin waited anxiously for the lights at the dock five hatch to change from red to green. As soon as the dock sealed and oxygen filled the bay, the 'hatch release' system activated.

Severin pressed the 'open' knob. The hatch made a series of noises when the locking mechanisms released.

Severin stared at Will pitifully. "You really want to do this now?" she asked.

"Yes, I do," he replied dutifully. "She needs to know that I'm there for her."

"Perhaps it's best I wait at the *Reaper*," she suggested to him.

"Thanks, Severin. I won't be long."

Will approached the *Leviathan* and waited.

The ship's hatch opened and Bastille stepped out. "Will, what are you doing here?"

"Why wouldn't I?"

"I just… It's a difficult… Never mind, they'll be out shortly."

Maya and Celine stepped out followed by Jack. He operating a motorized gurney with a large shape covered by a white sheet on it.

Jack paused in front of Will. They looked somberly at each other.

"Is this Shanna?" Will inquired nervously.

Jack placed his hand on Will's shoulder. "Yes, it's her. Goeth gave her the serum to stop the changes but she's struggling with the effects. She needs to rest."

"I want to see her," he said and approached the gurney.

Jack grabbed his wrist as he reached for the sheet. "She doesn't want you to see her like this."

"But, it's still Shanna! I don't care what she looks like."

Maya stepped in front of him. "Will, this is hard enough on her. I'm sure she knows you'll stand by her but she needs time to deal with this."

"Can I just touch her? She'll know how I feel."

Maya reluctantly stepped back. She motioned for the others to back away and give them a moment.

Will placed his hand on her shoulder through the sheet. "Shanna, no matter what, I will stand by you. If I need to change to be like you, I will. One way or the other, we'll always be together."

Will felt nothing from her and wondered why. He turned to the others. "Did you get the Crylum?"

"We sure did," answered Jack. "Now it's time for Prax to do his thing."

"I'm going to verify the location of the probes. I'll be back soon."

"Stay away from the *Widow Maker*, Will," commanded Maya. It's been a long time since I gave you an order. I'm giving you one now."

"I appreciate everything you all have done for us. Take care." Will exited the bay.

"Why do I think he'll do exactly that?"

"Go with him, Jack," ordered Maya. "Keep him safe.

"I will, Maya. Be safe."

"You, too."

Jack hurried after Will.

Bastille took over the controls on the gurney and guided it out of the bay. Celine and Maya followed.

**********

Shanna was taken to a cell modified for comfort. Jack and Maya brought in food and water for her.

"Don't give up hope, Shanna," said Maya confidently. "Prax will get the emulator operating that will return you to your old self."

Shanna sat up and pushed the sheet off. She stared at Maya and said nothing. She wanted to cry but her emotions were suppressed by thc mutation.

Maya sat next to her and placed her hand on Shanna's shoulder. "I wouldn't lie to you, Shanna. You know that."

"Maya, did you hear what Will said to me? I can't even cry!"

"You don't have to. He loves you very much."

"He said he would change into what I've become just to be with me."

"There's something I should tell you about Will."

Shanna became unnerved and stood quickly. She became angry and slammed her fist against the wall. "I knew it. Will was unfaithful again!"

"Shanna, stop it!" shouted Maya. "Sit down and listen to me."

Shanna leaned face first against the wall and moaned. "I can't control myself, Maya. I feel like I died and came back an empty shell."

"Goeth told us about the snake and how they found you," she related compassionately. "You've been through more than anyone can imagine."

Shanna turned slowly and faced her. "I thought I was dead. The snake – it swallowed me so slowly. I could feel its muscles flex and each time I would slide further inside it. I… I just wanted to die."

Maya went to Shanna and hugged her.

"You're not repulsed by me?" asked Shanna.

"Of course not. We're family and we'll get through this."

"So what is it that I need to know about Will?"

"Will was attacked and beaten badly. He nearly died."

"By whom?"

"We suspect Malduna and her thugs. To save his life we put him in the nanogenerator."

Shanna looked up with wide eyes. "You can't do that. Xerxes said it could be used only once!"

"He would have died if we didn't."

"So what is it you need to tell me?"

"His heart, Shanna," said Maya somberly. "It's very fragile."

"How fragile?"

"Any stress or excitement could kill him."

"Great. There goes our sex life."

Maya burst into laughter. "Shanna, you keep that attitude and everything will be fine."

"I hope so, Maya. This has gone on way too long."

"When I leave, I'm going to lock the door. Cintilla said that you'll have seizures and fits because of the serum."

"I understand. Will you come see me often?"

"Of course," replied Maya. "In fact, I'm going to see Prax right now and see if I can get a timetable for getting this machine of his running to cure you."

"I appreciate that. Please tell me if it won't work. I need to know."

Maya held her clawed hands in hers. "We won't let you down, I promise."

"I know you won't. I'm so scared."

"I know you are. Have faith." She smiled at Shanna and left the cell. The door slid shut and latched.

Shanna moaned as she realized her life and everything she cared about was slipping away.

**********

Will sat in the pilot's seat of the *Reaper* and stared blankly at the controls. Severin sat in the co-pilot's seat and strapped herself in.

"Are you alright, Will?"

"I'm still trying to accept everything that's happened."

"Let's focus on one thing at a time starting with the probes."

"You're right. I have to get it together now." Will powered up the ship's systems and waited as the computer ran a diagnostic.

Severin set the long range sensors for maximum sensitivity.

The *Reaper* exited bay three and departed the space station.

**********

The *Widow Maker* passed through its fourth portal and was confronted by over thirty Weevil fighters.

Malduna stood in front of the monitor and waited patiently until Polus' insect-like face appeared. She dressed in black leather battle garb with a spiked leather strap around her neck. Her eyes were underscored with black paint and a tear painted on each cheek.

"I thought you might have backed out of our deal, Malduna. I was thinking of how many different ways I could make you suffer."

"Don't flatter yourself, Polus. I have what you're looking for."

"The doomsday weapon?"

"If you prefer to call it such," she replied sarcastically.

"What's to keep me from destroying your ship anyway?"

Malduna held up a remote device for Polus to see. "I will give you the weapon only. One of your ships will escort me back to the edge of the portal. Once there, I will turn the remote over to the pilot."

"Very clever. Very clever!" said Polus as he erupted into laughter. "But what about Saris?"

"He's no longer a threat. I've seen to that personally."

"He's dead?"

"Of course."

"Then let us transact. Follow the fighters onto the command carrier. There we will accept the weapon."

"Don't double-cross me, Polus. You won't like what happens next."

Polus laughed and ended the transmission.

Malduna's son Victor approached her. "Permission to speak, mother."

"What is it?"

"How do we know the Weevil will leave the human worlds for us to control?"

Malduna stared psychotically at her son and reached under her vest. He retreated two steps from her. She held up a small tube with a cork on the end. Inside the tube was a small dart with a yellow substance at the bottom.

"A small present I will leave in Polus. The liquid is a nano-virus that can be activated by me at any time. If I even hear the word 'Weevil', Polus is a goner."

Victor smiled at her. "Father would be proud of you."

"Would he?" she replied eerily. "I must prepare for my meeting."

Malduna left the main quarters of the *Widow Maker*. Victor grinned dementedly and ascended the stairs to the pilots' cabin.

**********

The Weevil fighters entered through a large open bay in the battle star. The immense size of the ship dwarfed the *Widow Maker* as it housed many ships her size.

The *Widow Maker* docked at an empty pier while the fighters glided to the other end of the ship. Red lights lined the walls around the perimeter of the bay.

The bay doors closed slowly and oxygen flowed from giant ducts into the bay. Once the oxygen level was safe, a siren sounded briefly and green lights replaced the red ones.

The hatch for the cargo bay near the tail of the ship opened. Malduna stepped out first, followed by Victor and three big men. The men had long hair and piercings over their face and ears. They looked very intimidating.

Two men operated a small tractor with the coffin shaped case strapped on top. They brought the case onto the deck and waited.

Five Weevil entered the bay and approached the group. One of them looked just like Polus.

Malduna opened the small tube and removed the dart. She tucked it with the pointed end up inside her vest.

The Weevil stopped at the case and eyed it suspiciously. One of them approached Malduna. "Where is the weapon?"

"Inside the case. It was sealed to prevent anyone from tampering with it."

"Open it."

"No, you open it."

The Weevil resembling Polus approached the case and smashed the display screen with his claw. He pierced the recorder and used his clawed arm as a lever. After several attempts, he ripped the cover off the case. He turned around and faced Malduna. "We don't like games."

"Do you like what you see?"

The other Weevil examined the contents of the case. They were satisfied that this was the weapon they waited for. One of them nodded to him and he turned his attention back to Malduna. "We are done with the games, aren't we?"

"There's just one more thing I'd like to cover," Malduna said coyly. "What would you do for the body of Saris? He might make a nice snack."

The Weevil placed a clawed arm on her shoulder and snickered through his gruesome mouth. "You know where Saris' body is?"

Malduna removed the dart from her vest and stuck it into the Weevil's limb. The contents left the dart and emptied into him. She stepped back and laughed sadistically at him.

The Weevil looked at her curiously and waited for an explanation.

"I don't give a rat's ass about Saris!" she shouted triumphantly. "You're dealing with Malduna, Queen of the *Widow Maker*!"

Malduna tossed the remote to the Weevil. "Choke on this!" She returned to the ship with the others. They closed the hatch and prepared to depart.

The siren sounded and the green lights changed sequentially to red.

The Weevil hurried from the dock with the tractor and sealed the bay. The large outer doors opened and the *Widow Maker* departed the battle carrier.

Malduna stood behind her pilot and co-pilot on the flight deck and watched the sensors for any sign of Weevil pursuit.

The transmitter beeped much to her delight. She pressed the 'receive' button and Polus' face appeared on the screen.

"What's wrong, Polus? Feeling a little under the weather?"

"Ah, Malduna, Saris you will never be."

"And why is that?" she replied arrogantly.

"Because, you weren't smart enough to make sure it was me on the dock."

"Oh, I know it was you."

Polus pulled another Weevil in front of the screen. "This is my son. If anything happens to him, well, I think you know what to expect."

Polus burst into laughter and ended the transmission.

Malduna shrieked and punched the wall. She left the flight deck raving like a maniac. The pilot and co-pilot glanced uneasily at each other and accelerated quickly away from the Weevil battle star.

Victor met his mother in the main quarters. "Mother, what's wrong?"

"The Weevil played me for a fool."

Malduna stormed away and left the boy standing alone.

**********

The *Reaper* approached the Calamaari territory and shut down its engines.

Severin eyed Will curiously.

"You're wondering why I did that," said Will, somewhat amused.

"It did cross my mind."

"If Malduna did deliver the prototype to the Weevil, what do you think they would do with it?"

"Ah, you think they'll attempt to use it on the Calamaari."

"And," he continued. "I'm sure Malduna had to double-cross the Weevil to ensure she got away safely."

"But what's her fail-safe? There's nothing to guarantee that the Weevil would honor any kind of agreement."

"That's what bothers me."

Severin noticed a small dot on the long range sensor monitor. "Looks like we have a bite."

Will glanced at the screen and started up the ship's engines. He raised the power to fifteen percent.

The *Reaper* glided slowly toward the unknown ship.

"See if you can make out an ID on the ship," requested Will.

Severin pressed several buttons and entered a series of numbers.

Will placed the short range scanners on "rotational scan" and increased power to twenty-five percent.

The short range monitor showed four red dots, each spaced evenly from the others across a large distance.

The control panel beeped twice and an image of Malduna's man-o-war appeared on the overhead screen.

"It's that bitch, Malduna, in the *Widow Maker*!" exclaimed Severin. "Shall we pursue?"

"No, not today."

"But Will?"

"Keep an eye on that ship. Chart her course and speed."

Severin reluctantly focused on the monitor.

Jack entered the pilots' cabin and surprised both of them. "I can't believe I just heard that from you, Will."

"What, Jack?"

"You are shying away from an encounter for a logical reason."

"Things are a little clearer right now. I'm focused on our objective."

Will guided the *Reaper* towards one of the unknown dots on the monitor. As they approached, the short range sensor picked up an odd sound. Will turned up the volume.

The sound had a very low frequency and amplitude. Will activated the 'recording' mode on the computer.

"What the hell are you listening to, Will?" asked Jack.

"I think I know how they operate their portals! We're going back to the station, now."

"Son-of-a-bitch!" uttered Severin. "I see it, too."

Twenty-five small dots appeared on the long range sensors behind the initial dot. Severin was surprised by their quick appearance. "Looks like Malduna's got company."

Will programmed new coordinates into the computer and accelerated the ship to full power.

"Why are we headed toward the *Widow Maker*, Will?" asked Jack irritably.

"Watch and learn the art of deception," Will replied confidently. He activated the transmitter and entered several digits.

Thirty more dots appeared on the long range monitor from the opposite direction.

"Things just got a lot more complicated, Will," Severin remarked.

Will glanced at the monitor and frowned. He re-entered several digits into the transmitter control panel.

"I assume this is part of your plan," chided Jack.

"The plan just grew into something much bigger."

Will waited anxiously until the transmitter beeped. He toggled the short range monitor screen to 'display' and pressed the 'send' button.

Polus angry face appeared on the display. "Saris, you are alive!"

"Did you thnk I would ever leave without saying goodbye?"

"Our sensors have located you. This is the end for you."

"Not so fast, Polus. That device you received from Malduna isn't quite what you think it is."

"You're bluffing, Saris. You'd try anything to stop me from using this weapon on you and your Calamaari friends."

"Now, Polus, would I lie to you?"

"I'll launch the weapon now and I'll be rid of both you and that stupid bitch, Malduna."

"Perhaps you should give her more credit than that. She didn't give you the doomsday weapon. That's the prototype with a limited range."

"You're lying, Saris."

"Think about it, Polus. If she did, what leverage would she have?"

"Her leverage was a nano-virus she thought she injected me with. She failed due to stupidity as all humans are bound to."

"If you use that weapon on the Calamaari, you'll take out a small part of their force. Then she negotiates with the Calamaari for the real weapon. Their immediate reaction is to use it against you."

Polus glared back at Will but said nothing.

"I'll let you think about that while I try to get the real weapon from her. Thanks for being so attentive, Polus."

Will ended the transmission and breathed a sigh of relief. He entered another series of digits into the transmitter control panel and pressed 'send'.

Zorick's face appeared on the monitor. "Will Saris, to what do we owe this moment?"

"Zorick, Malduna gave the prototype of the doomsday weapon to the Weevil."

Zorick's face grew taut.

"It has a limited range but it's just as lethal as the real one."

"We are preparing to do battle with the Weevil at this moment," replied Zorick.

"Don't engage them unless provoked. I think they're going to have a change of plan any time now."

"What if they don't?"

"They will, for now. I'm going to try and force a meeting between Polus and Pinta. I expect that he'll use that opportunity to take out the Calamaari leadership. Meanwhile, Goeth and Cintilla will have the opportunity to regain control of your planet."

Zorick grinned at the monitor. "If the Weevil attempt to take out Pinta, we can justify her poor leadership as well. Even if she survives, no one will support her after an attempt like this."

"Now you get my drift."

"So who has the real weapon?"

Will hesitated and pondered what to say.

"Saris, I know all too well your history. You have the weapon, don't you?"

"I do, Zorick. I'm working on a plan to use it to take out the entire Weevil force, all the way back to their own planet."

"That's pretty impressive if you can do that."

"Look, Zorick, all I want is peace. The Weevil will never stop encroaching on worlds. They are parasites. We have their documented history from an earlier raid on one of their supply ships."

"So I should trust that you won't use it to annihilate both of us."

"Goeth and I have a bond of friendship. I saved his life and he saved the life of someone dear to me. That counts for something."

"If your plan works, I would like to sit down with you and discuss your methods. You have succeeded where many mighty leaders have failed. You surely don't fit the bill of any of those leaders."

"Sometimes wit and tact are more effective than strength. In the case of the Weevil, strength is necessary."

"What do you need from us?"

"If this meeting takes place, make sure your trusted commanders have an escape portal available. When the Weevil leave the meeting, they will likely detonate the prototype."

"And then?"

"You will be included in our plans to finish off the Weevil, I assure you."

"Then I will await some indication that your plan has begun."

"You'll know."

Will ended the transmission. He became pale and light-headed.

Severin unbelted herself from the seat and knelt by Will. As she checked his pulse, his breathing became irregular.

"Jack, take the controls!" she exclaimed.

Jack quickly took the co-pilots seat.

Severin paused by Will and ordered, "Don't you move, Will!"

Severin left the cabin and opened a locker just outside the door. She retrieved a vial and syringe. She filled the syringe with the contents and returned to the cabin.

Jack watched helplessly.

Will was incoherent and struggled to speak.

"Do something, Severin!" panicked Jack. "We're losing him."

Severin promptly injected the syringe into his carotid artery. She reached behind her into a cabinet and took out a bottle of water. She poured a small amount onto Will's lips and into his mouth.

"Just relax, Will. We're going back to the station."

Severin glanced at the long range monitor. The multiple shapes dispersed, leaving only the *Widow Maker* with a clean escape. She took over the controls from Jack and accelerated the *Reaper* to maximum speed back to the station.

The color slowly returned to Will's face. He sat up straight and his breathing returned to normal.

Jack slept on the floor in a sitting position.

Severin peeked at Will and placed the ship on 'auto-pilot'. She turned her seat and faced him. She could only stare as she realized he nearly died in her charge. A sick feeling came over her.

Will understood what she felt. He placed his hand on hers. "You saved my life. Thank you."

"Nice timing. I was about to compliment you on how you manipulated your way out of that mess and into another one."

"What do you mean?"

"Now the Calamaari know we have the fully developed PBU-57."

"For now," he replied weakly.

"What's that supposed to mean?"

"That's why we let Malduna escape. The real weapon is going to be her demise."

Severin sat back in her seat and shook her head in disbelief. "How do you work your plans with everything changing as fast as you can execute them?"

"It's a gift I inherited from my father. It's like chess. You have to be three moves ahead – sometimes four."

"Well you're damn good at it. Get some rest."

Will forced a smile and closed his eyes.

**********

As the *Reaper* approached Orpheus-2, Severin called in for assistance at the dock. She eased the ship into its berth and waited for the bay to seal and pressurize.

A medical team waited by the hatch with Maya. As soon as the hatch opened, they rushed inside.

Severin unbelted Will from his seat and lifted him to his feet.

"I'm okay now," said Will. "Let me walk."

"No you don't. We have people here to help you."

The medical team entered the cabin and moved Will into the main cabin. They sat him down in a chair and examined him.

Jack and Maya waited nervously at the hatch and watched. Jack informed her about what happened. They both were visibly upset over the incident.

Severin came to them and hugged them both. "I thought we were going to lose him."

Maya and Jack could feel her tremble.

"You saved him, Severin," said Jack appreciatively. "You did well."

"I can't do this again. I'm done traveling with Will," replied Severin with tear-filled eyes. "If I lost him out there, I couldn't live with myself. I won't do that again." Severin left the ship in a hurry.

Jack and Maya were shaken by her reaction.

"This is hard to take," said Maya sadly. "He's on a short leash for life."

Jack tried to comfort her and held her close to him. "Let's take it one day at a time. Will's got a history of cheating death."

"Not like this." Maya wiped tears from her eyes.

**********

Inside his office, Prax placed the blood sample inside the emulator and programmed the control panel for ten cycles. He removed a flash drive from his pocket and inserted it into a port on the device.

A small display screen came to life and prompted him to answer several questions about the blood sample. Once finished, Prax pressed 'enter' and the emulator hummed continuously.

The door burst open and Severin rushed in, startling Prax. She threw her arms around him and cried.

"What's wrong, Severin?"

"Will almost died right in front of me."

"How?"

"His heart. He was doing his thing with the Weevil and the Calamaari and when he finished, he …"

Prax hugged her tightly. It was the first time he ever saw Severin emotional.

The two sat down on chairs and Prax held her hand.

"Will handled things like a master manipulator and I could only watch," she blubbered. "He was so good at controlling them and then…."

"But that's Will."

"I felt so inferior to his skills out there in the heat of battle."

"Why would you think that?"

"I could only do what he did through force and tactical maneuvers. Will actually played with their minds."

"Will always was a little different," kidded Prax. "Is he okay now?"

"I think so. He was stable when I left him and the medics are with him now."

"Then everything is under control. Don't worry about it."

"Could you just hold me, Prax? I really need … I need …"

"I know," said Prax. "I'll hold you as long as you want."

**********

The medical team moved Will on a gurney into the clinic and parked him in the same spot as before. He was awake and alert when they attached the monitoring equipment to him.

"I need to see Bastille and Prax," demanded Will. He strained to raise his voice and emphasize the importance of his request.

"I'll get them for you," replied one of the technicians.

A doctor entered the clinic and stood by him. He studied the information on the monitors and frowned.

"What is it now, Doc?"

"Your heart may be in worse shape than we initially thought."

"I can't lay here like this. If I don't …"

The doctor motioned with his hand for silence and resumed reading the monitors. He scrolled through several screens.

"Alright, Saris, I'll give it to you straight. We're going to keep you somewhat sedated at all times. Any excitement or stress could trigger another episode with your heart and kill you. It's that simple."

Prax and Severin entered the clinic and approached Will. "I understand you needed to see me," said Prax.

"Yes, I did. I need to see Bastille as well."

"What's this about?"

"The Weevil portal system."

Severin turned away from Will with folded arms. She bit her lip as she tried to regain her composure. To see Will in his condition was too much for her.

"Before we get into that, I have some news for you," added Prax.

"Good news, I hope."

"Shanna's blood is being replicated by the emulator and I should soon have the necessary plasma to reverse the mutation."

"Does she know yet?"

"No. I thought you might want to tell her."

"Are you sure it will work?"

"Theoretically, it should. Xerxes was a genius with things like this and I have no reason to doubt him."

The doctor studied the wave patterns on the monitor as Will talked.

One of the technicians returned with an IV pole and a plastic bag containing a clear solution. He set up the IV and inserted the needle into Will's arm.

"I won't get goofey, will I, Doc?"

"No more than you already are. You should have never left this bed before."

The doctor and three of the four medical technicians left the clinic. The remaining tech sat at a desk and performed tasks on his computer.

Bastille entered the clinic and paused by the door.

Will was surprised by his reluctance to approach. "What's wrong?" he asked curiously.

"This isn't contagious, is it?" inquired Bastille.

Everyone was stunned by his question.

Bastille burst into laughter. "Come on, everyone. Lighten up."

Bastille gripped Will's hand in a friendly gesture. "How are you, my friend?"

"Good now. You had me going for a second there."

"So what can I do for you?"

"I want to talk about the probes that the Weevil use for setting up their portal system."

"Tell me you verified their locations," replied Bastille anxiously.

"Oh, yes, and more. They appear to operate off a low frequency, low amplitude signal. I recorded it on board the *Reaper*."

Bastille's eyes widened with excitement. "That's it! The frequencies of their ships' drives are what activate the portals. That's why we never see them coming."

"But we accessed their ports before. How come our frequencies worked?"

"The *Leviathan's* computers must have picked up the signal and adapted to it automatically without our knowledge. That's how we were able to get through."

"Can you develop small explosives to plant on the probes that can be triggered by a frequency change?"

"Why do that?" asked Bastille. "We can install a frequency generator on the explosive device to peg the frequency low or high. They won't be able to use the portals when we detonate the weapon."

"But we need to access the portal to escape before the probes explode."

"It's simple. When we're ready to pass through, we emit a frequency lower than the existing one. The detonator will be set to work on a rising frequency and amplitude."

"Let me know when it's ready and we'll plant them on the critical probes."

"We'll want a magnetic casing for attaching the devices," suggested Bastille. "Then you can launch the little buggers from the *Reaper* and they'll do their thing."

"Go for it, Bastille. Time's wasting."

Bastille left the clinic, excited about their new project.

"How about I bring Shanna in so we can give her the new plasma, Will?" suggested Prax.

"I'd really appreciate that. Can I give her the news?"

"Of course. I'll be back shortly with her." Prax left the room.

Severin followed him to the door but Will called out to her before she exited the clinic. She reluctantly paused in the doorway.

"Please, Severin, don't ignore me. I'm your friend."

Severin wouldn't turn around. Tears streamed down her cheeks. "I know, Will. And I'm yours. I just need time to recover from this." She exited the clinic leaving Will alone with only the technician to watch over him.

**********

Prax knocked on the door of Shanna's cell. He deactivated the lock and pressed the access knob for entry. The door slid open.

Inside, Shanna lay unconscious on the floor convulsing. Foam streamed from her mouth and strange noises came from her throat.

Prax rushed out to the hall and sounded the emergency alarm. A voice announced over the speaker, "Emergency personnel, dispatch to location C-16."

Prax returned to the cell and tried to lift Shanna into a sitting position. She was too heavy and in a limp position. He shook her by her shoulders repeatedly and shouted, "Shanna, can you hear me!" There was no response.

The emergency team arrived with a gurney, escorted by four soldiers. They placed Shanna on the gurney and rolled her out of the cell.

Two of the techs hooked up monitors which were mounted underneath the gurney. The other two checked her vitals.

As they waited for the elevator, Prax asked, "Is she going to be alright?"

"We don't know," answered one technician. "We have no experience with Calamaari."

"She's not a Calamaari! She's Shanna!"

"I'm sorry," replied the tech." She still has a Calamaari physiology right now and that complicates things."

The elevator doors opened and they hustled on.

**********

At the clinic, the emergency alarm startled both Will and the technician.

"What's happening?" asked Will anxiously.

"C-16 is the Isolation Ward."

"But that's where Shanna is. I have to go to her." Will attempted to get up but the technician forced him back down on the bed. The monitor alarmed and his heart raced.

"If you don't lie still, I'll knock you out," warned the technician. "If it is your friend, they'll bring her here."

The doctor rushed into the clinic. "What the hell are you doing to yourself now?"

"What's the emergency, Doctor?"

"They're transporting the mutant woman down here. Calm down and let us do our job."

"But, Doctor, I have to…"

The doctor pointed his finger into Will's face. "If I have to tell you one more time, you'll be tranquilized so that you don't know what world you're on. Now be still and shut up!"

Will reluctantly shut up and waited.

The doctor glanced back at him and repeated, "One more alarm off that monitor and it's la-la land. I'm not kidding."

"I got it, Doc," groaned Will.

The technicians arrived with the gurney and parked Shanna across the room from Will.

Prax entered the room from his office with a plastic bag filled with the nano-plasma solution that was synthesized by the emulator. "We need to get this into her ASAP," he instructed the technicians.

The technicians hesitated until the doctor authorized them to do so. The doctor glanced at Shanna and back at Prax. Finally he relented, "Do as he says. He probably knows more about her than I do anyway."

The technicians set up an IV and started the flow of plasma into Shanna's arm. After a few moments, the seizure subsided and she appeared calm.

"Is she alright?" asked Will anxiously.

"Looks like she's stable for now," answered the technician.

Prax remained by Shanna's side and observed her closely for any signs of change.

Jack and Maya entered the clinic and were relieved to see Shanna in a tranquil state.

"How long before we know if it works, Prax?" inquired Maya.

"I don't know. I think we'll see a change in her behavior before her physical features begin to change."

Maya sat on the edge of Will's bed. She held his hand for comfort and watched Shanna.

Jack paced back and forth as they waited for a sign that she was improving.

"Maya, could I discuss something with you and Jack?" requested Will.

"I'm listening."

Jack joined them and leaned against the bed. "This sounds serious."

"It is. I need a reason to make Pinta meet with Polus."

"Why would you do that?" asked Jack curiously.

"Because Polus would likely detonate the prototype to exterminate the Calamaari leadership, including Pinta."

"And most of the Calamaari forces with it," chided Maya.

"No, I spoke with Zorick, the Calamaari commander. He's aware that if this meeting takes place, he and his forces loyal to Cintilla should be prepared to escape by way of a portal as soon as the Weevil leave the area."

"What could we possibly do to make the two come together?" asked Maya.

"I told Polus that Malduna has the real weapon and would make a deal with the Calamaari. If Polus used the prototype, then Pinta would annihilate them."

"Okay, let's think about this," said Jack. "Pinta will deny having the weapon. Polus won't trust her. Why a face-to-face meeting?"

The three of them pondered the question.

"I have to get up," complained Will.

"Don't even think about it," warned the doctor.

"Can you move me next to Shanna?" he requested. "I'd like to be with her."

The doctor eyed the monitors. Will's heart rate was steady. "Alright, but if there's any sign of stress or anxiety, you'll get another dose of tranquilizer and we're putting you in a solitary room."

"I understand. I'm in control of my emotions now."

"No you're not. You're feeling the tranquilizer," the doctor replied. He glared at Will suspiciously as the technicians moved Will next to Shanna's gurney and chocked the wheels.

Will reached out and held Shanna's clawed hand in his.

"What if Pinta believed that Malduna was going to ambush her forces with the real weapon?" suggested Maya. "She might seek refuge from the Weevil."

"That would be too obvious," replied Will. "Malduna will have to be the reason for the meeting but why?"

Will felt Shanna squeeze his hand. Her eyes opened and she turned to Will. "Do I have to think of everything, Will?"

"Shanna!" exclaimed Will.

Shanna forced a smile and said, "Hello, Will."

"Are you feeling any pain?" interjected the doctor.

"My insides feel like molten lava."

The doctor prepared a syringe with a tranquilizer. He held it up and squeezed out a tiny air bubble. "This will relax you for a short while. Hopefully it will ease the pain."

Shanna's eyes appeared to regain their human colors. She also exhibited a human look about her. Will noticed immediately and was elated.

The doctor eyed the monitor and noticed Will's heart rate was increasing. "That's enough for you, champ."

"But Doc…"

The doctor nodded to the technicians and they moved Will's bed away from Shanna.

Shanna closed her eyes and drifted off to sleep.

The doctor whispered to Jack, Maya and Prax. They left the clinic.

The doctor increased the dosage of the tranquilizer and Will soon fell asleep.

**********

Arn sat in the Surveillance Control Center and studied designs and specs for the *Widow Maker*. As he searched for the ship's weaknesses, he noticed on the long-range sensor monitor a large green circle moving slowly at a fixed distance from the space station. He verified the signature of the ship as that of the *Widow Maker* and gritted his teeth.

"Come a little closer, you bitch," murmured Arn. "I've got some payback for you." He took a cigar from his pocket and lit it. He stared at the object with the look of a mad man.

The door beeped and slid open. Severin entered and took a seat next to him. Her eyes were red and swollen from crying.

Arn was pleased to see her. "What's wrong, Sev?"

"Will and I went out to scout for the probes. He did his thing with Polus and Zorick, you know the way he plays them all against each other."

"Go on."

"Things were going well until he finished his last transmission. He… He almost died."

"Good gracious! Is he alright?"

"I think so. I called in for a medical team and they took over from there."

"I've been so busy tracking the *Widow Maker* that I missed the announcement. I'm sorry, dear."

Arn led her by the arm into the hall. "Let's go for a walk."

"It sounds like Will has a real good idea how to play this – if he lives long enough," she explained.

"You care for him a lot?" inquired Arn curiously.

"Yes. He and I are so much alike but some things can never be."

"Maybe it's better that way. I noticed you have an interest in Prax as well."

"He's similar to Will but in some ways different. I'm used to being alone and taking care of myself. I'm seeing things in a different light now and it's scary."

They entered one of the spare transport bays. An old fighter was parked inside the bay.

"We're all afraid of being alone, Sev. It's human."

"Are you afraid, sir?"

"Look at me. My station has been attacked. Thugs have come aboard and stolen a critical piece of equipment. Worst of all, two people very dear to me nearly died. There was a time when I would have exacted revenge from everyone responsible for encroaching on me."

"Perhaps you've become diplomatic with age."

"No, I've withdrawn into a shell and left others to fight my battles." Arn pointed to the fighter. "Once upon a time, I was fearless and fought with reckless abandon. This was my baby." Arn caressed the side of the old fighter.

"I was once iron-fisted, sir. I think it wears you down over time. When it does, you feel naked and exposed."

"Perhaps that's what we've been reduced to – our true selves," surmised Arn.

"So what should I do, sir?"

"Follow your heart."

Severin hugged him and left the bay.

Arn puffed on the cigar and spit into a trash can. "We're a lot of things that we don't like," he uttered to himself.

# Chapter 8

## The Ruse

Inside the clinic, Shanna sat on the bed by Will's side. She wore a hooded cloak that hid her face and body from view.

Will twitched and opened his eyes. He knew it was Shanna and immediately tried to sit up. She held his shoulders down gently.

"Easy, Will. You've been through a lot."

"What are you talking about? No one's been through more than you."

"You've been out for quite a while since the operation."

"What operation?"

"They installed an electronic device in your heart to help regulate your heartbeat. You should be much stronger than before."

"And what about you, Shanna? How are you doing?"

"I'm slowly returning to my old self. Prax isn't sure if I'll revert completely to my original form or if there will be some differences."

"Why the cloak?" asked Will. "You don't have to be ashamed of your appearance with me."

"I've been through some things that I can never forget – horrible things."

"I'm so sorry, Shanna. This is all my fault."

"It's no one's fault. It's fate and it sucks."

Shanna turned away from him and fought to hold back her tears.

Will pulled the probes from the monitors off his arms and chest. He carefully slid from the bed onto the floor. After testing his first few steps, he felt confident that his strength had returned. He approached Shanna and placed his hands on her shoulders for moral support.

"Please, Will. Don't touch me yet. I'm still … I'm not the Shanna that you knew."

Will became angry and punched the wall. "Damn it, Shanna! What do you want from me?"

Shanna was startled by his abrupt outburst. "Time, Will. Just a little more time."

"Do you still love me?"

Shanna turned halfway around, her face still hidden by the cloak. "That's a stupid question. If I didn't, I wouldn't be here. All I thought about was you and how I couldn't live without you."

"That's all I needed to know. Thank you, Shanna."

Will exited the clinic wearing just a white gown.

"Will!" Shanna shouted but he continued down the hall.

Shanna caught up to him as he stepped onto the elevator. "What the hell are you doing?"

"We have to finish what we started. We have to get Pinta to meet with Polus. That's the key to getting out of this."

They stepped off the elevator as Severin was about to enter.

"Will! How are you feeling?" Severin asked.

"Much better, thanks."

Severin joined them and walked down the hall.

"You, uh, look a little drafty," she joked.

"Not for long. Where's Arn?"

"In the Security room. Why?"

"Ask him to meet us in the saloon as soon as he can. It's time to put my plan into action."

"Of course. I'll let the others know as well."

Severin turned right down another hallway. Will and Shanna continued to his quarters.

Once inside, Will tossed the gown against the wall and opened the closet door. Shanna glanced at his naked body and turned away. She feared they would never be together like they were before. Her emotions were volatile and she no longer felt like a woman. She was just a shell of her former self.

Neither spoke as Will dressed. As he straightened his shirt, Severin's voice blared over the intercom, and startled him. "Will, contact me at 1445. It's urgent."

"Here we go again!" groaned Will. "Some things never change."

Shanna just stood by quietly.

"Fourteen forty-five - that's the Security room. Let's go."

Will and Shanna hurried through two halls and descended the stairs to the lower corridor.

Severin stood nervously outside the Security room waiting. "Damn it, Will. Why didn't you call?"

"What's wrong?" asked Will.

"The General's gone."

"What do you mean 'gone'?"

"He took his old fighter and left the station. I think he's going after Malduna."

"Then we're going after him," replied Will. "You stay here and secure the station. Until he comes back, this station and everyone on it are your responsibility."

"Shanna, look out for him, please."

"Oh, I will."

Will and Shanna left for the transport bay.

Severin was stunned at the thought of being in charge of the station. She summoned the Captain of the Guard to lay out contingencies in case of an attack.

**********

Will and Shanna boarded the *Reaper* and promptly took their seats in the pilots' cabin. Will glanced over at her but the cloak still hid her face from him.

The bay depressurized and the large doors slid open. The *Reaper* drifted away from the dock until its engines ignited and launched it away from the space station.

Shanna set the long and short-range sensors. She scanned the areas around them for small energy signals that would indicate a dormant Weevil portal.

Will checked all the weapons stations and set the guidance system for 'standby'.

"Do you think we'll have company?" Shanna asked.

"I can't imagine the Weevil will let Malduna leave without turning on her."

Will toggled the transmitter to 'on' and entered a series of digits into the console. After what seemed an eternity of silence, the transmitter beeped three times.

"Is it Arn?" Shanna asked.

"Should be. I don't think there are any other ships out here that would match this signature."

Will pressed the 'send' button and waited.

A red dot appeared on the long-range sensor monitor.

"There he is, Will."

"Why won't he answer?"

A larger green dot appeared ahead of the red one.

"Look at this, Will! Arn's after something big."

"I'll bet it's the *Widow Maker*. He's trying to save face for what's happened on board the station."

"But that's suicide!" exclaimed Shanna.

"Yes, it is. He wants to go out with dignity."

The *Reaper* sped toward the fighter at maximum speed.

On board the *Widow Maker*, Malduna stood on the flight deck with two men. They watched Arn's fighter approach on a large monitor mounted on the wall.

"Who could this be - Saris, maybe?" queried Malduna aloud.

"I'll contact them and see what they want," replied one of the men."

"No, not yet. Let's wait and see what he's up to."

The two men grew concerned but stood back from the controls.

Malduna grinned as she eyed the approaching ship. "It doesn't look like Will's ship, does it?"

"No, ma'am," answered one of the men.

The transmitter beeped and startled them. Malduna calmly pressed the 'receive' button.

Arn's face appeared on a smaller monitor in front of her. She pulled up a chair and sat in front of him. "Well, General, isn't this unusual to find you away from the safety of your tin can station."

Arn puffed on his cigar and smiled at her. "You see, Malduna, I came all the way out here just to have this discussion with you."

"And what is it we are going to discuss today?"

"This..."

Arn fired six torpedoes from the underside of his fighter. Six red bursts of energy fanned out as they darted toward the *Widow Maker*.

"Deflector shields, fast!" she shouted. "Kill that bastard, now!"

"You see, Malduna, I've let you play with me for way too long. I studied the specs for your ship and if I don't get your crippled old ass, I'm sure the Weevil will."

The two men urgently operated the controls near each of them.

The ship rocked and the lighting dimmed. Emergency power turned on and powered the lighting and systems.

"Fire, damn it!" she screamed at them.

"Auto-fire is out, ma'am. I'm targeting him in 'manual'."

"Just get him!"

Arn chuckled as he watched her expression. "What's wrong, Malduna? Nothing to say to me?"

"Screw you, you fat-bellied bastard!"

"You know, Malduna, rumor has it that you're as cold as the outer hull of your ship. I'm kind of glad because the thought of being intimate with you, even after a number of drinks, makes me seriously ill."

The *Widow Maker* fired three torpedoes at Arn's fighter.

"Nice try," he taunted. "I'll just … dodge these little babies." Arn's face stared down from the screen briefly and then back up at her.

"You're a dead man, General."

"I hear you stole that kid of yours from some outpost whore. Word is you wanted to convince people that someone out there could impregnate a dead fish like you."

Malduna's face turned red. She glared at the man on her left. "If you don't destroy that ship, I'm gonna' rip you to shreds."

The man pressed several switches and changed the coordinates on the tracking system. He pressed the 'fire' knob.

Four bright bursts of energy shot from the *Widow Maker* and just missed Arn's fighter.

"Not bad for a fat-bellied old bastard, huh, Malduna?"

The man on her right noticed another ship drawing closer. "There's someone else out there, ma'am!"

"Ram this son-of-a-bitch, now!"

Twenty Weevil fighters appeared on the left edge of the monitor and approached the *Widow Maker* from the opposite direction as the *Reaper*.

"Ma'am, Weevil fighters! They must have come through a portal."

Malduna shrieked in anger. "Get us out of here, quickly," she commanded.

The *Widow Maker* turned and fled from the approaching Weevil fighters.

Malduna turned her attention back to Arn. "I hope you have friends in those Weevil fighters. You're going to need some." She snickered and ended the transmission.

Arn steered the fighter away from the attacking force and retreated from the area. The Weevil fighters gained quickly on him.

Will and Shanna were mortified as they watched what transpired on the monitor.

"We'll never get there in time!" Will exclaimed. "He doesn't stand a chance."

Shanna stood up and went to the door. "I'll man the cannons. Just like old times, Will."

Will looked at her with a concerned expression on his face. "You sure we want to do this?"

Shanna reached out to him and touched his cheek. "We need this. Let's do it." She left the cabin and closed the door.

Will felt renewed strength at the thought that maybe he and Shanna were one again.

Arn saw the *Reaper* closing from the other direction. He pressed the transmitter and waited anxiously.

Will's face appeared. "What were you thinking, Arn? This is crazy."

"No, this is long overdue. Go back, Will. There are too many of them."

"We're coming in hot. Stay to my left and we'll cover you."

"Forget it. The *Widow Maker's* firing system is damaged. They can only fire in 'manual'. She's all yours if you want her," Arn declared proudly. "Tell Severin that I know she'll do a fine job filling my shoes."

"Damn it, Arn! You're quitting on us."

"No, son. I'm going out like the warrior I once was. It's easy to forget what got you to the top. That makes you weak."

The fighter turned around and headed toward the fighters.

The Weevil fighters fired an array of cannon fire at Arn. He returned cannon fire and took out three fighters.

"Damn, that felt good, Will."

"Don't do it!" Will screamed at him

Arn smiled and puffed on his cigar. The transmission ended.

Arn's fighter was obliterated by an array of cannon fire within seconds.

Will felt a fire in him that was missing for some time. He piloted the *Reaper* at the Weevil fighters and used several evasive moves to create turmoil in the Weevil formation. The fighters fired randomly, sometimes striking their own ships.

Shanna was deadly with her aim as the number of Weevil fighters dwindled.

"That's my girl," said Will into the intercom.

"I see you haven't lost your touch for flying," she replied.

"Five left. Let's finish them off and get out of here."

"My pleasure," replied Shanna.

Will navigated the *Reaper* into a tight turn around the fighters. Suddenly, the ship lurched sideways.

"What the hell was that, Shanna?"

"We just got clipped by one of the fighters."

"Any damage?"

"Looks like we're leaking coolant out of the right side engine."

"Then let's make quick work of this."

Will veered in the opposite direction and took another tight turn. Two more hits to the right engine disabled it completely.

"Will…"

"I know. We lost our number two."

"Can we get back?"

"Yeah. We're limited to sixty-two percent power."

"Understood." Shanna meticulously picked off the remaining fighters, one by one.

Will checked the long-range sensors monitor for any sign of the *Widow Maker* but there was nothing.

"What do you say we head for home, Shanna?" Will suggested over the intercom. There was no response. "Shanna, are you alright?" Still, there was no response.

Will set the auto-pilot and hurried out of the cabin. He reached the turrets but there was no sign of her. "Shanna, where are you?"

He rushed through the main cabin and down the corridor to the rear of the ship. He opened the door to his cabin and burst through the door.

Shanna stood before him in a dress-shirt, unbuttoned down the front. Her physical features had returned with the exception of her hair. The long locks were gone but now she had a short blond crop of hair trimmed neatly to contour her head. On the floor was the over-sized cloak that she wore for so long.

Will stared in disbelief at her. "Shanna, is this really you?"

"I certainly hope so."

Shanna extended her arms to Will. He embraced her and kissed her hungrily, over and over.

"Why did you make me wait?" he asked.

"Something blocked my emotions from functioning properly. I couldn't feel love."

"And now?"

Shanna opened the shirt and let it drop to the floor. "Let me show you," she replied coyly.

She anxiously removed Will's shirt and pushed him down on the bed. Will pulled her on top of him and kissed her repeatedly.

"I don't want to ever let you go."

"You'd better not," warned Shanna. "Now make love to me, you fool."

**********

Will piloted the *Reaper* while Shanna checked the sensors.

"I know what you're thinking," said Shanna smugly. "Let's go after Malduna and give her a little heartache."

"That's my girl. It bothers me how the *Widow Maker* disappeared so quickly. At the very least, I'd like to find out how."

"Perhaps they have a portal system of their own."

"No way. I think they're exploiting some of the Weevil portals."

"I wonder if the Weevil were coming to attack Malduna and Arn just got in the way," Shanna pondered.

"Perhaps I can coax the answer from Polus."

Shanna entered coordinates into the transmitter control panel. "You know, Will, we just cost him another twenty or so fighters. He's got to be stewing."

"Yeah, that's more of a reason for me to speak with him."

Shanna transmitted a signal for the Weevil leader and placed the transmitter in 'standby'.

"I feel like I cheated death, Will. By all rights, I should be dead or seriously messed up."

"Why so, Honey?"

"I was nearly eaten by the snake; I was almost fully mutated into a Calamaari; I entered Pinta's own palace and beat the crap out of her then escaped; I survived a massive fall and then trans-mutated back to my original self."

"Do you feel anything that isn't you?"

"Yes. I feel stronger, more determined."

The transmitter beeped three times and interrupted their conversation. Shanna pressed the 'receive' button. Polus ugly face appeared on the monitor.

"Well, hello, Polus," said Shanna playfully. "We were just talking about you."

"Where's Saris? I know he's responsible for attacking my fighters."

"Sorry, Polus, that was me that shot up your force. Will was the pilot this time."

"So there are two of you who need to die a pained death."

"Oh, stop it. That is so old."

"Enough of the small talk. Where's Saris?"

Will set the ship on auto-pilot and slid next to Shanna. "Hello, Polus. It's nice of you to answer my call."

"I am coming for you, Saris. When I reach your little space station, I will dismantle it piece by piece, including your friends inside."

"Did you forget our previous conversation?" Will reminded him. "If you bring your fleet into our sector, Malduna will annihilate all of you with the doomsday weapon."

"I still don't believe you. She doesn't have it."

"Then who does - Pinta? Either way, you are screwed."

Polus looked irritated. His mandibles opened and closed repeatedly but he said nothing.

"Alright, Polus. I'll spell it out for you. Your fighters killed a friend of mine. You owe me."

"I owe you nothing!"

"I will try and board Malduna's ship. Once on board, I will find out if she has the weapon in her possession. Then I'll find out if she wants to make a deal for it. If Pinta has it, she'll want to detonate it and kill a lot of Weevil."

"Why do you care so much if she annihilates us?"

"Oh, I really don't. It's just that she's going to set it off at your portal by the space station and that means my friends will die as well. I can't have that."

"My patience is limited, Saris. What are you asking?"

"Give me some time to find out who has the weapon. Then we'll figure out how to get rid of Malduna and Pinta."

And what happens afterward?"

"You and I continue our game of cat and mouse just like before. I'm not a threat to your race, just a nuisance. I know it's just a matter of time before you take over the sector. I'm just trying to have a little fun before you do."

Polus' head bobbed as he chuckled. "Sometimes I really do like you, Saris. Not too often, but sometimes."

The transmission ended.

"I can't believe how you keep messing with their little alien minds," remarked Shanna. "They fall for it every time."

"I know. It will be sweet when Polus realizes that I set him up after all this."

"I think aliens have a difficult time with patience. When I was mutating, everything seemed time-sensitive. Waiting was never an option."

They returned to the area where the *Widow Maker* disappeared.

"Check for heat trails," requested Will.

Shanna activated the infra-red system and checked the screen for imaging. Four long red streaks from the *Widow Maker's* engines extended for a distance and vanished.

"That must be a portal at the end of the trail," concluded Shanna. She pressed several keys and the computer chirped when data transferred into the data base. "There's your coordinates, Will."

Will took the ship off 'auto-pilot' and navigated toward the end of the trails.

The *Reaper* glided toward the location and as it approached, a bright flash occurred. They suddenly emerged on the other side of a portal. Ahead of them were four man-o-wars.

"Oh, crap!" exclaimed Will.

"I'm headed for the turret. You'd better fly your ass off, Will." Shanna bolted from the pilots' cabin.

The transmitter beeped three times. Will acknowledged the 'receive' button and Malduna's face appeared, looking annoyed.

"So, Will you found our little safe haven. Congratulations."

"Why did you sell the weapon to the Weevil?"

"It's simple. Once the Calamaari are decimated, it will be years before the Weevil come looking for us. By then, we'll have newer, more effective weapons to fight them with."

"You have no conscience at all, do you, Malduna?"

"Why don't you come on board and we'll discuss it? You and I should get to know each other."

"The last time we met, you gave me a splitting headache," complained Will.

"You're a lot tougher than I gave you credit for. I thought we left you for dead."

"I'm a little tougher than that."

"We do, however, have some things to settle between us."

"Ah, yes. I forgot that Rourke was your hubby. He was a tough son-of-a-bitch."

"Not as tough as I've become, thanks to you."

"If it makes you feel any better, I didn't want to kill him. He left us no choice."

"How do you think my son feels every day he wakes up without a father?"

"How about we put that on the back burner for now and we discuss a brief alliance?"

"You must have brain damage, Saris. I would never ally with you for anything."

"What about getting rid of both the Calamaari and the Weevil? Then we can go about our business of getting even without all the distractions."

Malduna considered his suggestion but was reluctant to commit. "Why wouldn't you just sell me out to the Weevil?" she asked.

"What is it with women and Weevil? You can't trust either of them. Pinta hasn't learned and neither have you."

"And you are one to be trusted?" she replied mockingly.

"Look at it this way, your son will have a brighter future without the Weevil and the Calamaari hunting humans."

"So what is it you expect me to do for you?"

"We need to convince Polus that the weapon you gave him is a defective prototype. You have the real weapon."

Malduna grew interested in Will's proposal and dropped her sarcasm. "And then what?"

"If I can coax Polus and Pinta into meeting near the Weevil's primary portal, then I can trick him into detonating it to wipe out the Calamaari forces. He won't expect the weapon to take out all of his forces as well."

Malduna pondered for a moment. "You have sanctuary here while I discuss this with my commanders. I will contact you when a decision has been made."

"I trust your word is worth something out here."

"Of course it is. I don't want to blow up your ship. I want to see you suffer in an excruciating manner when the time comes."

"Then I feel much better about this," joked Will. He ended the transmission and lowered his head against the console, feeling somewhat fatigued.

Shanna stood behind him and rubbed his shoulders. "You play a dangerous game, Saris."

"And you are a dangerous vixen."

Will stood up and embraced her. They kissed passionately.

"Do you really think we can pull this off?" Shanna asked.

"Do you doubt me, my love?"

Shanna pulled back from Will briefly. "We're close to finishing this thing off. If it means we die, then so be it. We'll leave a better universe for Marina to grow up in."

"Uh, dying isn't in the plan right now, Honey."

"It's always in the plan, Will. Sometime, someplace, it will happen."

Will programmed the ship for a quick escape through the portal if needed. He set the 'weapons lock' alarm to trigger the 'auto-pilot' mode.

"Clever," remarked Shanna coyly. "Are you planning on leaving the cabin?"

"Do I really need to answer that?" He gave her an inviting look and left the cabin.

Shanna chuckled to herself and followed him.

*************

Will sat at the controls in the pilots' cabin with his feet up on the console. He ate peanuts from a tin can, wondering how much longer they'd have to wait for Malduna.

George, Will's monkey, scurried into the cabin and leaped onto Will's lap. Will was overjoyed to see him. He nestled the monkey affectionately against his shoulder.

The monkey slyly reached into the can and retrieved some of the peanuts.

"Where have you been, George? I thought you left me."

The monkey patted Will's cheek and took another small handful of peanuts.

The transmitter beeped three times and startled them. Will reached over to the console and pressed the 'receive' button. Malduna's face appeared, looking cold as usual.

"I thought you forgot about us, Malduna."

"I see you've found someone compatible with you, Saris."

Will tickled the monkey's chin. "George is really the brains behind my decisions," he kidded. "I couldn't have gotten this far without him."

"Well, I spoke with Polus and informed him of the defective prototype that he has in his possession. Is this true about the weapon?"

"Yes, it is," answered Will. "The compound responsible for making the blast zone so expansive doesn't work. In close quarters, it's very lethal. So, for being a doomsday weapon, it's far from it."

"I informed Polus that I kept the real weapon for insurance so if he double-crossed me, he's history."

"Did he buy it?"

"I think so. I informed him that I want him to use that weapon to annihilate the Calamaari or else."

"Very good, Malduna. I'm impressed."

"My people, although they trust you even less than I, have agreed that your plan has some merit. We'll shelve our little feud for now. So what happens next?"

"I'll go back and try to bait Pinta into meeting with Polus. Once they are all together, I'll tip Polus off that it's a trap and Pinta has the real weapon."

"I warn you, Saris, don't screw with me. If you do, I'll make sure you are the last to die after everyone you ever cared about is butchered to death."

"You're too tense, Malduna. Try and lighten up a bit."

Malduna grimaced at him and terminated the transmission.

Will and the monkey stared at each other briefly. "What do you think of her, George?" he asked playfully.

The monkey covered his eyes and shrieked.

Shanna stepped into the cabin wearing a silk nightgown. Her eyes were small slits and she looked tired.

"I see you and George are reunited."

"Yes, I thought he left us at the station."

"No, he was in one of the empty cabins. I heard him playing with the door switch."

"Have a seat, Honey."

Shanna sat down in the co-pilot's seat and rubbed her eyes.

"Are you feeling okay?" Will asked. "You've been asleep for a long time."

"I'm doing better. My body is finally acting normal again."

"We're going back to the station," announced Will.

"Malduna agreed?"

"Uh-huh. She already spoke to Polus and everything is in place."

"Then Pinta is the last piece of the puzzle."

"That's right. We'll have to think of a way to make her meet Polus for the last phase of this plan to work."

Shanna leaned forward and kissed him on the forehead. "I'm really proud of you, Will. We've come so far in such a short time."

Will activated the 'auto-pilot' controls. "I know," he jested.

The *Reaper* entered the portal and made its way back toward the space station at limited speed. The four man-o-wars remained behind.

**********

The *Reaper* arrived at the space station and pulled into one of the empty berths and powered down. The bay doors slid closed and the bay pressurized.

Severin and two guards arrived in the bay to meet them. They anxiously waited at the ship's hatch.

When the hatch opened, Will and Shanna stood somberly at the entrance for a moment before exiting.

Severin knew immediately that Arn was gone. Her eyes welled with tears as she stared in disbelief at them. Will tried to console her with a hug. Shanna stood by her side and placed a hand on her shoulder in sympathy.

"I'm alright now," replied Severin. "I knew it was coming."

"We're so sorry," Shanna said with tears in her eyes.

"You look good, Shanna," Severin commented shakily.

"Thank you. It's good to be back."

"How did he die?"

"Like a warrior," answered Will.

"By whose hand – Malduna's?"

"No. A Weevil fighter unit ambushed them. Malduna fled from the fight. Arn took them on."

"Did they pay for his death?"

Will turned to Shanna for her response. "Oh, yes. All of them paid."

"I need a favor from you, Severin."

"What is it?"

"The, uh, Reaper … It needs some repairs to the tail."

"What kind of repairs?"

"Just a little…"

Shanna glared at Will impatiently. "The number two engine is shot," she blurted. "Maybe your mechanics can repair it."

"I'll see what I can do."

"I hated to ask under the circumstances," Will added sheepishly.

"I can't believe he's gone," Severin uttered as her voice crackled in sadness."

"You're in charge, now," Will reminded her. "Our last transmission with Arn was that he knew you'll do a fine job."

Severin couldn't hold back her tears any more. She quickly left the bay. The two guards departed as well.

Will and Shanna followed them until they reached the clinic. The guards continued down the hall. Will and Shanna entered the clinic and knocked on Prax's door. There was no answer.

A single technician sat at the desk. "Well, Mr. Saris, it's good to see you looking well. And you, too, ma'am."

"Thank you," Shanna responded. She was pleased by his comments.

"It's good to be up and about," added Will. "Thanks for all your support."

"You were a handful, I must say."

"It seems so. Have you seen Prax anywhere?"

"Last time, I heard he was in the test lab two levels down."

"Thanks, again."

Will and Shanna departed the clinic. When they reached the test lab, the security door was locked and a red light flashed above it. Will pressed a button on the voice box.

"Who is it?" Prax's voice crackled from the speaker.

"It's Will and Shanna."

After a moment of silence, the door clicked and opened.

Will and Shanna passed through the security door and followed a long corridor. At the end were two sliding doors, one on the left and one on the right. The left door opened and Prax emerged. He was stunned by the sight of Shanna.

"I see the emulator worked its magic."

"Yes it did," replied Shanna. "Thanks so much."

"Come in. Bastille's here as well."

Will and Shanna followed him into a large warehouse-type lab.

"How are things' Prax?"

"I was about to ask you the same thing."

"Arn's gone. The Weevil ambushed him before he could get to Malduna."

"What a pity. He was a good man."

"Severin's in charge of the station now."

"How's she taking it?"

"She's upset right now but she'll be fine."

"I'd best check on her as soon as we finish here."

Prax led them to a large steel drum with thick windows. Inside the drum was a small quantity of brown powder, placed underneath the power source of a molybdium laser.

In front of the drum was a control console with three dials, two display monitors and a key pad.

Will and Shanna watched curiously as Prax powered up the console. He set the dials and entered a series of digits into the system. The power source emitted a purple laser which targeted the compound. After several seconds, the compound smoldered and gave off white smoke.

Prax dialed up the intensity of the laser and donned welder's glasses. He handed a set to Will and Shanna. "I suggest you put these on."

They no sooner placed the glasses on when it exploded with a white flash and a loud boom.

"It sounded good," kidded Will.

Prax removed his glasses and looked despondently at them. "That's about all it did." He pointed to one of the displays which read '4.62'.

"What are we hoping for?" inquired Shanna.

"Oh, about 11.6 or greater. I just can't get the formula right."

"Keep trying," urged Will.

"If I use up any more of the Crylum, there won't be enough for the final product."

"Then we've just lost the ace up our sleeve," complained Will. "We're screwed."

Prax reached over and took the welders' glasses off of Will and Shanna. "I received word from someone who can help."

"Who else would know anything about this stuff but .... Wait, you heard from Xerxes?"

"Yes, I did. He'll be here soon enough."

Will became excited like a little kid. "I can't believe we'll actually have the legendary Xerxes here at our station!"

"Easy, Will. He's just a human."

Bastille heard the commotion and crossed the lab from the far side. "Good news travels fast, I see."

"Depends," replied Will. "What do you have to tell me?"

"With a few changes, the *Reaper's* probes are now frequency-sensitive explosives that will magnetically attach to the Weevil probes."

"Will they impair the probes in any way?" asked Shanna.

"They shouldn't."

"Bastille, you impress me more and more. If I can ever do anything to repay you..."

"As a matter of fact, there is. I'd like to spend a few days with Celine to celebrate our anniversary."

"That's wonderful, Bastille!" exclaimed Shanna.

"Of course, you can have all the time you like," answered Will.

Bastille shook Will's hand and hugged Shanna. "After all our trials and tribulations, things are finally getting better for all of us," he said thankfully.

"Will placed his arm around Shanna's waist. "Yes they are," he remarked half-heartedly.

Bastille hurried out of the test lab.

Will looked around for Prax but there was no sign of him. "Where'd Prax go?"

"I guess he had something to do," replied Shanna.

"And so do we." Will took Shanna's hand and they left the test lab.

**********

Will and Shanna sat in the saloon at one of the tables. There were only a few patrons there and the mood was somber.

Jeanie came to the table with swollen eyes. "Is it true about the General? Is he really gone?"

Will looked up at her and nodded. "I'm afraid so. He fought valiantly."

Tears streamed down Jeanie's cheeks. "He was like a father to Heidi and me. We'll miss him."

"We're all going to miss him."

"Did you want something to drink?"

Will took Shanna's hand in his. "How about a toast to Arn, General and father to all on board Orpheus-2?"

"I think that would be appropriate."

"Would you mind if I joined you?" asked Jeanie.

"How about us, too?" shouted one of the customers at the other table.

"Of course."

Will stood up and addressed them. "The General was a proud man. He stood for everything we believe in and he stood for us."

"How did he die?" asked one of the gentlemen.

"He took on the *Widow Maker* and disabled her weapons system. Before he could finish her off, he was ambushed by a Weevil fighter group."

"Did they pay?"

"Of course they did. Every single one of them."

An elderly woman asked, "When will we put an end to the Weevil? We've incurred so many losses at their hands."

"We are working on the final details of a plan that we believe will put an end to the Weevil and this tiresome war, once and for all."

Everyone cheered at his remarks.

Severin and Prax entered the saloon and joined them. "Always working the crowds, Will," Severin quipped.

"I can see the end of this misery. It's not that far off."

"I hope you're right."

Jeanie returned with a dozen glasses of Arn's rum and distributed it to everyone in the saloon.

Will raised his glass and paused. The others raised theirs in response.

"To the General," he announced. "We'll never forget him."

Everyone took a swig from their glasses and coughed.

"Damn, that stuff gets stronger and stronger every time," complained Will.

Severin raised her glass, "I would like to make an announcement as well." She waited as everyone raised their glasses again. "The station will be dedicated to the memory of General Arn Adolpho for here we will soon take our stand against the Weevil for one final time. Whether we succeed or not, this battle will be remembered forever by our descendents."

Everyone cheered and drank. Severin finished her glass and slammed the glass on the table. Prax eyed her with a surprised expression.

Will looked at his half-empty glass humbly and quickly finished the contents.

"I think that's a proper way to do him homage," remarked Shanna.

"We talked before he left," Severin revealed to them. "He doubted his courage for letting so many things happen on his station. He felt that he owed it to us to be the man he used to be and not what he had become."

"I'm sorry, Severin. I didn't know he felt that way."

"So am I. If I stayed with him, he might still be alive."

"Don't blame yourself, Severin," Shanna said. "We'll all fight well and make him proud."

"That we will. I guarantee it."

"When Xerxes gets here, we need to talk about timing and if he can make this compound work," Will informed her.

"You have another problem with *Leviathan*," replied Prax. "She's got serious issues."

"Yes, I've heard. That figures into our plans as well. In the meantime, Shanna and I have a daughter to tend to."

"I can send a patrol out to install the new devices on the Wccvil probes," suggested Severin.

"Someone will need to guide them," suggested Shanna. "After the first two, you have to interpolate where the others are."

"I will go with them."

"But Severin, what if …?

"Forget it, Will. I'll take care of it."

"Very well. Holler if you need our help."

Will and Shanna left the saloon.

Severin took Prax's hand. "You and I have business to discuss."

"Yes, Dear," he replied.

The two of them left the saloon, hand in hand.

**********

Will and Shanna sat on a sofa in the main quarters of the *Reaper* with Marina and the monkey.

Marina rested her head on Shanna's shoulders and appeared disinterested in them. She stared at the monkey with tired eyes.

Shanna's eyes welled with tears as she stroked Marina's hair. "This is all I ever wanted, Will – my family."

"Maybe we're getting close, finally."

"We'll never be close. This is our curse."

Will placed his arm around her and pulled her close to him. He stared blankly ahead as he wondered if she was right.

George climbed on Will's shoulder and leaned against his head. The monkey seemed to understand the somberness of the moment.

"Arn's death made me realize how fragile all of this is," explained Will.

"When I was being swallowed by that snake, I felt so empty inside," explained Shanna. "I was helpless to say or do anything to let you and Marina know how much I love you before I died."

"I should have been there for you."

"No, I didn't want you to see me like that. I wasn't Shanna. I was something else."

"It doesn't matter. You were still Shanna to me."

Shanna wept.

"What is it?" asked Will.

"This could be our last night as a family," she blurted. "I feel something bad is coming."

"Is it the Eye telling you this?"

"No, it's something that I feel," replied Shanna. "We will be so close and it will be snatched away from us, just like all our enemies. They were so close to achieving their goals and we took it away from them."

"But they were evil. They had to be stopped."

"Will, the universe is not moral or immoral. It is a food chain and we are part of that chain."

Will stood up and paced the floor. "I refuse to believe that. We are on the side of right and we will defeat the Weevil."

"But at what cost? Will it be us? Our friends? Our family?"

Will sat down again and put his head in his hands. He wept as he realized she was right. "I should have listened to Maya on that first mission. I should have never taken things into my own hands."

"Then we would have never met."

"So what should I have done?" he shouted in frustration.

"Enjoy what we have, while we have it."

"Are you reading my thoughts, Shanna?"

"Sometimes. It comes and goes."

"Then we can't count on our telepathy."

"For our battle plans?"

"No, for support. I need you to help me through this."

"And I'll be there for you."

Marina fell asleep in Shanna's arms. She took her into the spare cabin and laid her in bed.

When she returned, Will was outside the ship. She stepped out and joined him.

The engine mechanics installed the repaired number two engine in the tail of the *Reaper*.

Will stared at the images painted on the ship: the skulls and wavering white shades, like ghosts trailing the ship.

Shanna placed her arm around his waist. "What are you thinking?"

"Those images – it's us. We're like ghosts chasing something unseen through space. No real home, no real life – just ghosts."

"Let's go inside, Will."

**********

Prax and Severin walked down the outer corridor along the transport bays, hand in hand.

"Are you sure you're okay with this?" questioned Prax.

"More than you'll ever know," answered Severin. "You're a lot like Will and Arn but you have a soft side that they refused to show. That's what I need in my life."

"Then I'm sure we'll have some interesting conversations when you meet Xerxes. He's my father."

Severin paused and held both of Prax's hands while facing him. "I don't care. It would be exciting to hear about Will's father and how you both tackled some of the alien issues."

"Oh, now you're asking for trouble."

Severin kissed his cheek and they continued down to the last hatch at the end of the corridor. The light above the hatch was red and sounds of air rushing through pipes distracted them briefly.

Severin leaned against Prax and held his arm. This was a new sensation to her as she never took time to be with a man before. Her whole life was committed to a military career and she excelled at it but at what cost.

The whooshing sound stopped and the light turned green. The two of them approached the hatch and Prax pressed the 'open' knob.

The chain linkage emitted a grating noise as the hatch swung open. Neither one took particular notice of the sounds before but today was different. They were in love. Everything seemed clearer for some reason.

Prax and Severin entered the bay.

A small dart-shaped transport rested at the dock. Hydraulic pipelines emerged from the wall and automatically attached to ports in the ship's hull. The ship's hatch opened and Xerxes, a short, albino man, exited carrying a small attaché case.

Prax extended his arms toward him and hugged him tightly. "Father, it's good to see you!"

Xerxes stepped back and looked Prax over, "You haven't changed at all, boy," he said affectionately. "I heard you might need the help of an old geezer out here."

"What took you so long?"

"It wasn't easy getting away from Earth. So many problems on that planet."

Prax gently pulled Severin in front of him. "Dad, this is Severin. She's a very special friend."

"It's a pleasure to meet you, dear," said Xerxes. He took her hand and kissed it.

The three of them left the bay and proceeded to the saloon. Xerxes was amazed at the architecture of the saloon as it reminded him of one of the western bars he had seen in Arizona.

As soon as they sat down, Jeanie came over from the bar. "Hello, everyone. What can I get you today?"

"Just a water," answered Severin.

"Water! This is a celebration!" exclaimed Xerxes.

"Oh, alright," she relented. "Three rums."

Jeanie smiled and left them.

"Rum, eh," quipped Xerxes.

"It's home-made from a close friend of ours. He was recently killed in battle by the Weevil," explained Prax.

"My sympathies," replied Xerxes. "So, you solved the riddle of the PBU-57s I understand."

"Yes, we did and not a moment too soon. The prototype was stolen by mercenaries thinking it was the real deal."

"The mercs left a large explosive device of their own on board the station," added Severin. "We were lucky that Prax knew how to disarm it."

"Have you solved the mystery of the compound yet, son?"

"It's funny you should ask. I've tried everything but I can't get it right."

"You saved enough of the compound for me I hope."

"Of course. I couldn't afford to ruin our chance to annihilate the Weevil because I couldn't get the right blend."

"Then let us see what you have."

Severin grabbed Prax's arm and interrupted, "I have to go. I'll check in with you when we get to the portal."

"Be careful. I don't want anything to happen to you."

"I will," Severin replied and kissed his cheek.

Prax eyed her as she walked away.

"Very nice lady," commented Xerxes.

"Yes she is. It's been a while since I met someone like her."

The two men stepped onto the elevator and proceeded to the lab. When they arrived, the disarmed bomb was still in its case. Xerxes grew uneasy as they walked past it.

"Relax, Dad. It's disabled."

Prax and Xerxes stopped at the large steel drum with thick windows.

On the steel table next to it was a notepad filled with formulae and data. Xerxes picked up the pad and studied it. He frowned as he read the concentrations. Prax watched curiously.

Xerxes removed a pen form his pocket and marked up one formula. He set his attaché bag on the table and opened it. Inside was a transparent case with seven vials. He opened the case and removed one of the vials.

"I think you'll find that this will improve your results significantly," said Xerxes. Also, you'll need to modify the laser's intensity a bit."

After combining the new element with a sample of the compound, Prax placed a small quantity of the new compound inside the drum under the laser. He powered up the console and entered a series of digits into the system.

Xerxes dialed up the intensity of the laser. Prax donned a set of welder's glasses. He handed a set to Xerxes who quickly donned them.

The power source inside the tank emitted a blue laser beam instead of the purple beam that Prax used earlier. After several seconds, the compound flashed into a bright white light. The light was self sustaining for twenty seconds and then faded.

Prax looked at Xerxes and waited for his reaction.

Xerxes nodded to him and replied, "You now have the most powerful weapon in the universe at your disposal."

"So it worked?"

"Better than the original. Now all you have to do is use it against the Weevil and bye-bye Weevil."

Prax carefully blended a portion of the substance in the vial with the actual compound. He then placed it inside a centrifuge and operated it at low speed.

"Dad, can I ask you a question?"

"Sure, Son."

"Why did you send the weapon in a coffin? I thought you were dead."

"As I told you earlier, things are really bad on Earth. I faked my death to elude mercenaries and the world government."

"But why you?" Prax inquired. "Did you do something wrong?"

"Heaven's no. It's all about the lousy weapon."

Prax looked down at the floor sadly. "My heart broke when I found it. I didn't know what to think."

"It doesn't matter now. I'm here, safe and sound." Xerxes hugged him. They were an odd sight as Prax was much taller than Xerxes. Prax always took after his mother. She died in battle against alien insurgents when he was very young.

Prax stopped the centrifuge and poured the compound into a glass canister. Once he secured the steel cap on top of it, he placed it in a vault at the back of the lab.

"We have much to share with the others," Prax declared excitedly. "Everyone has waited a long time for good news about the compound."

"Well, now they have it," replied Xerxes.

**********

Will and Shanna entered the *Leviathan* with Marina. They were surprised to find all of their friends gathered in the main quarters.

Jack and Maya sat at one table with their two girls. Bastille and Celine sat across from them. Many of the others sat at the bar and on couches along the walls.

Prax and Xerxes sat at the table next to Jack and Maya.

Xerxes stood when Will entered. "Will!" exclaimed Xerxes. "It's good to see you again."

"Welcome, Xerxes. I can't believe you're here."

Will introduced everyone to him by name and their roles in his successes. When they finished, Prax announced that they successfully tested a sample of the compound and were ready to install it into the PBU-57B when the time arrived to strike at the Weevil. Everyone cheered at the prospect of finally ending the war.

Xerxes told stories of the early decades of the alien alliance before the Weevil entered the picture. He told of Will's father's adventures and how he changed the history of mankind.

Shanna proudly related how Will, much like his father, has continued in his father's footsteps.

"I've been dying to ask you something, Will," Xerxes remarked sheepishly."

"Anything, Xerxes."

"Do you turn into a furry creature like your dad did?"

Will looked at Shanna and the two burst into laughter.

"Not in a while but it has been done. So can Shanna."

"How did that come about? I didn't think males could pass that trait to a female."

Will deferred to Shanna for an explanation.

"Well, Xerxes, it happened that I come from a tribe of shape-shifters just like Will's mother did. My mother was queen just like her."

"So you and Will are royalty?"

"Please, Xerxes, we're trying to forget that part," complained Will, faking a pained expression.

"I'm impressed. Will, your mother was one of the bravest souls I ever met."

"Were you there when she died?"

"Not quite. We arrived too late to save her but those who escaped, thanks to her, told of how she fought while outnumbered against a vicious race of aliens so valiantly to the end. Those were trying times."

"Not much has changed. Just different circumstances."

The remainder of the evening was spent discussing the *Leviathan's* degrading circuitry and how they might save her.

**********

The next morning, Will and Shanna sat at breakfast in the station's crowded cafeteria with Marina.

Shanna beamed as they finally had a chance to enjoy family life for a change. She knew it would be short lived when the new security officer entered and spotted them. He promptly came toward them with a somber expression.

Will immediately knew something was wrong.

The officer leaned close to them. "We have a situation that you should be aware of," he said in a low tone to prevent others from overhearing. "Severin and her crew have been captured by the Calamaari."

Will and Shanna looked mortified.

"How do you know this?" inquired Will.

"Because Pinta contacted us to show them off. She wants to speak with you soon or she'll kill them."

Will glanced at Shanna.

"I'll join you later, Will," said Shanna as she wiped Marina's face clean.

"Thanks, Honey." Will replied and followed the officer out of the cafeteria.

When they reached the Surveillance Control Center, Pinta's face was displayed on the large monitor. She appeared pleased to see Will. This was a pivotal moment in Will's plans as Pinta now had a bargaining chip to use against him.

"Well, Pinta, what a surprise this is," said Will cynically.

Pinta chuckled in a twisted, garbled series of sounds and backed away from the monitor. Behind her, Severin and six crewmen were chained to a wall.

Pinta walked up to one of the men and eyed him fiendishly. The man trembled and pleaded for mercy.

Will watched with disbelief as he knew the message she would send.

Pinta bit into the man's neck and slurped greedily on the warm, pulsing artery.

Will bowed his head helplessly. The security officer pounded his fist against the wall and paced angrily. Will motioned for him to calm down.

Pinta returned to the monitor, blood smeared over her ashen face. "Ready to talk, Saris?"

"Alright, Pinta, you made your point. What do you want?"

"I know you have the real doomsday weapon. I also know that the Weevil have a prototype that doesn't work."

"I wouldn't say it doesn't work, Pinta. It just doesn't have the bang they think it does. What do you want in exchange for my friends' lives?"

"I want you and the doomsday weapon. I'm not feeling very patient right now if you know what I mean."

"There's a little problem with that."

Pinta left the monitor and approached another crewman. She glanced back at the monitor as she was about to bite into another throat.

"Wait!" shouted Will. "Let me explain."

Pinta returned and stared defiantly at him. Will tried to come up with a tactical response that wouldn't undercut his original plan.

Shanna entered and waited by the doorway. She tried not to distract Will and stayed out of Pinta's view.

"Look, Pinta, I'm tired of fighting," explained Will. "I have a plan to use the weapon to annihilate the Weevil. That's a win-win situation for both of us."

"There's just one problem, Saris: I don't trust you."

"The weapon is part of the *Leviathan*, Pinta. We integrated it into the ship's structure."

"That's ridiculous!"

"No it isn't. We already had the prototype stolen. Why would we chance the finished model being stolen as well?"

"Then you need to turn over that ship and yourself. If not, I will be eating well today."

"Don't give in, Will!" shouted Severin.

Pinta rushed at her and held a clawed hand to her throat.

"Hold on, Pinta," pleaded Will. "Let's talk."

Pinta returned to the monitor.

Will continued, "If I surrender the *Leviathan* and myself to you, will you sign a truce with my people?"

"I might consider it if we throw that beauty of a mutant into the deal, too. I owe her for a little visit she made to my palace."

"Let's leave her out of this."

"I'll bet she's looking real good to you, isn't she?"

Shanna stepped into view behind Will and placed her hands on his shoulders. Pinta was aghast at the sight of her.

"Thank you for the compliment, Pinta. Not only did I retain my looks, I have skills and strength I never had before. I welcome the opportunity to meet you face-to-face once again and show my appreciation for what you've given me."

Pinta was silent as she considered this new twist.

"Well, Pinta, there's your answer," said Will. "We'll bring the *Leviathan* and meet with you. In return, you'll transport our people on board an alternate ship."

Pinta still said nothing. This was all too easy.

"I'll make arrangements to leave immediately," Will informed her.

"Wait! How do I know you won't detonate the ship once you arrive?" questioned Pinta.

"Then let's leave the ship out of it," suggested Will. "You release my people and they leave on it. I'll instruct them to keep you informed of their plans for the Weevil."

"I want the ship destroyed. Dismantle the weapon and bring it and the mutant bitch to me. That's my final offer."

"I understand. There will be two ships coming; *Leviathan* and a smaller ship."

"I'm looking forward to tasting your flesh, Saris."

"And I'm looking forward to tasting yours, Pinta," interjected Shanna. "Since our encounter, I've developed an insatiable hunger for alien flesh." Shanna burst into sadistic laughter.

Will promptly ended the transmission and glared at her. "What was that all about?"

"Intimidation. Now she's distracted."

"I don't like it!" shouted the security officer.

"We don't have a choice," replied Will. "Unless you want to see a lot of people die, this is our only way out."

Will and Shanna barged out of the room. The security officer kicked the chair over and slammed the door.

In the hall, Shanna complained, "I already don't like this guy."

"Let it go. We have bigger problems."

**********

Inside the lab, Will and Shanna pondered over the unexploded ordinate left by Malduna's mercenaries. Prax and Xerxes entered the room.

"I thought I'd find you here. Security said that you were in the middle of something insane."

Will didn't respond.

"Severin's been captured," replied Shanna.

"What? They didn't tell me that!" exclaimed Prax.

"By whom?" inquired Xerxes.

"The Calamaari have her. We're working on a plan to get her back."

Prax stood next to Will and looked down at the explosive device. "What can I do to help?"

"Make this look like a doomsday weapon. You'll need Bastille's help."

"We're on it, right away."

"Let me know when it's ready," requested Will.

"Let's go, Will," ordered Shanna. "We need to talk."

Will followed Shanna obediently back to the saloon. Shanna went to the bar while Will took a seat at the table. She returned with two drinks and sat across with him.

"Look, Will, this is our chance to solve one of our problems."

"What if we fail?"

"We won't," assured Shanna. "Now let's put our heads together on this."

"I don't understand why Goeth and Cintilla haven't made a move yet," fretted Will.

"We can't worry about that. Are we really taking *Leviathan* out to Calamaar?"

"We have to."

"Then let's make Pinta come out to us."

"What good does that do?"

"We can do a lot of things. Detonate the ship. Board her ship while they board ours."

"We need a ship for Severin and the others to return on. I also want the *Reaper* for a fast escape."

"What about this damn doomsday weapon?" asked Shanna.

"It stays here. We'll take the dummy. After that …"

"After that," interrupted Shanna, "we'll play it by ear. There are too many possibilities."

"But what if we're caught?"

"We're going in fighting and we're coming out fighting. Just like the good old days."

Will tapped his glass against hers in a toast. "I knew there was a reason I married you."

"And I'm still trying to remember the reason why I married you," she teased.

**********

Bastille and Celine met Jack and Maya at the jet way to the *Leviathan*. Together they boarded the ship and entered the main quarters.

Will and Shanna sat somberly on one of the couches. He leaned forward with his head in his hands. Shanna nestled against Will for consolation.

"What's wrong?" asked Bastille.

"Problems with the Calamaari," replied Shanna.

Will looked up grimly. "I need you and Celine to pilot *Leviathan*. You're carrying the *Reaper* and a second ship for our escape."

"She's not coming back with us?" asked Bastille.

"Probably not. We're doing a tricky exchange to get Severin and her crew back."

"Well, she's done herself proud," replied Bastille. "I'm gonna' miss her."

"I'm surprised that's all they want," quipped Jack.

"It's not. They want me and Shanna as well."

"You're not giving up, are you, Will?" asked Maya.

"No, but we have to look like it. Is the new weapon on board, yet?"

"Yes it is. It doesn't look like a missile but it does look like an intricate bomb."

"That works. I told Pinta that we integrated the bomb into the ship's structure."

"When do we leave?" asked Jack.

"Now."

Bastille and Celine sensed his urgency and went directly to the flight deck.

Jack and Maya waited for additional details from Will.

After pondering for several moments, Will stood up, looking quite somber. "Shanna and I will go aboard Pinta's ship. I want the two of you to come right after us but to a different location."

"What's the point of that?" asked Maya.

"Surprise. I don't expect Pinta to let them go. I don't expect her to let us go. The two of you will figure out a way to get us out of there."

Jack and Maya look stunned.

"That's a hell of a plan Will," chided Maya. "Didn't you forget something like 'how are we going to do that'?"

"I won't lie. We're going to wing this one."

"Well, at least you're honest for once," said Jack cynically.

# Chapter 9

## The Winds of War

The *Leviathan* glided toward Calamaar with the *Reaper* and a support ship docked inside its huge bay.

Will sat with Shanna, Jack and Maya in the main quarters. They discussed various scenarios for dealing with Pinta.

A dozen Calamaari fighters appeared along with a battle star from a portal and shadowed the *Leviathan.*

Celine spotted the ships on her long distance monitor. She informed Bastille and they prepared for evasive maneuvers.

Bastille announced over the intercom to everyone that the Calamaari ships were sighted and requested Will contact him for instructions. Before Will could respond, the transmitter beeped.

"This can't be good," uttered Bastille. He pressed the 'receive' button and Zorick's face appeared.

"I need to speak with Will," demanded Zorick "Is he on board?"

"Give me a moment," replied Bastille. He called Will over the intercom and requested he come immediately to the flight deck.

Will burst through the cabin hatch and saw Zorick's face on the screen.

"What are you doing, Will?" inquired Zorick. "You can't surrender to Pinta like this!"

"I have a plan. Have you heard from Goeth or Cintilla?" asked Will.

"No, we haven't. I fear they may be dead. Now, what are you trying to do?"

"Pinta is holding several of my friends prisoner. I'm going to rescue them."

"That's insane! You'll be killed."

"That's a risk I have to take."

"Pinta is waiting for you when you cross through the portal to Calamaar. She's in the battle star. It's surrounded by six cruisers and numerous fighters."

"Can you pull some of them away from her?"

"I'll see what I can do? Perhaps a Weevil skirmish might require extra support."

"Just give me some space to execute my plan, Zorick. If things go wrong, well, you'll know."

"I hope you know what you're doing. We're counting on you."

"I know you are. I won't let you down."

The transmission ended. Will departed the flight deck without any comment or instruction, leaving Bastille and Celine baffled over his intentions.

Will returned to the main quarters and revealed the details of his discussion with Zorick.

The *Leviathan* passed through the portal and encountered the Calamaari fleet just as Zorick warned they would.

Will activated the local communications control panel and entered a series of codes.

Shanna, Jack and Maya watched quietly, wondering what he had in mind.

Pinta's face appeared on the monitor. "I see you've kept your word so far, Saris."

"I said I would. How are we going to do this?"

"I'm sending three of my officers over to inspect the weapon. If they are satisfied, I'll send the prisoners over next. You and the wench will come on board my ship now."

"We have a problem there, Pinta," replied Will. "We'll return with the officers and the weapon."

"You are in no position to bargain, Saris. I think I'll kill one of your friends to prove it."

"Wait! I'll come over. Shanna will come with the officers."

"Perhaps I'll allow it to show that mutant bitch of yours how little I think of her."

Shanna bristled with anger off to the side. Maya and Jack restrained her.

"I'll lock onto your flight deck for transport."

Pinta hissed and gurgled in Calamaari laughter. The transmission ended.

Will left the main quarters briefly and returned with a sword strapped to his waist. He hugged Shanna and kissed her. "This will work," he assured her.

"Jack. Maya. I know you'll do your best to help us," Will said somberly.

Jack hugged him tightly with a man hug. Maya kissed his cheek and squeezed him against her. "Be safe, Will," she pleaded. "Please, be safe."

They hugged Shanna and exchanged looks of concern for each other.

Jack and Maya left the main quarters and hid in a nearby cabin. Shanna stood by Malduna's explosive device and waited nervously. She tried to smile at Will but her eyes welled up.

Will stepped onto the transport platform and vanished. No sooner had he disappeared, three Calamaari officers arrived.

The officers inspected the weapon meticulously for several minutes. One of them asked, "What is it that makes this weapon so deadly?"

"It's in the compound used to trigger the reaction," replied Shanna. She wanted to attack the officers but she couldn't risk jeopardizing Will's safety.

One of the officers approached her uneasily. His eyes indicated that he wasn't her enemy. "Why would you give in to Pinta's demands?"

"Because we have no choice."

"Pinta's going to kill him, you know that."

"Not if I can help it."

"We were instructed to kill you as soon as we confirmed the weapon is legit. If not, we were to take you hostage."

"So, what's it gonna' be? It's your shot," she said arrogantly.

"We don't support Pinta. We also don't want the weapon falling into the wrong hands."

Shanna stared at the weapon and contemplated whether or not to trust them. "Alright, this isn't the weapon. We have it and intend to use it against the Weevil. Now, what about Will?"

"We'll take you to Pinta and choose our moment to overtake her."

"Very well. You do realize that this may be the last and only chance to do this?"

"Yes, we do. We have taken other precautions as well to ensure our success,"

"Then let's go."

The officer contacted Pinta and announced their return. He also informed her that the weapon was a fake.

On board Pinta's battle star, Will was surrounded by Calamaari guards. Pinta was seated at a control console when she received the information. She gritted her teeth and fangs until brown blood seeped from between her lips.

Will sensed that something was wrong. Pinta got up slowly and approached him with extreme prejudice in her eyes.

"You thought you could play me, Saris. Now, it's time to pay."

Four Calamaari guards escorted Severin and five of her crewmen onto the flight deck.

Severin glared at Will. "What the hell are you doing, Will? This isn't negotiable."

"Shut up, Severin," ordered Will.

Pinta raised her claws and approached Severin. "You'll be the first to go," she declared.

Will drew his sword and prepared to take on the guards despite being outnumbered. The guards drew their pulse pistols and took aim at him.

Pinta turned her attention back to Will and howled humorously. “Put the sword down before you hurt yourself, Saris. You don’t stand a chance.”

One of the doors to the flight deck slid open and Shanna marched in with the three officers. They held their pulse pistols pointed at her as if she were in custody.

“This is just beautiful!” uttered Pinta. “I want the mutant bitch first, then I’ll deal with the others.”

“I’ve waited a long time for this, Pinta,” Shanna said with a devious smile.

“No, Shanna, you can’t!”

“Relax, Will,” she replied confidently.

She raised her arms, stretching and straining.

Everyone gazed in awe as Shanna transformed into a mutant Calamaari.

She looked human in many ways but became muscular with clawed hands and long legs. Her pullover shirt stretched and split in several places. Her pants bulged in the butt and shortened at the ankles. She yanked her boots off, revealing sharp, pointed nails at the end of her toes. Her skin and hair remained unchanged but she clearly looked intimidating.

Pinta stared in surprise while the guards appeared ready for an entertaining event.

“Come on, Pinta. Something bothering you?”

Pinta lost control and took a fighting stance. “Yes, you bother me. You insignificant mutant freak!”

Will cringed when he saw the rage build inside Shanna.

Shanna and Pinta charged at each other and fought tenaciously. Shanna inflicted wounds on Pinta’s face, more frequently with each rush. They tumbled across the floor as Shanna gradually wore down Pinta.

Pinta made a desperate lunge but Shanna caught her by the throat and slammed her to the floor.

Four guards quickly surrounded them and held their weapons against Shanna's head. She reluctantly released her hold and backed away.

The three officers trained their pistols on the guards.

"Stand down," ordered one of the officers.

"What is this treachery?" Pinta screamed.

"We are leaving and the prisoners go with us," explained Will.

"I don't think so," Pinta replied.

Ten guards entered the flight deck and surrounded the officers.

Shanna transformed back to her human form. She sidled over to Will.

The door opened and in came Jack, Maya, Cintilla and Goeth. They aimed their weapons at Pinta.

"You lose Pinta," announced Cintilla.

Goeth questioned the guards as to who they accepted as their true leader. They supported Pinta.

Suddenly, the ship rocked. The power flickered several times.

"What's going on?" shouted Pinta.

The flight officer replied, "We're under attack. There are Weevil fighters all around us."

"Then you are on your own," announced Goeth.

Goeth assembled all those who pledged loyalty and they transported off the ship.

Will's party retreated from the flight deck and closed the door. Goeth left with them.

Jack contacted the *Leviathan* and promptly had their group transported off the Calamaari ship as well.

Once on board *Leviathan*, Will rushed to the flight deck.

Bastille piloted the ship while Celine operated the weapons system. Both looked panicked.

"What's going on?" asked Will.

"The weapons system is shutting down!" shouted Celine in a panicked voice.

"We'll give you some cover with the *Reaper*. Get out of here as quick as you can," instructed Will.

"It looks like some of the fighters are turning back," said Bastille. "That's strange."

Will leaned over Bastille's shoulder and studied the monitor. The wave of green dots migrated away from them."

The red dots representing the Calamaari cruisers pursued them, leaving only the battle star.

"What is Zorick doing?" groaned Will. "He's going to get in the way."

Down in the main chamber, Goeth and Cintilla spoke with Zorick on the communications panel. She instructed him to order all commanders loyal to her to report back to Calamaar immediately.

Will descended the stairs and ordered, "Shanna, get on board the *Reaper*. Everyone else, go with Goeth and Cintilla on the transport ship. We'll meet you back at the station."

"What's wrong with this ship?" inquired Cintilla.

"The weapons system just shut down. We need to move fast."

"What about the Weevil?"

"Zorick's forces chased half of the fighters away. The others are attacking Pinta's ship."

He hurried after Shanna to the cargo bay.

"Let's go," ordered Jack. "We've got to go."

Jack led the remainder of the group to the transport ship.

Within moments, the *Reaper* darted from the open bay door at the rear of *Leviathan*, followed shortly after by the second ship.

Will guided the *Reaper* back toward the Weevil fighters. He set up the weapons control panel and prepared to do battle.

Shanna entered the pilot's cabin and sat next to him. She took over control of the ship, giving Will a breather.

"Something's not right, Will."

"What do you mean?"

"The Weevil could have finished us all off. Instead they left half their fighters to be slaughtered. Why didn't they?"

"And why did the others flee the area?" he pondered aloud. "Oh, no!"

Will accelerated to maximum speed after the Weevil fleet.

"You don't think ...?"

"Yes, I do, Shanna. They're going to detonate the PBU-57A. We have to get through their portal."

"What about the others?"

"Tell them to get the hell out of here as fast as they can."

Shanna contacted Bastille and warned him of the pending danger.

The *Reaper* raced into the Weevil portal and fired selectively at several fighters.

Many of the fighters landed inside three large battle stars, which moved away from the portal as well.

Will contacted Zorick and warned him of the pending threat.

Zorick turned his forces around and fled the sector through two portals.

The transmitter beeped and startled Will. Polus' face appeared, looking sinister and gleeful.

"Say good-bye to your world, Saris. Now, you'll have no place to hide."

"I told you, Polus, that is not the weapon you think it is. It's just a small scale prototype."

"We'll see about that."

On the other side of the portal, the Calamaari fleet loyal to Pinta regrouped to protect the battle star. They approached the portal en mass.

One of the Weevil fighters fired a missile into the portal and veered away.

Pinta watched the large monitor anticipating an easy victory over the fleeing fighters.

A sleek red missile emerged from the portal and darted toward them.

"Destroy that missile, now!" screamed Pinta.

It was too late. The missile exploded into a bright white light.

All the Calamaari ships that remained with Pinta were decimated including hers. That region of the sector became a dark void.

**********

Severin and Goeth sat at the controls of the small transport. They discussed the successful escape from Pinta's ship and the events leading up to it.

Suddenly, the *Widow Maker* and three other man-o-wars burst through a portal. They fired every one of their cannons at the *Leviathan.* The ship was defenseless as it was pummeled mercilessly by Malduna's battle stars.

Severin and Goeth were shocked by the onslaught. Goeth immediately accelerated the ship away from the battle and raced toward the space station.

Severin tried to contact Will but there was no reception. "I can't reach them, Goeth!"

"That could mean the Weevil detonated their weapon."

"Then Will could be…"

"One problem at a time," interrupted Goeth. "Let's get out of here before they hunt us next."

**********

"Shanna, see if you can locate the source of Polus' transmission," Will requested.

Will stared at Polus on the monitor and shook his head disappointedly at him. "I told you that was only a prototype, you fool," said Will mockingly.

"It served its purpose," replied Polus. "Now you'll serve yours."

"Did you think I would come here empty handed, Polus?" taunted Will. "I have a special delivery for you."

Polus' expression became somber as he realized that Will might have the real doomsday weapon.

Will piloted the *Reaper* straight for Polus' battle star. He activated the weapons control panel and waited for Shanna's response.

"I've got him, Will. He's on board the ship on the far left."

Will locked onto Polus' ship and armed six torpedoes.

"You couldn't set the weapon off," countered Polus. "The reaction would engulf your people as well."

"Not if we shut down that part of your portal system."

"You wouldn't."

"This is your last chance for peace, Polus."

Two dozen fighters shot out of the battle star and raced toward them.

"Bad move, Polus. Think about it. If they shoot me, then we're all gone. Either way, your race becomes extinct."

"You don't have the real weapon," shouted Polus nervously.

Just as the fighters were within range of him, Will launched the six torpedoes toward Polus. "You were right this time, Polus," he taunted. "Next time will be different."

Four torpedoes struck a force field around the ship and exploded harmlessly while two struck the unprotected fighter bays. A large fireball erupted from the side of the battle star and vanished, leaving a large crater in the battle star's hull.

Will changed direction and went after the fighters. Once the *Reaper* was among them, it became a difficult target to hit. Four fighters were promptly destroyed by their own fire as the *Reaper* stayed in close quarters to the attackers.

Shanna took over the weapons system and selectively targeted fighters with torpedoes.

Squadrons of fighters emerged from the other battle stars. They were still distant from the battle.

Will maneuvered in and out of the fighters and circled around the battle star several times. With only five fighters left, the armament panel flashed 'empty'.

"We're out of torpedoes, Will. I think it's time to leave the party."

"I think Polus got the message."

Will turned the *Reaper* toward the portal and accelerated to maximum speed. The fighters from the other battle stars had no chance of catching them.

The *Reaper* burst through the portal and headed for the space station. An alarm sounded and the short-range sensors picked up large pieces of debris around them.

Will slowed the ship and used the outside cameras to monitor the large chunks of metal.

"Something's wrong, Shanna."

"I know. That debris wasn't there before." Shanna immediately tried to contact the *Leviathan* but to no avail. She changed channels and sent signals to the transport ship.

Finally, after several attempts, Severin responded. "Shanna, the *Leviathan* – she's gone!"

"What!"

"The *Widow Maker's* after us. We're taking fire."

Shanna glanced at Will. His eyes welled with tears.

"Severin, it's Will. How close are you to the station?"

"Not close enough. I've called for help but we're running out of time."

"We're coming. I'll see if I can distract them."

"Please hurry, Will."

Will pounded the console and screamed. Shanna rubbed his shoulder and tried to calm him.

"They're going to pay!" he cried.

Will returned to maximum speed and pursued the *Widow Maker*.

"Remember, Will, we don't have any torpedoes," Shanna reminded him.

"Damn it! Everything's falling apart."

Will sent a signal out to the *Widow Maker*.

Malduna's face appeared immediately on the monitor. "Well, Saris, you did well. Now the Calamaari are gone. That makes my job a whole lot easier."

"No it doesn't. You and I have personal business. I'm coming for you."

Malduna laughed mockingly and ended the transmission.

Shanna kept an eye on the long range sensors. A large green dot and a small green dot appeared at the edge of the screen. "We have them, Will."

The large dot veered away from the smaller one and vanished. "They've vanished!" exclaimed Shanna.

"I figured she would. She wants me to suffer a while longer."

Will lowered his head and sobbed. Shanna knelt next to him and comforted him. She, too, felt the loss of their friends, Bastille and Celine.

Will slowed the ship down and set the 'auto-pilot' feature. He got up and left the pilots' cabin. Shanna hesitated a moment and then followed him.

"Will, are you okay?"

"No! At this rate, it won't matter if we destroy the Weevil. No one will be left."

"Don't say that."

"We're going to bring this thing to an end and it's going to happen real soon."

"We're running out of options."

"No we're not. I'm going to put that PBU-57 right up Polus' fat ass."

"And I'll be there with you. Try and calm down. I know this is tough but we have to stay focused."

The transmitter beeped, irritating Will all the more. Suddenly, the short-range monitors picked up a large Calamaari force.

Shanna acknowledged the 'receive' button. Zorick's face appeared on the monitor.

"I'm sorry, Will. We couldn't get here in time to save your friends."

"Malduna's going to pay for this."

"Then let's go after her. We're with you."

"Thanks, Zorick. We'll lead."

Will smiled at Shanna. "Maybe there is justice out here somewhere."

"I'll get the cannons. That's all we have for defense."

"That's my girl."

Will picked up the *Widow Maker's* heat trails on the infra-red scanner. He piloted the *Reaper* through the portal with forty seven Calamaari cruisers behind him.

As soon as they cleared the portal, four man-o-wars attacked for them.

The cruisers raced in a large circle around the battle stars and fired inward at them.

The man-o-wars fired their cannons repeatedly back at the cruisers.

Will watched the battle on the monitor and realized what the Calamaari were doing. They targeted two of the man-o-wars until they were crippled. Then they focused on the remaining two.

The man-o-wars destroyed over twenty of the cruisers but were left with only one able to fire.

The remaining Calamaari cruisers pounded the two crippled man-o-wars until they exploded and vanished.

Ten more cruisers were destroyed, leaving only seventeen.

The cruisers focused on the man-o-war with firing capability. Three cruisers were damaged and flew kamikaze-style into the man-o-war's bridge. The flight deck blew out in a brief but bright flash and the man-o-war split in half. Its wreckage drifted aimlessly through space.

Will contacted Zorick by transmitter.

"What is it, Will?"

"We've done enough. I don't want you to incur any more losses."

"Understood. We're breaking off the battle."

"Zorick, thank you."

"My pleasure."

Will announced over the intercom to Shanna, "We're going home."

"But there is still one left! It could be her."

"We're going home," he affirmed.

**********

The next day, Severin called an all hands meeting. She announced that two of their patrols sighted a large Weevil force entering the sector. She ordered all commanders to prepare their ships for war.

Afterward, Will approached her to discuss the move. Severin ordered Will to back off and let her handle things.

"Those ships will be massacred, Severin," warned Will. "You can't send them out there."

"I appreciate all you've done for me, Will, but we can't expect you to do everything."

"At least give me time to speak with Cintilla and see what support they can give us."

"Then do it fast. This looks like the Weevil invasion we've feared would come one day."

"Then the timing could be perfect. I'll get back to you soon."

Will hurried out of the large meeting room and met Shanna in the hall.

"How did it go?" she inquired.

"Not good. The Weevil force is entering this sector and Severin's going to send every ship she has out to intercept them."

"She can't!"

"I know. Can you find Prax and see what the status of the weapon is. I have to speak with Cintilla."

"She's not here."

"What?"

"She and Goeth went back to Calamaar."

"Damn! I guess we're going solo."

They hurried down the corridor to the lab. Three guards stood at the entrance.

"I'm looking for Prax and Xerxes," said Will.

One of the guards pointed inside. "They're in the rear by the elevator," he replied. He sensed their urgency and opened the security door for them.

Will and Shanna entered the test lab and proceeded past several tanks, tables and table-sized centrifuges.

Prax operated a chainfall with a long thin assembly made of transparent material. Inside at the nose section was the brown compound. In the middle was a series of silver rods with red fluid flowing around them. At the tail end was the detonation circuit. Displayed through the transparent cover was a series of blinking lights and a bar graph indicator reading "20 percent".

Xerxes held the aft end of the assembly as Prax lowered it into a red missile body.

Will and Shanna watched anxiously as the assembly seated neatly inside of the missile.

Once the chainfall was removed from the device, Prax and Xerxes turned their attention to Will and Shanna.

"Please tell me it's ready, Prax?"

Prax calmly put his hand on Will's shoulder. "We guarantee it will work as expected. Thanks to my father, we've perfected the compound."

"So all I have to do is launch this baby?"

"Yes, and most importantly, get the hell out of there."

"Don't worry," replied Shanna. "I'll take care of that part personally."

"I'll let Severin know it's coming down. Her people will load it into the *Reaper's* weapons inventory."

"Will, thanks so much for rescuing her. I don't know how I could ever repay you."

"I think your dad saved my life once or twice along the way."

"It's funny how intertwined our paths are, going back to your father's life and now through yours," commented Xerxes. "He'd be proud of you."

"Thank you Xerxes. That means a lot."

"Your destiny is so much like his was."

"Once we finish the Weevil off, I want to hear all about him from you."

"I'd be happy to tell you."

Will and Shanna hugged the two men. They stared teary-eyed at them and left the test lab.

"I'm afraid we'll never see them again, dad," said Prax sadly.

"Don't think that way. Of course we'll see them."

**********

Will and Shanna sat in the briefing room. Severin and her security officer sat across from them.

"You can't do this alone, Will. It's suicide."

"All I need is for your ships to cover me until I get into the portal. After that, I want them to get away as quickly as possible."

"I know the two of you are damn good pilots with that craft but you'll never make it through a force that large."

"If only the Calamaari were able to help us," said the officer regretfully.

"We don't have time to track down Goeth and Cintilla. It's now or never."

"Are you sure the explosives are planted on the correct probes?" Shanna questioned Severin.

"I'm sure. That's why I went with them. We planted sixteen devices. That should take out the three portals in our sector."

"If you set them off too soon, a portion of the Weevil force will be trapped on our side of the portal," the officer warned. "Then we'll have to deal with them."

"You said they are already in the sector?" asked Shanna.

"Yes, they are. That means there are only two portals between us and them."

"You don't have much time, Will," Severin reminded him. "If this doesn't work, I'm launching a full scale attack."

"Stay calm, Severin," Will pleaded. "Don't do anything unless you are absolutely sure."

The security officer received a call and left the room.

"I have a bad feeling about this," Severin said somberly. "I'm worried about the two of you. We've lost a lot of friends and I don't want to lose you, too."

The three of them stood. Severin hugged Will and Shanna tightly. "Good luck to you both. Come back safe."

"We plan on it," answered Will.

"You make sure you wipe out any strays that get by us," Shanna instructed Severin.

"You have my word. I want these bastards gone for good."

"Keep an eye out for the *Widow Maker*," warned Will. "It's the only man-o-war left in Malduna's fleet."

"I want to see that bitch die a horrible death," Severin uttered vindictively. "If it weren't for her, the General might still be alive."

They gazed at each other one last time before departing.

**********

Jack and Maya waited with their two girls and Marina in the main quarters of the *Reaper*.

The girls played with the monkey. Jack and Maya held hands and watched them.

"What if this doesn't work, Maya?"

"Then nothing matters. The Weevil will destroy everything and everyone."

"And what if we don't make it back?"

Maya stared at him for an instant and burst into tears. They nestled against each other. Jack's eyes filled as he looked down at the girls.

Will and Shanna entered and saw them. Their eyes filled with tears as well.

Shanna picked up Marina and held her tightly. Will wrapped his arms around both of them.

Three women arrived inside the ship to retrieve the girls. Jack and Maya picked up their girls and hugged them. Maya kissed the girls repeatedly. Finally, they gave up the girls to the women.

Jack closed the hatch behind them and leaned against the hull. He wondered if it would be the last time they'd see the girls.

"The ship is 'weapons ready'. Our 'red death' is located in the 'six' position' in the tubes," announced Maya confidently. "Whatever you do, don't select it until you're ready."

"Thanks, Maya," replied Will. "You and Jack don't have to go with us. We'd understand."

Jack turned around and joined them. "Will, we've been through a lot over the years," he explained. "There's no way we'd let you two go out there alone."

'We couldn't live with ourselves," added Maya.

"Then let's go exterminate the Weevil race!" shouted Shanna. The four of them put their hands together as a sign of unity.

"Jack and I will man the cannons," Maya informed them.

"We'll leave the intercom open if you want to talk," replied Shanna.

Everyone took their positions in the ship. Will powered up the *Reaper* and waited as the bay doors opened. Shanna performed diagnostic checks on all the ship's systems.

Jack and Maya activated their turrets and performed functional checks. The turrets pivoted and the cannons moved along their tracks. They donned their helmets and powered up the miniature control system in each.

The *Reaper* glided out of the bay and away from the station. Forty ships of various sizes joined them. Among them, ten man-o-wars and one battle star.

Will took note of the size of their fleet on the monitor. "They should be able to hold off the first few waves of fighters. Once the Weevil battle stars arrive, they're in trouble."

"Can we deliver the missile in time to stop them, Will?"

"I hope so."

The fleet raced toward the first of the two portals separating them from the Weevil.

The transmitter beeped, indicating an incoming transmission.

"Who could this be so soon?" pondered Will aloud.

Shanna pressed the 'receive' button and Goeth's face appeared on the screen.

"Were you planning on leaving us behind?" chided Goeth playfully.

"Goeth! It's great to hear from you. How did things go on Calamaar?"

"Very well. My mother is back in charge and she's committed our entire force to support your operation."

Will and Shanna saw a multitude of green dots appear on the short range screen.

"Well, we're damn glad to have you."

"Our scouts tell us that the Weevil are sending their entire force through the portals."

"We've heard. We have the weapon and we're going to give it to them, once and for all."

"What do you need from us?" asked Goeth.

Cover us until we get through the second portal. Whatever you do, don't follow us through or you'll be caught in the blast."

"I understand. Good luck to you, my friend. Thanks for everything you've done for us."

"My pleasure, Goeth."

The transmission ended. Will's attitude improved dramatically over the addition of the Calamaari to their forces.

"Your diplomacy paid off," remarked Shanna.

"It sure seems so."

"I just have to ask, what were you thinking when you took your sword on board Pinta's ship."

"It was a distraction."

"Are you sure that was all?"

"Yes. Why?"

"I almost burst into tears, I wanted to laugh so hard. So did Pinta."

"Well, thanks a lot. That really does a lot for my self-confidence."

"Well, I thought it was cute."

Numerous red dots appeared on the long-range monitor. "Here comes the first wave of fighters, Will."

"Save the torpedoes for the other side of the portal."

"We'll handle them with the cannons," said Jack over the intercom.

"Make me proud, buddy," Will replied.

A dozen Calamaari cruisers passed over the *Reaper*.

"Looks like our friends don't want us to get hurt," commented Maya over the intercom.

"They're clearing a path for us," replied Shanna.

Will focused on the monitor and navigated behind their escort. "We're passing through the first portal," Will announced. "Get ready."

As soon as the Calamaari ships cleared the portal, they were besieged by dozens of Weevil fighters.

"This is where we split," Will informed them.

The *Reaper* broke away from the battle and headed toward the battle stars.

An immense battle ensued as Calamaari and human ships appeared from the portal to take on the Weevil force.

"The second portal is coming up," announced Will. "It's showtime!"

Will reached over and held Shanna's hand. "I love you, Shanna."

"I love you, too. How about we make a social call to Polus for old times' sake?"

Will grinned playfully and sent a signal to Polus' ship. After several tries, Polus' face appeared on their monitor.

"I can't imagine what stupid idea is in your head right now, Saris."

"I told you, Polus, the next time you see me, I'll have the real 'doomsday' weapon."

Will pointed to Shanna. She launched five torpedoes toward Polus' ship. Five bursts of red energy darted from the *Reaper* toward Polus' ship.

Polus laughed at them on the monitor. "That's funny, Saris. Keep trying."

Fighters emerged from the battle stars and soon swarmed around them.

Jack and Maya fired the cannons at the fighters as fast as they could maneuver the turrets.

The five torpedoes struck a force field around the battle star.

"Nice try, Saris," taunted Polus, "but you lose."

"Screw you, Polus and your whole race!" Will turned to Shanna and decreed, "Do it for our daughter, our friends and those who died to help stop these rodents."

"My pleasure." Shanna fired the doomsday missile.

Will turned the *Reaper* around and immediately broke for the portal.

Polus was immediately interrupted by one of his Weevil officers who whispered something in is ear. Polus turned his attention back to Will.

"If you detonate that missile, you'll die, too."

"No, you stupid, inferior creature. That's why we're shutting down your portals. The impact will be confined to your side of the portal – all the way back to your home planet!" Will laughed sadistically.

Polus ordered all fighters to target the missile and fire.

The *Reaper* darted through the portal. Will initiated the frequency transmitter and detonated the portal's probes using the designed frequency. Something strange happened. The probes for the portal in front of them exploded but the probes for the portal behind them did not. They were trapped in the impact zone.

"Will, what's going on?" Maya shouted frantically.

"The wrong portal collapsed!"

Shanna used the computer data base and accessed a star chart for the area.

"There's a small planet not far from here, Will. We can make it."

"Give me coordinates!"

Shanna entered the coordinates and the computer responded with the recommended course.

The Weevil fighters fired furiously at the missile until it exploded. A bright flash flooded the area and spread back through the Weevil portal system all the way to their home planet. Every ship and Weevil was incinerated within a second.

The Reaper circled behind the frozen planet just as the flash struck the tail of the ship.

Will and Shanna were thrown hard against either side of the pilots' cabin and rendered unconscious.

Jack and Maya were both knocked unconscious in the turrets. Both sustained head injuries and were bleeding.

The *Reaper* was pulled into the gravitational field of the atmosphere of a frozen planet called *Ithaca*. Light gravity prevented the ship from being destroyed upon landing plus the added cushioning of snow helped keep the ship intact when it crashed on the surface.

On the other side of the first portal, the Calamaari and humans battled the Weevil fighters until the last one was destroyed. They attempted to find the portal to search for the *Reaper* but to no avail.

Will came to and tended to Shanna. He called over the intercom, "Jack! Maya! Are you there?"

"Did we do it?" replied the weak, trembling voice of Maya.

Will glanced at the long-range sensor monitor and it was blank. "I think we did! There's no sign of them anywhere!"

Shanna stirred and awoke. She smiled at Will and asked, "Is it over?"

"Yes, it is."

They hugged each other.

"Jack, are you alright?" asked Will over the intercom.

"Damn!" he responded. "Where did you learn how to fly?"

The four of them laughed, despite their condition.

**********

The *Widow Maker* appeared through a portal and searched for the *Reaper*.

Malduna paced the flight deck with her son, Victor, nearby.

"Now, Victor, we will avenge your father's death. I will show them no mercy."

"Yes, mother," he replied.

One of the technicians at the control console called out, "We've found them, ma'am."

Malduna hurried to the console and saw for herself. The infra-red scan of the planet's surface clearly showed the heat from the *Reaper* in red against the frozen background of blue.

"Prepare to transport us as soon as you have a lock. Place us in the main quarters of the ship."

"Yes, ma'am."

Malduna motioned for Victor to follow her. They left the flight deck for the transporter room. Malduna ordered the operator to dress them in cold weather gear. When they were ready, they entered the transporter room and stepped onto the platform.

The 'ready' light flashed green.

"It is time for justice," she announced.

The four soldiers stepped up on the platform, then Victor.

A nearby display flashed a countdown, "Three, two, one." The green light turned red and they vanished from the platform.

Malduna, Victor and four soldiers arrived on board the *Reaper* dressed in cold weather gear. They removed their hoods.

Jack and Maya descended the ladders from the turrets. They recognized the intruders immediately.

Jack drew his pistol and fired. Two soldiers were struck and killed. Maya, still dazed, reacted more slowly. Malduna and one soldier fired at her. She collapsed to the ground, badly wounded.

Malduna pushed Victor into a rear cabin away from the gunfire.

Jack fired again and struck the remaining two soldiers. Malduna stepped out and fired at Jack, striking him in the head. He collapsed next to Maya. He grabbed for her hand and gave her a fading gaze before dying.

Maya desperately reached for her pistol on the floor but Malduna kicked it away. She stepped on Maya's wrist and held her pistol to Maya's head. "Any last words before you die?"

Maya tried to speak but could not. She raised her head and gave a scornful and defiant glare to Malduna and died.

Malduna contacted the ship and ordered the dead men transported back to the ship. She and Victor donned their hoods and dragged the bodies of Maya and Jack outside the ship.

When they returned, Victor questioned Malduna, "Why did we put the bodies outside?"

"You see, Victor, I want them to die in fear. I want them to die in agonizing fear."

"Does it matter?"

"Oh, yes, son. It matters very much."

Unaware of their intruders, Will tried repeatedly to contact any of the ships for help but there was no reply.

"Why wouldn't they answer us?" asked Shanna uneasily.

"Maybe the second portal blew later than the first one?"

"Or maybe someone detonated it to keep us here?" suggested Shanna.

"We'd better get down there just in case."

Will helped Shanna to her feet in the pilot's cabin.

Malduna hid in the cabin with Victor and waited patiently.

As soon as the door opened, they saw blood stains on the floor.

"Jack!" shouted Will. "Maya!" There was no answer.

They checked the turrets but there was no sign of them.

"Oh my God!" cried Shanna. "Where are they?"

Will became pale and sweaty. He became unsteady.

"What is it, Will? Are you okay?"

Will shook his head 'no' and held his hand over his heart.

Malduna entered and aimed both her pistols at them.

"Well, well, well. Look at this."

"I'll kill you, you bitch!" shouted Shanna.

"You can't kill me. I died a long time ago."

"Then you should have stayed dead."

You took everything from me: my world; my husband; my fleet. Now I'm going to make you suffer in your dying moments."

"Not if I rip your lungs out and tear your face off!"

Shanna felt the urge to transform into her mutant form but resisted. She needed to be smart.

Will fell to one knee and breathed heavily.

Shanna dove for Maya's pistol and rolled. She quickly fired two shots. Malduna was struck in the chest with both shots. Red blotches appeared on her cold-weather suit. Shanna leaped on her and pounded her face repeatedly while sobbing hysterically. She gouged at Malduna's face and clawed chunks of flesh from her.

"Shanna," called Will weakly.

Shanna stopped her attack and turned her attention to Will. She helped him to his feet. "It's all right, Will."

Victor watched in horror as Malduna lay dead on the floor. He placed his hood back on and crept from the cabin.

Shanna held Will in her arms. "Hold on, Will. I'll find a way to get us out of here."

"It can't end like this."

"It won't, Will. It won't."

"I'll always love you, Shanna."

"And I'll always love you."

Victor rushed to the hatch and pressed the 'open' knob.

Shanna saw the hatch open and was horrified. She set Will down and ran to the hatch but it was too late.

The temperature in the room quickly dropped to sub-zero. She and Will immediately succumbed to the cold and froze.

Victor stared at them sadistically through the hood on his suit. He studied the look of horror on Shanna's face and felt a degree of satisfaction. He dragged their bodies outside the ship and laid them in a row next to the others in the snow.

Victor used Malduna's transmitter to call for help. He and Malduna's bloody corpse were transported back to the *Widow Maker*.

Three of Malduna's officers waited in the transporter room when Victor arrived with his dead mother. They immediately tried to administer first-aid but Malduna was dead.

Victor announced, "I am in command of the *Widow Maker* as successor to my mother and father."

"What of Will Saris?" asked one man.

"He is no more. This is the end of the Saris era and the beginning of my era. Any questions?"

The men were silent.

"Then let us return to Yord where I will assume the throne that should have been my father's."

**********

Severin waited anxiously for word on the mission. Her security officer stood behind her. Finally, she received an incoming transmission.

Goethe's face appeared. "The mission was a success. The Weevil have been exterminated."

"What about Will and Shanna?" inquired Severin anxiously.

"There is no sign of them or the portal."

"Can we open it up again?"

"It's gone. We can't open what isn't there."

"Then what can we do?"

"Hope. If they are alive, they may one day return."

"And until then…?"

"The Calamaari will forge an alliance with your people in appreciation for all that Will and Shanna did for us."

"That would be a very generous token of your gratitude."

The transmission ended.

Severin stared at the blank screen.

"What is it, ma'am?" asked the officer.

"There are three orphaned children down stairs. How do we tell them their parents are gone?"

"Who will raise them?"

"Perhaps we can send the girls to a temple. They can be raised by the priestesses."

"I think they'd agree with your decision."

"It's ironic but with Will's rise came the rise of the hostile alien races and with his demise, the wars ended."

"Do you think he's dead, ma'am?"

"I think Will would have sacrificed whatever it took to end the Weevil domination. If that meant his life, then he would surely give it. I think he destroyed that portal."

**********

Severin presided over a service for all that were lost in the war and included prayers for Will, Shanna, Jack and Maya, wherever they may be.

In addition, Prax and Xerxes spoke of Will's legacy and the commitment that he and his father had for the peace and well-being of all humans.

Three priestesses stood nearby with the three orphaned girls. They exited the area first with the girls.

Severin eyed Marina and concluded the service with the closing comment: "Perhaps one day, there will be another as worthy as Will and Shanna to lead us."

Severin stepped outside the temple on the top floor of the station. She was met by Zorick, Goeth and Cintilla. They gave personal condolences over the loss of life of their friends.

Severin thanked them and left for her quarters. She sat on the bed and drew her pistol. She stared at it for several moments, and then placed it in her mouth.

The door slid open and Prax entered. "Severin!"

Severin burst into tears. She tried to pull the trigger but didn't have the courage.

Prax took the gun away from her and cradled her in his arms.

"They're all gone!" she cried.

"But I'm not. I'll do anything for you, Severin."

"I want a family. You and me. We can raise Marina."

"But Marina's gone."

"That's the least we can do for Will and Shanna."

"Sev, it's too late. They've been taken away."

"Then I have a station to run," she said coldly. Severin stood up and straightened her uniform. She stowed the pistol and walked out of the room.

Prax's transmitter beeped. "Hi, Dad," he answered. "No, wait. I'm coming with you."

Prax stowed the transmitter and left Severin's quarters. He walked sadly down the hall in the opposite direction.

**********

Severin stood on the bridge of the station and stared out at the stars. "I should have died with you."

A passing officer heard her and paused. "Are you alright, ma'am?"

"That's a stupid question."

# Other books by Michael D'Ambrosio

**The Space Frontier Series starring Will Saris, the son of Billy Brock, Fractured Time Series.**

Eye of Icarus, Book One

Dangerous Liaisons, Book Two

The Devil's Playground, Book Three

## About the Author

Michael is a lifelong resident of the Philadelphia area and a graduate of Widener University with a B.S. in Technical and Industrial Administration. When he isn't writing novels or screenplays, Michael can be found at one of many conventions around the world. With The Fractured Time Trilogy, Night Creeps and now the conclusion of Space Frontiers, look for Michael to expand his fan base overseas in the coming years, particularly in the UK., where science fiction is more popular than anywhere else in the world. Visit Michael's site at www.fracturedtime.com to see details on the progress of his screenplays and his next writing project entitled Princess Pain.

CPSIA information can be obtained at www.ICGtesting.com
Printed in the USA
BVOW04s1446090415

395392BV00005B/12/P

9 780983 010968